'Kevin Holohan's wickedly funny debut novel, set in a rundown Dublin religious school where the spirits are low but the Gaelic pride runs high, will make you laugh almost as much as it makes you weep, for beyond their almost comical [illegible]mpetence and a thin veneer of piety the Brothers who [illegible] place are sad, flawed men, whose weaknesses range [illegible]dism to depravity. They educate by cudgel and dole o[illegible]cipline with a leather strap, while protagonist Finbar S[illegible] and the other long-suffering students bear it all with [illegible]d of wise-cracking cynicism, irreverence, and pranks that one would expect at that age.'
-— Preston L. Allen, author of *Jesus Boy*

'[illegible]*others' Lot* is a screamingly funny indictment of the cul[illegible] of repression and abuse that has plagued Ireland for gen[illegible]ons, but it is much more than that. It is a brilliantly t[illegible]le, compassionate and brutal. Most important, it [illegible]tes the spirit of reckless bravery and rebellion, the sp[illegible]hat draws back the curtain on iconic institutions to [illegible]al the frailty of an ecclesiastical house of cards.'
[illegible] McLoughlin, author of *Heart of the Old Country*

THE BROTHERS' LOT

A NOVEL BY

KEVIN HOLOHAN

NO EXIT PRESS

First published in the UK in 2011
by No Exit Press, an imprint of
Oldcastle Books Ltd., P.O.Box 394,
Harpenden, Herts, AL5 1XJ

www.noexit.co.uk

First published in the U.S. by Akashic Books, New York, 2011

A CIP catalogue record for this book is available from the British Library.

ISBN
978-1-84243-505-2 (paperback)
978-1-84243-507-6 (ePub)
978-1-84243-506-9 (Kindle)
978-1-84243-508-3 (PDF)

Printed and bound in the UK by Cox & Wyman, Reading, Berks.

For all the kids who never had a chance to answer back

Whatsoever you do unto the least of these
my brethren, you do unto me.
—Matthew 25:40

Prologue

With a start Brother Boland woke. He had dozed off while praying at his cot. His coarse tweed undershirt was soaked in sweat. Around him pressed the deep silence of night.

He had been dreaming. He was flying through the air. He could see the school below him. He could hear a voice in the wind. It came from everywhere and nowhere and was filled with a strange harmony of anger, dust, and the smell of wood.

Brother Boland had started to circle lower over the school and suddenly, all lightness sucked from him, he began to fall toward the roof of the monastery. That was when he woke.

He got up off his knees and stared around the surrounding dark of his cell. Everything was as it had been for his last sixty years as a Brother. The statue of the Infant de Prague stood where it always had on the windowsill. His trousers hung on the chair as usual. His cassock hung on the back of the door as always like some outsized crow carcass. Everything was as it should be, yet not. Brother Boland could not put words on what it was, but there was something. He stepped into his slippers and threw on his cassock.

His slippers made a dead fish sound on the highly polished wooden floor as he tiptoed along. The half-light from the street slid through the windows and cast shadows everywhere. From his perch in the return of the stairs, Venerable Saorseach O'Rahilly, the founder of the Brotherhood, seemed to cower uncertainly back into the shadows, so unlike his stern, disciplinarian, daylight demeanour. Brother Boland nodded and blessed himself as he passed the statue and wisped down the stairs to the ground floor like a tattered black fog with the shakes.

In the monastery kitchen he checked all the doors and windows. Locked tight all of them. He ghosted through the ground-floor Biology lab. All secure there. He paused and leaned a moment against one of the big desks.

Satisfied that all was safe downstairs, Brother Boland twitched back up the stairs as fast as he could. At the top landing he wrestled with the stiff, heavy door. He opened it with a jolt. His hand spidered its way over the musty wood of the inner stairs until it found the light switch. He flicked it. Nothing. The darkness inside seemed to intensify in retaliation against his attempt to dispel it.

The air stank of damp and neglect. The narrow spiral stairs protested under Brother Boland's feet as he cautiously ascended. The air was chill yet oppressive and Brother Boland laboured to find enough oxygen to keep going.

The stairs led to another small landing. There Brother Boland paused and peered up into the gloom. He could just about make out the dull sheen of the bell above him. He paused, unsure whether to head up the ladder. He shivered. He brought his breathing to a minimum and listened. In the nearby flats a dog barked the bark of one who lives from dustbins. From closer came an answering howl hoping to reduce its desperate straits by sharing them. Such foolishness! He had not come all the way up here in the middle of the night to listen to dogs barking and speculate on how they found food!

He moved to the corner of the landing and reached down. His hands found the familiar boxy contours. This was his safe haven. This was where he came when the bad things closed in around him. This was his retreat.

Here he kept his tea chest. This was how he had arrived at the school: five months old, in the bottom of a tea chest with whatever clothes he owned thrown over him, left on the steps of the monastery by his unfortunate mother. There had been a note too, or so Brother Boland had been told, but that was long gone, as were the clothes. Yet he still had the tea chest, he still had his roots.

He sat on the edge of the chest and slowly rocked to and fro. He clutched each elbow and held himself close. As he felt his unease begin to subside, he reached out and ran his hands over the surface of the chest. He luxuriated in the familiarity of its shape and lovingly rubbed the rusted edging strips. His talonlike fingers felt love in the rough metal surface. He pressed at the tiny nail heads and sensed the love pulse into him. Brother Boland squeezed his eyes shut and ran his fingers faster over the metal edges of the box.

He emptied his mind. All he was aware of was the persistent tick-ticking of his middle finger on the side of the tea chest. He tried to listen behind that. There it was. There, just on the edge of the silence, was the sound of something different. Not new, but changed, differently evident. Boland shuddered. He felt a white light invade him but would not breathe for fear of putting the silence out of focus. He then felt a jolt as the silence slipped away from him. He tensed and twitched and with one final spasm he snapped into catatonic rigidity, unmoving as the walls around him.

When he woke the crows cawed harshly in the trees. The early trucks hauling toward the docks ground their gears like prophets' teeth. Dogs barked their secret plans for the new day and softly the blinds and curtains of the early risers were drawn to admit the new dawn. In the early pubs, the dockers and the bona fides drank in uneasy alliance, all of them, either by choice or necessity, on a different timetable to the rest of the city. The tide shrugged out of the Liffey bringing in a cacophony of gulls to pick at the sludge in its shallows.

Brother Boland carefully placed his tea chest back in its corner and ran his hands lovingly over its surface. Whatever had haunted his night was gone. He glanced at his watch. He had two minutes to get to the bottom of the stairs and ring the bell for morning mass. He removed his slippers and tiptoed silently down the stairs.

1

"Finbar! Declan! Wake up, boys! It's time to get cracking!"

His mother's voice drifted in from the fuzzy outskirts of Finbar's dream. It registered in his head for a few moments and then faded back into the muffled waking world.

"Finbar! Get up, will you, for the love of God!"

It was closer now. From out of nowhere light leapt at his eyelids. He scrunched his eyes shut and felt the covers being pulled off. He clutched at them but they slid from his grip.

"Now, Finbar! I won't tell you again! Lord knows I have enough to be doing! Come on, love, please . . ."

His mother's voice trailed off and he finally opened his eyes. She was standing there at the end of his bed, biting the knuckle of her index finger and staring at the wall.

"All right, mam, all right. I'm up!" he said brightly, and swung himself into a sitting position on the side of the bed.

Mrs. Sullivan nodded and smiled weakly: "That's a good boy. I'll just get Declan up then."

In the bathroom Finbar ran the water. Stone cold. He splashed it on his face. Outside he could hear them at it already.

"Declan! Get up!"

"Yeah, yeah, yeah."

"Declan! I'm turning the light on now. Come on!"

"Yeah. Fine. Just leave me alone, will you?"

"Leave you alone, is it? Well, I'm sorry, Mr. High and Mighty, but you have to get up just like the rest of us. Finbar's already up."

"Well, isn't he the little saint then?"

"Declan, that's quite enough lip out of you. Just get up, can't you?"

"I didn't ask to go."

"Not this again! Look, we're going and that's that. We're not having this argument again. Now, get up out of that and stop your nonsense!"

"What if I don't?"

"The movers will be here in half an hour."

"Well, maybe I'll get myself a flat then."

"You will not! You don't have two pennies to rub together. I'll not have any more of this talk. We've heard enough of it out of you."

Her voice was getting louder and shriller. Finbar sat on the toilet and ran the water in the sink as hard as it could go. He didn't need to hear all this over again. There'd been weeks of it already and with each week Declan had become more disagreeable to the point where now he hardly spoke to anyone in the house, not even Finbar. All because that stupid Sheila Barry had dumped him or run away from home or whatever: no one was too clear on it.

"Yeah? And why not? I can do what I want!" yelled Declan.

"Not while you're under my roof."

"And who says I want to be under your roof? I didn't ask to be part of this family. I didn't ask to be born into this."

"Oh, Sacred Heart of Jesus, Declan, stop it!"

Finbar heard the front door slam.

"What the hell is going on up there? Ye can be heard out on the street!" called his father from the bottom of the stairs.

"Nothing," called Declan, the fire suddenly gone from his voice and replaced by a damp, leaden resignation.

"Well, fine then! Get up so! I got some sausages and bread from Mrs. Morrissey. Breakfast in ten minutes!" shouted Mr. Sullivan.

"Finbar, are you nearly finished in there? Declan has to wash himself," called Mrs. Sullivan as she made her way back downstairs.

Finbar reached over and slowly turned off the water in the sink.

Once breakfast was over and the dishes washed, dried, and packed into the car, Finbar sat on the footpath outside the house and watched the movers load the furniture into the back of the truck. His father hovered around them, mostly getting in the way and making their job more difficult, but Jack Sullivan was not the type of man to trust hired workmen to do a good job unless he was breathing down their necks.

"Finbar! Give me a hand with these few things," his mother called from the front door. He took the box of photographs and ornaments from her and put it in the car. Declan stormed out of the house full of gangly seventeen-year-old bad temper and flopped into the backseat of the car. He sat there with a face like a curse on him and glared out the window at nothing in particular.

Mr. Sullivan oversupervised the movers loading the dining table and then ran back into the house. Finbar went in after him. The house echoed weirdly under his footsteps. Even the lino was gone. It had so quickly turned from his home into a shell of brick and floorboards. He watched his father stand at the top of the stairs and stare ruefully out the small window at his garden below. He went out to the car and sat in the backseat beside the silent, fuming Declan. Separated only by three years, they might as well have been from different planets. Finbar couldn't be bothered even trying to talk to him and picked his own patch of nothing in particular to stare at and sighed.

"Will ye stop that sighing like an old woman, ye little prick! Just cos you're going to miss the first day of school. Stupid sap," hissed Declan.

"Ah, get lost you," answered Finbar.

Declan rolled down the window and spat onto the street.

"Right so!" called Mrs. Sullivan as she came out of the house and pulled the door behind her. Its familiar clunk followed by the little rattle of the knocker and the letter box jabbed at Finbar with little pins of "not going to hear that sound again, boi!" He clenched his teeth and stared away down the street.

Mr. Sullivan slid into the car and foostered around under the seat trying to move it back from the steering wheel. His brother Francie, whose car it was, was a much thinner man than he. "Stupid fecking thing!" he muttered, and then gave up. Mrs. Sullivan got into the car and settled herself with a tug at her skirt and another quick, hollowly cheery "Right so!"

As they headed across Cork to the Dublin Road, Finbar peered out the window at all the familiar sights. *Off to Dublin!* he thought with scorn. A scorn that, ironically, his parents had spent most of his early years inculcating in him. Why the hell were they now taking him from the Real True Capital of the Country all the way to Dirty Dublin where they knew no one? He didn't want to leave Cork. It was stupid, that's what it was. It was just fecking stupid and thick. "That's the why and there'll be no more talk about it!" was not a reason.

2

"Jesus wept! Get away from the window, will you?" shouted Mr. Laverty, the French teacher, as he banged on the frosted staff room window where the two grey shadows were sitting. Reluctantly the two shapes moved away. "Desperate, isn't it?" he lamented to the crowded but mostly silent staff room. He went to his bag, took out his thermos, and poured himself a quick cup of coffee, then lit a cigarette and stared dejectedly through the dirty glass at the sliver of cloudy sky visible above the monastery. He wrinkled his nose, and his droopy moustache and small rheumy eyes momentarily moved closer together. September already. Where did the summer go? It seemed only a few days ago that they had finished up, looking forward to the long, easy summer.

Now, gazing out through the grubby window, hemmed in by the growing noise of the boys outside and surrounded by the heavy tired sounds of all the other teachers in the staff room, it all seemed so desperately far away and long ago, like something that had happened in someone else's life.

"Another year in this kip," he moaned.

"Ah, feck off with ye now, Laverty. The last thing we need is your complaining to add to it," chided Spud Murphy, the History teacher. Spud flashed a big, crooked, nicotine-stained grin and puffed on the pipe that he hoped would finally help him give up cigarettes this year. His mischievous eyes wrinkled mockingly at Laverty through the cloud of smoke.

"Piss off, Murphy," snapped Laverty, and winced at the smell of the pipe.

Slowly all in the staff room became aware that it was getting loud, very loud, outside in the yard. The white noise of the boys' voices seemed to be pressing against the windows like some incredibly heavy fog. It was a weighty, mirthless sound filled with the hollow laughing and horseplay of boys trying to distract themselves from the long-dreaded day that had hung over the latter part of the summer like a toxic mist. It had finally come: the first day back at school.

"What time is it at all? My watch has stopped," called Laverty.

"Ten to nine," announced a bronchitic voice from the silence.

"Jaysus, but they're eager, the little bastards," replied Laverty, taking a deep, despairing drag of his cigarette.

"Eager, my arse," huffed Mr. Devlin, the Biology teacher, from the doorway. "They're just early cos they don't remember how to be late from last year." Mr. Devlin popped two more mints into his mouth and breathed on his hand to see if the dead beer smell was still there. He had only intended to have a couple of pints and get to bed early but then the night had spun a little out of control.

"Good morning, gentlemen! Nice of you to turn up on time for once, Mr. Devlin. We hope this is a new leaf," clipped Mr. Pollock's angular vice principal's voice. He was right on Devlin's heels. "Here are the class lists. To the hall with you now!" He dropped the sheaf of typed pages on the table, whisked around on the ball of his right foot with a mousey squeak of his brothel-creepers, and was gone.

"Poxy creep!" muttered Spud Murphy under his breath.

Mr. Barry, the Chemistry teacher, picked up the lists and started dealing them round the staff room like a stacked tarot deck that contained nothing but death cards.

In the monastery common room, Brother Kennedy pursed his thin cracked lips and ran his hand over his balding skull, smoothing the wisps of white hair over the bright red parchment of his scalp. He looked up briefly as the door creaked open and Brother Boland jittered his frail frame into the room. Boland's watery blue eyes cowered in their sunken sockets and darted about the room as if expecting some sudden attack. The man had jittered for as long as Brother Kennedy could remember. Brother Kennedy was in his seventies and Boland seemed to him to be at least a generation older. School lore had it that when Brother Boland was in his thirties, one of the sixth years had dropped a desk on him from a third-floor window while allegedly trying to knock dirt out of the inkwell. The boy had been dispatched to Saint Loman's Reformatory and later escaped to London. Brother Boland was never quite the same after it.

Brother Kennedy rarely exchanged words with Boland. It was too slow and arduous an undertaking, particularly first thing in the morning when the man's speech was still staggered and hesitant.

"Ge-ge-ge-ge-ge-good morni-ni-ni-ni-ni . . ."

"Good morning, Brother Boland." Brother Kennedy snapped his newspaper and went back to the Gaelic football results. His county, Mayo, were not doing too well but he still held out hope that they would make the Connaught finals. More hope than he could ever hold out for the pathetic school team. The scholarship boys, mostly from the local flats and tenements, had the audacity to show their ingratitude to the Brothers by being good at soccer only. It was typical of bloody Dubliners. The more malleable boys who came from the suburbs because their parents were under some illusion about the reputation of the school were just not rough enough for Gaelic football, try though they might.

New Roof for Mullingar Dog Track in Jeopardy, Bishop May Intervene, Brother Kennedy read with interest.

Brother Boland checked his watch against the wall clock and left the common room with a reptilian urgency.

Francis Scully turned into Greater Little Werburgh Street, North. There, on the corner with the West Circular Road, stood The Brothers of Godly Coercion School for Young Boys of Meagre Means, or "De Brudders," as it was more commonly known.

The sun was shining somewhere, but not anywhere near where Scully was. A dark shroud of despair surrounded him. The long summer of drizzly days with scattered outbreaks of sunshine lay lost behind him; it was now time to go back to school.

He looked up from the ground and the appalling sight of the dead end of Greater Little Werburgh Street, North, and the heavy school gates greeted him like a bout of stomach cramps.

Forty shades of grey was the only way to describe the schoolyard. The school buildings and the monastery that surrounded it on three sides were grey. Even the windows seemed to be grey. The concrete surface of the yard was grey. The sky above it was grey. The boys' shirts, sweaters, and trousers were grey. The only thing that broke the uniformity was the occasional black school blazer. The yard was a variegated fugue on the theme of grey. Had it been music, it would have been slow, mournful stuff played on a bassoon, a tuba, and the pedals of a church organ.

Scully turned heavily into the yard and looked around. It was exactly the same as last year, but even familiarity with the scene could not lessen its soul-sapping effect. The dull murmur of subdued teenage voices only added to the overall gloom.

"Scully, ye bollix! Are they lettin' ye back in?"

Scully looked over to see Lynch and McDonagh sitting beside the bin in the small covered shed. He walked over and stood in front of them.

"So?" asked McDonagh.

"So, nothing," muttered Scully.

"Yeah, right," agreed McDonagh.

"Shite," added Lynch meaningfully. He extended his cupped hand and Scully took the lit cigarette it contained. He took a long drag and exhaled slowly so as not to cause a cloud.

"Now, you boys!" It was Brother Loughlin, the Head Brother. He was on the steps of the monastery. "You will all go to the hall and get your class assignments there. First years will report to Mr. Laverty, second years to Mr. Devlin, third years to Mr. Skelly, fifth years to Mr. Murphy, and sixth years to Mr. Barry." Such menial tasks as calling out names were beneath the Brothers and left to the junior lay teachers.

No one moved.

"To the hall!" shouted Brother Loughlin. He started down the steps in a wave of cruel blubber, smoothed his eyebrows—apart from his nasal hair the only visible hair on his whole person—and took his leather strap out of the special pocket of his cassock.

Slowly the grey, reluctant sludge of boys began to ooze out of the yard and across the big yard to the hall. Scully, Lynch, and McDonagh fell in with the flow when they saw Brother Loughlin swing his leather and start in on some third years who were leaning against the wall in a manner unbecoming of boys who should be on their way to the hall.

"Jaysus! Bollocks Pollock for form master. What is that for?"

"He's a complete bastard."

"It's cos of the fire in the basement."

"Can't prove anything."

"No. But . . ."

Scully, Lynch, and McDonagh thus examined their fate as they walked back from the hall. It had been good fun for a bit, pretending not to be able to hear their names called out, answering for other people, calling out that others weren't coming back this year because they had been taken away by zombie spaceships, but there was no escaping it: they were going to have Pollock as their form master for the rest of the year, which at that moment felt pretty much like the rest of their lives.

"Yeah, and what is Smalley Mullen doing in our class?"

"Don't know. Maybe we're the new A class."

The three of them burst out laughing.

"In ainm an Athair agus an Mhic agus an Spiorad Naomh, Amen." Mr. Ignatius Pollock, the first lay vice principal in the history of the school, finished blessing himself in the tongue of the Gaels, and the prayer, probably a Hail Mary from what the boys could gather, was done. Mr. Pollock reflexively and pointlessly smoothed his wispy ginger hair over his bald spot, pursed his thin lips, and proceeded to call the roll.

"... McDonagh?"

"Here. I mean, anseo."

"Mullen?"

"Here, ehm, present, ehm, anseo."

"O'Connor?"

"Anseo."

"Rutledge?"

"Here, eh, anseo."

"Scully?"

"Anseo."

"Sullivan?"

Who was Sullivan? The only Sullivan anyone knew was Kieran Sullivan and he was in sixth year. There had been no Sullivan in third year with them last year. Mr. Pollock looked up from the roll book.

"Finbar Sullivan? Fionnbarr Ó Súilleabháin?"

Still no answer.

"We go to the trouble of making last-minute arrangements to fit him in and he does not even deign to turn up on the first day," Pollock complained to no one in particular. From the top pocket of his time-shined suit jacket, he removed a red pen and tut-tutted to himself in disapproval as he marked Finbar Sullivan absent.

He carefully examined the boys before him. Suddenly he spun around and furiously wrote the days of the week across the blackboard: *Dé Lúain, Dé Máirt, Dé Céadaoin, Déardaoin, Dé hAoine*. Down the side he wrote the times in fifty-minute intervals from nine through half past three.

He turned around and looked inquiringly at the boys, his eyebrows raised.

McDonagh raised his hand. "Sir! Sir! Sir! Sir! Sir! Sir! Sir! Sir!" he implored breathlessly, as if there were stiff competition to volunteer an answer.

"An tUasal, Mhic Donnacha!" announced Mr. Pollock, and gestured to the boy.

"Irish words, sir," answered McDonagh with a false enthusiasm you could have bottled. That was McDonagh's thing. It was a subtle and relatively safe form of disruptiveness, that and being able to faint at will. He was a reasonably good farter too but not one of the best, not up there with Lynch who could play simple tunes out of his arse.

"Ní thuigim," announced Mr. Pollock.

McDonagh looked crestfallen. He stood up slowly, walked sadly to the door, opened it, went outside, and softly closed it behind him. Mr. Pollock stood rooted to the spot. He was momentarily at a loss. He roused himself, went to the door, and opened it. McDonagh turned and looked at him, his face a caricature of contrition. Mr. Pollock motioned him back inside the class and stared at McDonagh questioningly.

"You told me to get out, sir."

"No, sor. I told you that I didn't understand. Ní thuigim. I don't understand. Understand?"

This was one of Mr. Pollock's favourite ways of slighting the boys. "Sor" in Gaelic meant louse and it was the custom during colonisation for the tenants to take what little pleasure they could get by addressing their rack-renting landlords with the word.

McDonagh saw a great opportunity for further confusing the issue by asking if "Ní thuigim" meant "I understand" or "I don't understand," but something glinted dangerously in Mr. Pollock's eyes and he thought the better of it. Just as he was about to answer, Mr. Pollock suddenly turned sideways and his leather was out and he was smacking McDonagh hard across the right hand.

"Ní thuigim. I don't understand. Ní thuigim. Repeat!" he shouted at McDonagh, each syllable punctuated with the sharp sound of the leather on the boy's palm.

"Ní thuigim, I don't understand," said McDonagh tonelessly.

"Suigh síos," barked Mr. Pollock, and then watched McDonagh as if defying him to deliberately misunderstand that one. McDonagh walked sullenly back to his desk and sat down as instructed.

The heavy post-leathering silence settled down on the boys like dense soot. The lines were drawn. No messing around. It was true what they'd heard. Pollock *was* a complete bastard. He was as bad as any of the Brothers. This was the shape of the year to come.

Grimly they copied down the timetable Mr. Pollock wrote on the blackboard, dismayed to see that Mondays, Tuesdays, and Wednesdays were going to start with double Irish with him and last thing Friday was Religion with him.

Mr. Pollock walked around the class checking that they were copying correctly. "You would want to take more care of your handwriting, Mr. McDonagh," he said pointedly as he passed the boy's desk. McDonagh said nothing and went on writing with his swollen, throbbing hand.

"Now, we will walk silently down the stairs and proceed to the hall for the mass," announced Mr. Pollock when he had completed his circuit of the class.

3

Father Flynn cleared his throat nervously. This was his first school mass as chaplain to the Brothers of Godly Coercion. As the newest priest at Saint Werburgh's parish, this extra duty had fallen to him. He had trimmed his beard three times the previous night. The uneven growth he now presented to the world was what he determined to be his most youth-friendly, approachable, and understanding face.

He smiled broadly at the hallful of boys in front of him and let rip: "We are all God's family. And He has asked us to go on a journey with Him. As we begin this new school year, we are like pioneers in the cowboy films that I am sure you boys like so much. You know the ones with the covered wagons going across the desert in search of their promised land. Well, Jesus is like our scout. He rides ahead of us and checks the way and then comes back to warn us of any dangers that might lie ahead."

"Deadly! Jesus and the Holy Ghost trying to sell crucifixes and holy medals to the Apaches," whispered Scully.

Lynch started to chuckle. That was always dangerous and Scully knew it. Lynch had one of those soft, shaking, crazed chuckles that was really contagious. With anyone else Scully could pass off his remarks and keep a totally straight face himself, but if Lynch started to giggle . . .

"Many times when Jesus returns from His scouting missions we are too busy or proud to listen to Him. Many things can get in the way. Sometimes we are distracted by our children crying or we are worried about finding food or water, or sometimes we are working out how long we will have to save up for those new football boots. Sometimes we don't listen to Our Lord and insist on walking into danger . . ."

"And then the Apaches cut yer balls off and wear them round their necks on a string." Scully couldn't help it. It just came out.

Lynch started to shake in the plastic chair beside him. Scully was starting to go too. He was chugging with silent hysterics and starting to sweat.

"We must try to listen to Our Lord when He warns us of the dangers. We must open our hearts to Him . . ." continued Father Flynn.

"Shut up, ye wanker, or I'll open yer head for ye," muttered Lynch. It wasn't funny, but it was enough. They were both now giggling helplessly. Lynch tried to cough his laugh away. That made Scully worse. He tried really hard not to listen to any more of Father Flynn's sermon. Another crack and they would be laughing out loud and then there would be trouble.

Scully put his fingers in his ears and started to hum softly: anything not to hear Father Flynn say something stupid like "The Lord is there to save our scalps," anything but that. He felt Lynch's rocking beside him subside and decided it was safe. He took his fingers out of his ears. The sermon was over. They were on the home straight. Soon it would be lunchtime.

Mr. Pollock then struck up on the warped, untunable school piano. He launched into "The Lord Is My Shepherd" with far more gusto than ability, hitting bum notes with artful and oblivious incompetence. Lynch started to sing along, following Mr. Pollock's bum notes. That did it. Scully was in hysterics. His shoulders shook violently as he tried to stifle the laugh.

Suddenly, out of nowhere, the bulk of Brother Loughlin burst through the sea of plastic chairs. Scully saw him coming but there was nothing he could do; he was caught. Lynch put on his most angelic face and continued to sing tunelessly along with Mr. Pollock's playing. Brother Loughlin grabbed Scully by the strands of hair above the ear and dragged him out of the hall.

"So, Mr. Scully? Something funny about 'The Lord Is My Shepherd' then, is there?"

"No, Brother," mumbled Scully as the words *The Lord Is My Apache Wearing Loughlin's Balls Round His Neck* flashed momentarily across his mind.

Somehow his face betrayed a hint of inner smirk. In a surprising blur of speed for someone so bulky, Brother Loughlin whipped his leather out of his sleeve and smacked Scully across the face with it.

The boy's face smarted and tingled. He had been caught completely off guard. His eyes watered but he stared at Loughlin as steadily as he could. He would not give the bastard any satisfaction.

"So, Mr. Scully? Anything else to say for yourself? Any smart-alecky remark you would like to make?"

"No."

"No, BROTHER!" shouted Brother Loughlin. He grabbed Scully's right hand and began to leather him, punctuating each word with a blow. "I'll! Teach! You! Manners! You! Little! Thug! Now get back to your seat and no more messing out of you!"

Brother Loughlin pushed Scully through the doors into the hall.

"Go in peace now to love and serve the Lord," intoned Father Flynn from the altar on the stage as he blessed them all. Mr. Pollock struck up the last hymn, "Nearer My God to Thee." It was one of his favourites. That only increased the mauling he subjected it to.

Scully walked slowly back to his seat and stood beside Lynch, who looked sideways at him with the minimum of head movement.

"Fucking bastard! Fucking fat bastard!" hissed Scully under his breath.

Lynch nodded and went back to annihilating the hymn with tuneless gusto: "Neeeeerer my Gooooodddd toooooo Theeeeeeeee, neeeeeeeeyrer toooooooooo Theeeeeeeeeee. Eeeeeeeeen tho it beeeeeee a crossssssssss . . ."

Scully smiled wanly and rubbed his hands together to deaden the stinging. "Fat fuck, he's dead," he continued to mutter under the strains of half-hearted hymn-singing around him.

There were still two verses to go when the lunch bell rang out from the yard. Mr. Pollock's playing seemed to slow down. Lynch gave up his derisory singing and started to shift agitatedly from foot to foot. It was one thing to waste what would have been a double math class with this mass, but it was very much another to start messing with the lunch break. Lynch felt very strongly about this.

With a final chord that could only be described as G-demented, Mr. Pollock put "Nearer My God to Thee" to uneasy rest and the mass was finally over.

"All boys will assemble outside with their form master and return to their classes and gather up their things. Today being Friday, we will be granting you a half day. Monday will follow the timetables you have been given," announced Brother Loughlin from the stage.

There was no cheering or whooping to celebrate the half day. All energy was expended in getting outside as quickly as possible. As Mr. Pollock and his class were close to the back, they got themselves organised and reached the school first. The first boys stopped suddenly and stood at the edge of the yard.

"What's wrong with you boys there? Move on!" snapped Mr. Pollock from the back of the group. He stepped forward and then he too stopped in his tracks.

The grey concrete of the yard was littered with another, different grey. Strewn around were shattered roof slates that lay there like birds that had suddenly turned to stone and plummeted from the sky. There was not a breath of wind. As they watched, another slate slid from the roof and sailed to the ground where it smashed into pieces with a weird metallic crash.

Mr. Pollock looked cautiously up at the roof of the school. He could see nothing.

"Right, you boys, stay close to the wall. Get your things from the class and go straight home. Straight home! No loitering about the yard!"

They ran for the door and up the stairs.

"Deadly! The place is falling to bits!" shouted McDonagh.

"Wonder who done them slates. I'd never've thinkin' of that," remarked Lynch admiringly.

As they left they saw Mr. Pollock supervising proceedings, letting one class at a time go up and get their things. His voice was a brittle whine as he shouted instructions and lashed out with his leather at the inattentive and the overeager.

* * *

Conall McConnell, School Janitor, Grade IV, sat quietly in his shed behind the school hall waiting for the kettle to boil. As first days went, this had not been a bad one. There had been no mess-ups in classes or desks, and while they were all at mass he had been able to patch the puncture on the back wheel of his bicycle.

McConnell pulled his milk crate over to the door and sat watching the sparrows pick at the moss on the twenty-foot wall that separated the school from the adjoining Lombard Street Jezebel Laundry. It was still not too cold and he could sit beside the open door and enjoy his tea. From the yard he could hear the muted sounds of the boys drifting home. A nice cup of tea and then he could head home by way of Stern's, the butchers, and get a few nice bits of lamb's liver for the tea. Mrs. McConnell was very partial to the bit of liver.

From the pocket of his overalls he removed a small notebook and a stubby pencil that he had taken from Hackett's, the bookmakers at Binn's Bridge. He stared at the sliver of sky above the wall that divided the school from the laundry and wrote:

In the autumn of desire
Screeds of cloud flow tear
Across the mind's eye
Billowing, billowing
Filled with the rain
Of promise.
How many autumn breezes
Have promised to keep
Close to—

"Mr. McConnell, I want you to look at the roof!"

Brother Loughlin was standing over him looking down at the notebook with profound distaste. It was all very well for a member of the working class to know how to write, but one who did it for recreation was deeply suspect in Brother Loughlin's estimation.

"And what might be the matter with the roof, Brother?"

"There are some slates that have fallen off on the school side. The yard is littered with them. You might want to take a look at it now that we have given the boys a half day. Best get it fixed before they all come back on Monday."

"But I'm not a roofer. I'm a janitor."

"I am well aware of that, Mr. McConnell, but where do you expect me to find a roofer at this hour on a Friday afternoon?"

"It's all the same to me."

"Are you saying you won't fix the roof?"

"Ah, no. That wouldn't be exactly what I am saying. What I am saying is that it would probably be better to get a certified, accredited roofer to look at it. I could see if there's any of the lads I know would take a look at it for you."

"Mr. McConnell! I don't have time for this hairsplitting! Either get up on that roof or find yourself another position!"

"But Brother, I could be sanctioned for crossing over demarcation lines. Brannigan Brothers could blackball me. You know they run the whole shebang. I'd love to fix the roof for you but I'm a janitor. I can't be doing that. Imagine if there were roofers wandering in here off the streets to mop out the toilets or lock the gates or—"

"The roof, Mr. McConnell!"

"All right. All right. I'll take a look at it."

"Good, and don't be too long about it."

Before McConnell could say anything else his kettle started hissing and spitting, threatening to extinguish his kerosene stove.

"I didn't know you had a stove in here, Mr. McConnell," said Brother Loughlin archly, every syllable implying that there probably shouldn't be one in the janitor's shed.

"I said I'll go and look at it now."

"Well be quick about it then!" replied Brother Loughlin and strode away.

"Ah, go ask me arse, ye big fat fucker!" muttered McConnell, then turned off the stove.

"Ah, for fuck sake!" exclaimed McConnell when he finally made it on to the roof. While sitting in his shed bloody-mindedly finishing his tea, he had convinced himself that the roof would be a minor matter of a few loose slates. A couple of nails and a couple of bits of plywood to patch the holes and he would be off home.

Now, as he stood unsteadily on the steeply pitched roof, he saw that the slates had not all slid from the same part of the roof. With almost mathematical precision the slates had fallen from roughly fifty different spots and the area of damage spread over the whole west side of the roof.

"I'll be here all fucking day!" McConnell moaned aloud and turned to make his way back down to collect the necessary tools. As he moved he noticed the roof joist in one of the nearby holes was almost completely rotted through. "No way I'm fixing that as well." He made his way carefully back to the gable end and climbed down.

4

Whatever tiny bit of excitement Finbar might have had about going to a new school had been severely damaged by Saturday's encounter at the corner shop. He had spent all day Sunday just moping around the house, refusing to go out after mass while his father tried to unpack and brighten the tiny cement backyard with fuchsias and geraniums he had brought from their garden in Cork.

Redneck, *Culchie*, *Bogman*, *Muck Savage*, they had shouted at him in bad Cork accents and then followed him down the street imitating his walk.

"Finbar! Come on! I won't tell you again. You don't want to be late," yelled Mrs. Sullivan from the bottom of the stairs.

From the other bed Declan glowered groggily at him: "Get up before I split you, you little prick!" Declan was unemployed and seemingly unemployable. The army had already turned him down in eight different counties.

"Ah, go feck off. Get up yourself and get a job, ye lazy shite," muttered Finbar. This was awful. On top of everything else he had to share a room with Declan now. In Cork he'd had his own room. Dublin was just bloody perfect.

"Finnnnbarr!" called his mother again.

"I'm up! I'm up!" he snapped.

"Well get up and get the fuck out then," mumbled Declan from under the covers. Finbar scowled at the hump in the other bed but said nothing. He braced himself and then whipped back the covers and leapt onto the cold floor. He shivered and dressed hurriedly. He put on the scratchy grey nylon shirt, the itchy grey trousers, and the stupid clip-on tie. He grabbed the sweater and looked at it: grey. Just like the rest of the stupid uniform. Just like this stupid house and this stupid street and this stupid city.

"Ah, Finbar, did you comb your hair at all? You look like you were dragged backward through a bush," fussed his mother when he walked into the small dining room. They had still not unpacked much and the room was lit by a bare forty-watt bulb that seemed to create its own special kind of gloom. His father stood by the kitchen sink hastily munching on some toast.

"Do you want an egg, Finbar? Will I boil you an egg? It won't take a minute. It'll be done by the time you're finished your porridge."

Finbar shook his head and ground his teeth. He moved the porridge around in the bowl and took a couple of mouthfuls. It tasted like dust. He took a bite of toast and slurped down some tea. More dust.

"Do you want another cup of tea, Jack?"

"No, I'm fine. Will you stop fussing? I don't have time. It's me first day, I can't be late," replied Mr. Sullivan as he grabbed his overcoat from the back of the kitchen door.

"Well, good luck."

Mr. Sullivan nodded and walked slowly out of the kitchen. "Be good at school, Finbar," he said softly as he left.

Finbar ran upstairs and collected his schoolbag from the bedroom. He slammed the door hard on his way out.

That'll help Declan's lie-in, ha!

A jagged blade of pure horror drove itself into his chest when he saw his mother standing at the bottom of the stairs in her coat and headscarf and holding her good handbag. Suffering Jesus! She was coming with him!

Singly or in small groups of two or three, grey-clad boys slouched down the West Circular Road toward The Brothers of Godly Coercion School for Young Boys of Meagre Means on Greater Little Werburgh Street, North. Muted drums and horses wearing black crepe drawing gun carriages would not have seemed out of place, such was the pall of gloom and despair that hung heavy over the road. The first fully fledged Monday of a new school year.

In the IRA shop (so named for the riot of Irish Republican Army paraphernalia that covered the walls) Scully counted out his change. He pocketed two of the loose Woodbines and put one behind his ear.

"You going in today?" asked Malachy from behind the counter.

Scully looked carefully at the man. It was rare that Malachy ever said anything so it was a safe bet this was not a casual question. Last March when Scully had skipped school, he had spent the day with Malachy packing Easter lily badges to be shipped to Chicago. He received ten Woodbines and a sick note for his troubles. Scully had wondered about the wisdom of getting tangled up with Malachy. Still, it was good to be in with someone in the Ra, even a very minor someone. Also, Malachy had a wonderful repertoire of parent-shaped handwriting.

"Yeah. It's only the first week. See how it goes," replied Scully.

"Suit yourself," said Malachy mysteriously.

"Good luck," called Scully as he dashed out the door.

"Take it handy. Tiocfaidh ár lá!" muttered Malachy, and went back to restocking the Banana Cola Taste Blasters, one of the more glamorous of his fundraising activities in the struggle to reunify Ireland and end British occupation of the North.

"Ah, go ask me arse!" Scully shouted at a honking motorist as he dodged through the traffic. He could see Greater Little Werburgh Street ahead. Judging by the pace of the grey bodies turning into it, it was still only about ten to nine. Plenty of time for a smoke.

"Now stop dawdling, Finbar, we'll be late!" chided a shrill country voice behind Scully. He felt himself involuntarily cower at the words, so expertly laden were they with that artful mixture of love, exasperation, self-sacrifice, and guilt-inducing sadness. He vaguely remembered how his own mother had used this tone on him before she went astray in the head and stopped talking to anyone in the house.

"We won't be late! Will you stop rushing? I can go the rest of the way on me own!" protested a boy's voice. To Scully's ears this voice was redolent of turf smoke, bogs, tractors, parish priests with hawthorn sticks and no front teeth, céilí dancing, mucky Wellington boots, and all other things backward and primitive that he associated with life beyond the confines of Dublin city.

"Excuse us," the shrill mothering voice instructed him. Scully moved closer to the wall and let them pass.

"That boy is going to be late," Mrs. Sullivan observed to Finbar as they bustled past him. "You wouldn't want to be late on your first day now, love, would you?"

Scully could see the boy in front of him shrink at his mother's words. He lit his smoke and saw Mrs. Sullivan's shoulders stiffen—he could sense that she was about take him to task for this filthy habit. But just as she slowed to turn around, a harsh, nasal Dublin accent came crashing into her tidy headscarf-and-overcoat world and successfully distracted her from the evils of smoking.

"Yeauw, Scully, ye manky shite!"

Scully, Mrs. Sullivan, and Finbar all looked up to see the maniacally grinning Lynch hanging off the back of a truck as it hurtled toward the docks—*scutting*, as it was known in the parlance, a much-frowned-on mode of transport punishable by automatic expulsion.

"Oh, look at that boy, Finbar! Isn't that disgraceful behaviour? He must be one of the boys from the Technical School," pronounced Mrs. Sullivan.

Finbar made no reply. Scully didn't bother to shout back; Lynch had already turned his attention to some girls from Windsor Street Convent in a passing bus.

"Vulgar boy! Should be ashamed of himself! I'm surprised even the Technical School will have him!" huffed Mrs. Sullivan, instinctively reaching for her son's hand.

Finbar awkwardly twisted away but she caught him by the collar of his blazer.

"Don't you ever let me catch you carrying on like that, do you hear me?" she scolded as they moved further ahead of Scully and turned onto Werburgh Street.

A moment later when Scully rounded the corner, he watched them: instead of heading down to the end of the street and turning into the school, they went in the main entrance to the monastery. *She'll probably offer him up as an apprentice Brother*, thought Scully.

"Fuck sake! Missed the light! Nearly ended up on the docks! Give us a drag, ye bollix!" shouted Lynch as he ran up behind Scully. His round, impish face and tiny eyes were afire with mischief.

Scully handed him the almost done butt and the bell ground out hollowly from the yard inside.

"You goin' in?" asked Lynch.

Scully nodded matter-of-factly. Lynch took one last drag, shrugged, spat, and the two of them walked slowly through the heavy lead-coloured gates.

5

"Mr. Scully, sor, you can stay standing. I think we will have a change of environment for you, eh? Keep you close to hand, out of the way of pernicious influences, where you can come to no harm, ha?"

Mr. Pollock's face belied any levity that might have been deduced from the words coming out of his mouth. He had obviously seen Scully's encounter with Brother Loughlin at the mass.

"Mr. Farrelly, take your bags, chattels, and belongings and change places with Mr. Scully."

"But sir, I can't—"

"No ifs, buts, or wherefores, Mr. Farrelly. Move yourself!" Pollock cut in.

Farrelly, who had chosen to be near the front because of his weak eyes, reluctantly took his things and moved to the back where Scully had been sitting. The desk beside Smalley Mullen remained empty.

"McDonagh?"

"Here. I mean, anseo."

"Mullen?"

"Anseo."

"O'Connor?"

"Anseo."

"Rutledge?"

"Here. Eh, anseo."

"Scully?"

"Anseo."

"Sullivan?"

"Still no sign of the elusive Mr. Sullivan."

Mr. Pollock finished the roll and then went to the large cupboard. He opened it wide to reveal stacks and stacks of tattered books. A gentle tapping on the glass of the door caught his attention. He tilted back his head in acknowledgment and strode to the door. He opened it and, turning to raise his eyebrows in preemptive warning to the class, stepped outside into the corridor.

After a few moments Finbar Sullivan walked in, followed closely by Mr. Pollock.

"Bye now, love, be good!" came Mrs. Sullivan's voice from the corridor. Finbar's guts turned to dust in embarrassment. He glanced cautiously at the icily scrutinising sea of faces in front of him.

"It appears we have found the mysterious Fionnbarr Ó Súilleabháin," announced Mr. Pollock and moved to his desk. He sat himself on his high stool and tucked his black gown around him like some balding ginger-haired bat. He reopened the roll book and started to make some notes in it. Finbar stood at the top of the class feeling very exposed. There was not one welcoming chink of light as his eyes darted from one face to the next.

A new boy presented all sorts of possibilities. Even the most picked-on and bullied boys in the class could entertain the hope that here was someone weaker than them, with a limp or a worse stutter or bigger ears; anything that might put him at the bottom of the totem pole and move them up a notch. Finbar felt himself begin to go red under the intensity of this scrutiny.

From outside in the corridor his mother's voice echoed

around mercilessly: "He's a very good boy, Brother, very bright and always has good reports. A lovely hurler, a fine footballer, and very well-behaved and mannerly. Brother Morrissey in Cork was very sorry to lose him. He was a well-liked boy. Indeed he was. I'm very sorry that Finbar missed the first day of school. I hear there was mass. It's a pity Finbar missed that. He was an altar boy, you know."

"Indeed. I'm sure he will fit in very well here, Mrs. Sullivan. I'm afraid I must leave you now and attend to pressing school matters. Good day to you now," concluded Brother Loughlin emphatically. Finbar breathed a sigh of relief and went back to trying to suppress his beetroot blushing.

Out of the corner of his eye he saw two of the boys in the front near the windows point to the door and laugh. Silently, almost telepathically, the signal passed through the class and more boys began to look toward the door. With a horrid dread in the depths of his spirit, Finbar turned to see his mother grinning and waving enthusiastically at him like she was at a parade. He made an odd movement combining a reluctant return of her wave and a gesture of barely suppressed fury shooing her away.

"Mr. Sullivan, you will take a pew at the back there beside Mr. Mullen," said Mr. Pollock without looking up from the roll book.

With huge relief Finbar hurried to the desk and sat down. Mullen did not even look at him. Finbar was now far enough down the class to be spared the sight of his mother at the door. There was little doubt that she was still there, and when Mr. Pollock finally looked up from the roll book he was compelled to wave farewell before she would leave.

"Fionnbarr Ó Súilleabháin?" he called.

"Anseo, a mháistir!" answered Finbar.

Mr. Pollock made a tick in the roll book with an extravagant flourish. The respectful and fluent-sounding "a mháistir," equivalent to a gratuitous "here, master," when a bare "here" was all that was required, brought an approving glance from Mr. Pollock. Perhaps there might be a pearl among these swine, he thought. Unsolicited and unaided use of the vocative case showed promise.

In direct and pointed contrast to Pollock's approval, Finbar could feel the air around him bristle with hostility and suspicion from the boys in the class. He put his head down and stared hard at the top of his desk. He felt his ears burn and a prickling feeling in his eyes assured him that he was indeed feeling miserable.

"Now, back to the matter of books," said Mr. Pollock from his perch on the high stool behind his desk. Before he could begin to distribute the books there was another knock at the door. Mr. Pollock beckoned the caller in.

A first year of diminutive size with outlandishly large ears entered bearing a note. He wore a uniform that he was obviously expected to grow into sometime in the next decade. A perceptible ripple of derision ran around the class. Finbar, glad for a moment to have someone else be the focus of malign attention, joined in the feeling of superiority to this hapless first year.

"Well, what is it?" clipped Mr. Pollock.

"Ehm, ehm, ehm, a note, sir," stammered the poor unfortunate.

"From whom?" pursued Mr. Pollock.

"From the Head Brudder, sir."

"And who is the Head Brother?"

"Ehm, ehm, ehm, I don't know, sir."

"And what is your name, Mr. Ehm, Ehm, Ehm, I Don't Know, Sir?"

"Anthony, sir."

"Well, *Antney, sir*, Brother Loughlin is the Head Brother."

"Ehm, ehm, ehm, Brudder Loughlin, sir," repeated Anthony carefully.

Mr. Pollock took the note from the boy's trembling hand and nodded grimly while he read it.

"Go raibh maith agat. Tell Brother Loughlin they will be there in a moment," said Mr. Pollock.

"Yes sir," answered Anthony, and darted from the class in relief.

"Mr. Bradshaw, I see by the smirk on your face that you enjoyed that little interlude. Let us see how you enjoy your visit to Brother Loughlin's office. Out! Now!" barked Mr. Pollock.

Bradshaw stood up and slowly moved toward the door.

"And you can join him, Mr. McDonagh," added Mr. Pollock.

McDonagh got up and he and Bradshaw left. The puzzlement abroad in the rest of the class was not evident in the two boys. They had a pretty good idea of what they were in for.

Mr. Pollock managed to kill the rest of the double class by inspecting all the books in the cupboard and making each boy sign for what he received. A collective sigh of relief greeted the bell that signalled the ten minutes of morning break.

6

Outside Brother Loughlin's office was not a pleasant place to be. There was nowhere but Mrs. Broderick's adjoining office to wait in. She had been at the school longer than anyone. Even Loughlin was a little scared of her. Some of the more articulate sixth years had christened her Only the Good Die Young.

McDonagh, Bradshaw, and Slater from 5-F stood awkwardly half in and half out of her office. Mrs. Broderick ignored them and harrumphed her way through whatever it was she did to pieces of paper to keep the school running. Slater and Bradshaw rubbed their palms together behind their backs to work up some heat that would dull the inevitable leathering they were going to receive. Small break had come and gone and still nothing had happened. The waiting was the worst. They knew it. Brother Loughlin knew it. It wasn't subtle but it worked.

McDonagh, Bradshaw, and Slater were not new to this experience, but this was one of the more severe raps they had been got on recently, even counting the fire in the toilets that had never been conclusively pinned on them. This time they were in for it. The three of them had been seen at the end-of-year sports day in June carrying Mr. Laverty's tiny car into the middle of the waste ground beside the Saint Francis Industrial School sports field. What annoyed Mr. Laverty more than the moving of his car were the sticky multicoloured spits they had left on the door handles and windshield.

They watched the brown door behind Mrs. Broderick's head. On the right-hand side was a little gadget with lights on it. At the moment the red light read *Engaged*. When it changed to the green *Enter* they would have to go in. They were unsure if it would be a group beating or if they would be broken down individually. Their hearts sank as they heard the unmistakable hurried squeaking of crepe-soled brothel-creepers approaching. Mr. Pollock entered, glowered at them, and wiped the sweat from his head.

Seconds later a gaggle of angry Brothers crowded into the doorway.

"I told you I would deal with this," Mr. Pollock snapped at them.

"Out of the way!"

"This is an emergency!"

"We have to see him now!"

"Brothers! Gentlemen!" weaseled Mr. Pollock in a pitch honed to cut through even the most uproarious cacophony of voices.

Brother Tobin, the Physics and Geography teacher, broke past Mr. Pollock and barged into Brother Loughlin's office waving the newspaper. "Take a look at that then!" he stammered, his tobacco-stained shock of grey hair standing up in alarm.

Brother Boland and Brother Kennedy followed Brother Tobin and soon there was a shouting match going on. Mr. Pollock strode into Brother Loughlin's office and closed the door behind him with a sickening vacuum-like *clunk*.

The boys could make out the agitated rising and falling tones inside Brother Loughlin's office but none of the words. Mrs. Broderick too was obviously trying hard to hear what was going on, but as soon as she noticed the boys were aware of this, she glowered at them contemptuously and went back to stapling bits of official-looking paper to other differently coloured bits of official-looking paper.

Mr. Pollock's head suddenly appeared in the crack of the open door: "You boys, yes, you boys there, back to your classes! We'll deal with you later."

A reprieve? No way. They were dead. It was just a question of time. Whatever was going on, it was just temporary. Nonetheless, they were all pleased by the worried look on Mr. Pollock's face. They were so elated, in fact, that on the way back to class they stopped in the outside toilets for a smoke.

"Well, what do you say to that?" challenged Brother Tobin as he pushed the paper into Brother Loughlin's pudgy hands. Brother Loughlin and Mr. Pollock went into a little managerial huddle over the paper and read:

> *We, Fionn and Patrick Sweeney, hereby make known our application for planning permission for development on the site of The Brothers of Godly Coercion School for Young Boys of Meagre Means at Greater Little Werburgh Street, North, in the city of Dublin (Lot #867-3D/9A, Folio 4287 of the Register of Freeholds) for the construction of a storage and warehouse facility to service the nearby port and docks on this day of September nineteenth . . .*

"This is outrageous," blustered Brother Loughlin. "This cannot be right. There must be some mistake. We'll get to the bottom of this and there will be no more about it!"

"They're out to destroy the Brotherhood," hissed Brother Boland.

"Who's they?"

"Those Sweeneys and their cronies, whoever they are."

"Probably with the Labour Party."

"I don't remember ever teaching any Sweeney at this school."

"Brothers, Brothers, stop this nonsense! I will take care of this. It is some silly clerical misunderstanding. I'll get to the bottom of it," cried Brother Loughlin above the din.

"When?" asked Brother Boland, unconvinced.

"Now! So please get back to your duties and I will take care of mine." Brother Loughlin waved his hand imperiously toward the door.

"I don't like the sound of it, I tell you, not one bit," worried Brother Boland as he left.

"No, that's fine, I'll wait . . . Yes . . . Thank you," Brother Loughlin muttered into the mouthpiece of his telephone. This was his fifth call.

Mr. Pollock paced the room nervously and looked out through the wire-reinforced glass onto the drab street and the burnt-out garage across the way. Brother Loughlin was finding the slow, badly oiled wheels of local government a little trying. He was on his third cigarette already and he normally waited to smoke until after lunch when Mrs. Broderick brought him his two o'clock cup of tea.

"They're putting me onto someone higher up," he informed Mr. Pollock, who was not at all concerned by this apparent threat. He was convinced it was a prank. He just wanted to be sure so they could wholeheartedly get back to dealing with McDonagh, Bradshaw, and Slater. It was the best excuse for vindictiveness that had come his way since May and he was not going to let it slip by. It was always healthy to start off a new year with a good punishing of recidivist troublemakers.

7

Right then, you ungovernable rabble. Settle down!" Brother Kennedy strode up and down in front of the boys. He was not at all happy about this, but the Conclave of Brothers Superiors had decided that if the Department of Education was going to insist on Physical Education classes, it could not be trusted to a lay teacher to administer them in a manner guaranteed to preserve the Brothers' ethos. Brother Kennedy had been selected by lot. His knowledge of Physical Education was limited and extended little further than the precepts laid down for the Brothers in a recent circular from the National Conclave that exhorted them to abstain from:

1. The use of intoxicating drink.
2. The wearing of soft hats (berets and birettas excluded).
3. The public fondling of young boys.
4. Peering into trams, omnibuses, hansom cabs, taxis, or other public conveyances likely to cause impure thoughts.

A quick survey of the list left Brother Kennedy with two fairly uncontroversial if useless principles to impart as a philosophy of Physical Education.

"How many of you here wear soft hats or peer into trams or buses?" he asked suddenly. No one moved. Experience had taught them that open-ended questions without clearly defined consequences attached to the answers were best avoided. No one even dared to point out that trams had not run in Dublin for years.

"Well, let me tell you that whether you do or don't do either of those things, if you are not vigilant you will find yourselves drifting into such depraved activities. It may begin with soft woolly hats, but mark my words, it will not end there. Then there will be the trilby, the fedora, the soft slouch, or any number of feeble pieces of millenary, and before you know it, you will find yourself peering into public conveyances with lustful intent, and that way lies sickness and depravity and the path to Hell and damnation."

Brother Kennedy paused for breath. His bald head was already glowing bright red with the exertion of his discourse.

"You, boy, what is your name?"

"Vincent O'Connor."

"Vincent O'Connor, BROTHER!" Brother Kennedy barked.

"Vincent O'Connor, Brother," O'Connor replied.

"What sports do you play, O'Connor?"

"Ehm, football, relievio."

"Define football."

"Soccer."

"Soccer, BROTHER!"

"Soccer, Brother."

"Soccer, ha! Bloody vile foreign garrison game! And what is relievio?"

"You have two teams and one tries to catch the other and put them in the den, but if you get in the den without being caught and shout *Relievio*, then all your team are free again," explained O'Connor.

"That is not a sport! That is a corner boy's street game! Out to the line!"

As they were standing in the middle of the gym hall, no one was quite sure where the line was supposed to be. O'Connor took a guess and started walking toward the stage.

"Not over there, you fool," cried Brother Kennedy and swooped toward him. He grabbed the boy by the hairs above the ears and dragged him over to the side of the hall near the climbing ropes. "If you don't know what you are supposed to be doing, ASK!" he shouted, and delivered a couple of strong raps to the boy's head to enforce his point. "You, boy! What's your name?"

"Francis Scully . . . Brother."

Brother Kennedy arched what traces of eyebrows he had at him. "And what sports do you play, Scully?"

"Pullin' me prick," whispered McDonagh behind Scully.

"Pullin', ehm," began Scully. McDonagh drew in his breath sharply. There'd be murder. "Ehm, what do you call it, Brother? Pullin' me, ehm, the rope, like, tug of war!" announced Scully triumphantly.

"That is not a sport, you stupid amadán!" shouted Brother Kennedy.

"But it's in the community games, Brother," protested Scully.

"I'll community-games you! Out to the line!"

Scully joined O'Connor beside the climbing ropes. They both started rubbing their hands together behind their backs.

"You, boys! Hands by your sides!" called Brother Kennedy across the hall. He knew well what they were doing. He had not spent thirty years leathering recalcitrant thugs without learning a thing or two.

Scully and O'Connor sullenly complied.

"You, boy, there, what's your name now?"

"Finbar Sullivan, Brother."

"Oh, the new boy. Quite a Gaelic footballer and a hurler, I believe," mused Brother Kennedy approvingly.

Finbar felt himself severely on the spot. He could sense the swell of scrutiny press around him. He had to do something or he would be marked as a "good pupil," and it would be doubtful if he could make it through the week.

"Only when the soccer season is over, Brother," he found himself saying. It was like someone had gotten inside his head and was finding new circuits in his makeup that he had never known before. It was by equal measure exhilarating and frightening.

Brother Kennedy stared at him in disbelief. This was inconceivable. It was all very well for Dublin guttersnipes to know no better than the street game of soccer, but for a boy from the noble County of Cork to not only know how to play Gaelic games but to turn his back on them deliberately in favour of the foreign evil of soccer was beyond perfidy.

"Out to the line, you ingrate!" he barked, the veins in his forehead showing dark blue against the bright red of his skull.

In twenty minutes all except Maher, who'd had polio and wore braces on his legs and thus could not reasonably be victimised for his lack of sports playing, at least not on the first day, were standing on the line.

Brother Kennedy contemplated the group. He walked right up to Finbar, his eyes gleaming malevolently. "Go to Brother Loughlin and ask him for the extra leather," he hissed, and frog-marched Finbar to the door. "And no delaying or I'll have your guts for garters."

Finbar stood outside Mrs. Broderick's office and tapped lightly on the door frame.

"What is it you want?" Mrs. Broderick lifted her head and brought the full force of her cold, empty stare to bear on him.

"Ehm, Brother Kennedy sent me to, ehm, get a leather, the extra leather."

"Brother Loughlin is in the monastery." She pointed across the yard with her twiglike fingers and offered no further explanation.

"But, but—"

"No buts, young man. You were sent to Brother Loughlin and to Brother Loughlin you will go. I'm sure he'll have some words of advice for you."

Finbar walked heavily across the yard and past the downstairs lab. He edged in the door, and just beyond the corridor that led to the back lab he saw the big double door to the monastery. He pushed it open carefully and was assaulted immediately by the smell. The predominant odour was one of floor wax, but within it were tinges of old cabbage, sweat, and whatever toxic thing Mrs. McCurtin, the housekeeper, used to polish the brasses. Finbar breathed as shallowly as his mounting unease would let him. His shoes squeaked on the polished floor. The silence around him seemed to be weighing the moment, gauging when the best time would be to pounce and devour him.

Finbar glanced down the dim corridor toward the end, where there seemed to be some kind of atrium presided over by an altar to Our Lady of Indefinite Duration, a sort of theological by-product of Heisenberg's Uncertainty Principle and much beloved of the Brotherhood. He had no idea where he was going but the atrium seemed to promise more light than any of the other options and certainly the stairs to his left did not seem at all inviting.

He tiptoed down the corridor to minimise the squeaking of his shoes. He froze when he heard the soft sounds behind him. It sounded like a small bird trapped in a cardboard box. He pressed himself against the wall; his mind blanked. The weird fluttering stopped. The subsequent silence was if anything more eerie. Almost on the edge of hearing, Finbar noticed a light rustling sound. He slid back along the corridor toward the bottom of the stairs. Through the banisters he saw a shape on the stairs hugging the wall.

Finbar watched aghast as Brother Boland whispered and cooed to the wall while he ran his hands lovingly over the mortar between the large granite stones. He inched back from the stairs as quietly as he could.

"You, boy! What are you doing there?"

Finbar spun round to see Loughlin striding down the corridor toward him. Behind him he heard Brother Boland flutter back up the stairs on his feet of ashes.

"Brother Kennedy sent me for the extra leather."

Loughlin slowed his pace to a menacing stalk and it was then that Finbar saw Father Fury coming out of what was presumably the refectory and fidgeting down the corridor toward Brother Loughlin. Father Fury moved in short, angular motions with more energy than seemed necessary. He had the wiry build of a lightweight boxer and his thin lips pursed at regular intervals, the only animation in his narrow, suspicious face. He looked like a bad-tempered, constipated ferret.

"Ah, Father Fury. You finished your tea. Good. Just in time. I have here before me one of our specimens who seems to be hell-bent on ending up in a reformatory. Brother Kennedy sent him for the extra leather."

Father Fury nodded solemnly at this news: "I saw many of his ilk when I was chaplain here, Brother Loughlin."

"You did indeed, but you stood for no nonsense. And how are the boys at Saint Bodhrán's?"

"No better, no worse. Deaf or blind or both."

"I'm sure that keeps them out of trouble."

"You'd think it would. They find their own ways of devilment."

Brother Loughlin nodded understandingly and returned his attention to Finbar: "Well . . . Mr. . . . uhm . . ."

"Sullivan," Finbar volunteered.

"Ah yes, the new boy. Seems you're already contagioned by the blackguardism abroad within these walls. Falling in with the wrong crowd already, I'll bet!"

Slowly Loughlin took the extra leather from the side pocket of his cassock.

"Let me warn you, my young bucko, that if you start out this way here, it will be a very short trip to the Industrial School for you. Do you understand?" spat Loughlin as he gave Finbar two rapid stinging belts on each hand. "Mind your step, or I'll mind it for you." Loughlin held the leather out to Finbar. "Now take that to Brother Kennedy with my compliments."

Finbar took the leather and felt its weight in his hot, throbbing hands. He left the monastery and walked back toward the hall feeling with each step more humiliated by carrying the leather that would soon be used to beat him.

Finbar walked back into the hall and Brother Kennedy sent him to the end of the line. "We shall save the best for last," he taunted, taking the extra leather from him. "White vest!" *Whap!* "White shorts!" *Whap!* "White socks!" *Whap!* "White running shoes!" *Whap!* "Next week!" *Whap!*

Brother Kennedy went along the line and gave each boy five stinging tastes of the leather on the right hand and reminded them of the correct attire to bring along for Physical Education class the following week. Twice he had to pause to catch his breath. Finbar got an extra final belt called "Ingrate" for his supposed betrayal of his noble rural heritage for the pernicious influence of soccer.

"Tell him you only play soccer and he'll put you on the special line," whispered Lynch to the bunch of third years who entered the hall as they were leaving.

"You're a bastard, Lynch," said McDonagh.

"Yeah, and you're a farty little bollix," answered Lynch.

"What time is it?" asked Scully.

"Twenty-five past," answered McDonagh.

"What's next?" asked Lynch.

"French, with Laverty," interjected Finbar, who was walking out behind them.

Scully turned and stared coldly at him. He shook his head and turned away again. Finbar was not worth a confrontation.

8

Bawn jourz mayzsewerz!" drawled Mr. Laverty as the boys bundled in the door. "Veuwz ets arreevayz trays tard. Poor kwoh?" His best qualification for being a French teacher seemed to be that he cycled a lot and his wife was French. He spoke the language with his own drawling nasal Dublin accent, pronouncing all the letters in a way that one is not really supposed to do. As far as anyone in the school was concerned, that was the way French was spoken. Of course, the Brothers would have much preferred that the language be taught with a nice Galway or Kerry accent, but they had to take what they could get.

"Brother Kennedy kept us back," ventured McDonagh, guessing at what Mr. Laverty was talking at them about.

"Oh, did he now?"

The boys nodded.

"Sit down."

The boys moved to their seats.

"Hey yew?"

Finbar stopped in his tracks and turned around.

"Me, sir?"

"Yeah, yew, sur. Commont sappellaayze vouze?"

"Je m'appelle Finbar Sullivan, monsieur professeur."

Even Mr. Laverty could not fail to notice that out of this exchange Finbar sounded more like the one capable of speaking French. "Right, Meester Sullivan. Sit down then," he said sharply and eyed Finbar suspiciously.

Mr. Laverty stood awkwardly in front of the class. It was useless for him to even attempt to cut an imposing figure. He had a big chalk stain on his nose and wore the jacket and trousers of two different cheap blue pinstriped suits. Both were tatty and ingrained with years of chalk dust and shiny grime. He distributed the French books from the cupboard and had the boys sign for them.

"Right, now, you're going to write a short essay entitled 'Mon ay tay,' my summer." He looked at the clock. "Youse have thirty minutes."

With that he sat back at the desk and started to write in some important-looking papers. He was filling out a job application for Southwell, the Jesuit school. It was something at least, something to attempt to quell the lung-hardening sense of dejection and purposelessness that took over the moment he set foot in Werburgh Street. It only got worse when he found himself standing in front of these reluctant faces with no interest in Maupassant beyond, at best, writing English translations between the lines.

"Sir, sir, sir!" implored McDonagh.

Mr. Laverty glanced up wearily. "What is it, McDonagh?"

"How do you say 'The woman from the dole with the broken briefcase came to see me da'?"

"Use something else simpler," sighed Mr. Laverty.

McDonagh nodded enthusiastically and then drew an exaggerated look of puzzlement across his face.

"What is it now, McDonagh?"

"How do you say 'woman,' sir?"

"Get outside the door, McDonagh."

That was sometimes Mr. Laverty's thing. If he was feeling sporting, he didn't actually send you to Brother Loughlin. He just put you outside the door, and if you happened to get caught then you got a hiding. It was a game of roulette and gave the boys, Mr. Laverty felt, a fair chance and took all responsibility away from him. McDonagh closed the door softly behind him and pushed himself into the alcove where coats were supposed to hang.

Mr. Laverty opened the door. "Out against the wall where I can see you," he hissed into the reverberating emptiness of the corridor. McDonagh reluctantly moved to the other side of the corridor where he knew he would be visible from either end, thus increasing his chances of being caught. "Ye pays yer money and ye takes yer chances," observed Mr. Laverty and returned to his class.

The hands on the clock crawled round their course as the boys flipped through their French books looking for sentences they could use. There seemed to be no lessons in this course that concerned scutting on the back of speeding trucks or smoking loose cigarettes in laneways or inventing lies about feeling up girls or any of the other activities that had occupied them over the summer.

A perfunctory knock at the door announced the intrusion of a Brother into the class of a lay teacher. This was always done with the minimum of ceremony or apology, as if to remind the lay teachers that they were only there on sufferance until the inevitable upsurge in vocations to the Brotherhood.

"Mr. Laverty, a moment of your time," announced Brother Mulligan imperiously as he entered.

Mr. Laverty smiled coldly and went to sit on the windowsill.

Brother Mulligan was by all conservative estimates in his late nineties. He was only recently retired from teaching and now spent his time collecting pennies for the Missions, selling scapulars, medals, and rosary beads, and conducting other minor evangelical tasks. He wobbled and shimmered like someone who was not quite real; you could not look at him for too long without feeling that the film you were watching had stuck in the projector and was about to burn to bits.

"Mr. Laverty, I think it would be helpful if that boy outside the door was returned to the class so he could hear this with the rest of them."

Mr. Laverty slouched over to the door and yanked it open: "McDonagh, get in here and stand in the corner and listen to what the Brother has to say."

Brother Mulligan placed himself under the crucifix that hung above the blackboard and cleared his throat theatrically. "Now, you boys are approaching a point in your lives when you must begin to make decisions for yourselves. This can be a difficult and frightening time. Do I join the Electricity Supply Board? Do I try for junior clerical assistant in the Department of Fisheries? Do I acknowledge who I really am, abandon notions of uppitiness, and leave school to get an apprenticeship in one of the trades or a delivery job with a prosperous grocer? These are all important questions. But there is another question that it is time for you boys to ask yourselves: Do I hear a call? Do I feel the need to give something back in gratitude for what I have received?

"Do I think that with the help of the Holy Ghost, Our Lady of Indefinite Duration, and Venerable Saorseach O'Rahilly, I could make the commitment to the Brotherhood? Do I think I am ready for such a challenge?

"Look deep inside. Sit for a few moments and see if you hear a calling. Close your eyes and picture the Holy Ghost. You, boy! You, boy, there, with the big ears! Close your eyes now! I will tell you when to open them again! Now, repeat after me: Oh Lord, if it be Your will that I waste my life in penury and uselessness, then send not the Holy Ghost to guide me to the Brotherhood where I can atone for the sins, original, venial, and mortal, that damn my soul to the fires of Hell.

"We will now sit in silence and wait for an answer to our prayers for a vocation."

The silence that followed was punctuated by sporadic giggling, two operatic farts, a couple of warning hisses from Mr. Laverty, and one brief two-stroke leathering that Brother Mulligan administered to Bradshaw for no discernible reason. As leatherings went, those meted out by Brother Mulligan were hardly vicious but they did not really create an atmosphere conducive to a visitation by the Holy Ghost or any other supernatural entity.

"Now open your eyes, you boys!"

Mr. Laverty threw a piece of chalk at Scully to wake him up.

"Now, every boy will take a small piece of paper. If you think you may have a calling you will write your name on that piece of paper. Every boy will hand one up. If you are not interested, leave the paper blank. This will be conducted in strict confidence and writing down your name does not bind you into anything final. No one else will know if you have a vocation or not. Is that clear?"

The boys nodded and started rummaging for paper.

"Brother, what size paper should we use?"

"Any size, you fool!"

"Brother, if the Holy Ghost came to me but about something different, should I write my name down?"

"Only if you think you might have a vocation."

"Brother, will the Holy Ghost be able to read my name in Irish?"

"The pieces of paper are not for the Holy Ghost, you stupid amadán!"

"Brother, does it matter what colour pen you use if you aren't writing your name?" asked Lynch, eager to outdo.

"God help me!" gasped Brother Mulligan.

"Get out and join McDonagh in the corner, Lynch," drawled Mr. Laverty.

Lynch stood up with a look of total innocence comically plastered across his face. He stood beside McDonagh in the corner and looked hard at the floor.

"The Holy Ghost is colour blind, ye sap!" whispered McDonagh. Lynch looked even harder at the floor. They could easily get a fatal attack of the giggles at this stage.

"Now then, fold the papers twice and pass them to the front. If I see anyone looking at them there'll be trouble, I can tell you. Ha, Mr. Laverty?" babbled Brother Mulligan.

"Oh yeah, trouble, Brother," agreed the teacher tonelessly.

Brother Mulligan gathered up the papers and counted them to make sure that everyone had given him one and then shuffled out, leaving the door wide open behind him.

Mr. Laverty turned to Lynch and McDonagh. "What're we going to do with these two eejits? Sit down, yiz pair o' goms," he commanded, and shut the door with a crack.

Hardly had Mr. Laverty started back into his application form when Brother Mulligan was back at the door, this time accompanied by Brother Cox. "Brian Egan!" announced Brother Cox.

Egan stood up, dumbfounded. "It wasn't me! I didn't do anything! I swear, Brother, I didn't! It couldn't have been me! I wasn't there! I didn't do it!" he pleaded.

"Yes. Yes. There's no trouble, Brian. We just want to have a little chat."

Egan stood rooted to the spot. Brian? What the fuck?

They never, ever called you by your first name. Then a jolt of understanding smacked him in the face. Some stupid shithead had put his name down for a vocation. He peered around the class, searching the faces for the telltale signs of having set him up. Scully met his eyes and smiled mischievously.

Bastard! mouthed Egan at him.

Scully gave him an ironic thumbs-up.

"Brian, we'll step outside where we can chat in peace," murmured Brother Cox. Brother Mulligan beamed broadly in a way that made Egan feel very uncomfortable. Dazed, he followed them out the door.

"In strict confidence. That's a laugh!" muttered Mr. Laverty to himself. "Youse have five minutes to finish your essays," he informed the class, and went back to embellishing his résumé in the hope of wrangling his way onto the junior staff at Southwell. Anywhere, anywhere but here.

"Sir, how do you say 'My brother found a gas mask in the canal' in French?"

"Just use something else." Christ on a crutch, would this class never end?

A slight commotion outside the door caught Mr. Laverty's eye. Evidently Brother Mulligan and Brother Cox had lost all interest in using Egan's first name because they were now hitting him with all their limited strength and pushing him toward the stairs.

"A joke? A joke? I'll show you a joke!" shouted Brother Mulligan as he ineffectually flailed at Egan with his leather. "Get down those stairs in front of me!"

"Settle down," snapped Mr. Laverty as a ripple of murmurs made its way round the class. He folded up his job application and put it in his bag. He glanced at the clock and the Angelus bell rang out from the yard below. "Pass your essays up to the top of the row, the angel of the Lord declared unto Mary . . ." he said, waving his right hand in front of his face in a barely discernible blessing motion.

"And she conceived of the Holy Ghost," mumbled the boys as they stood up and passed their tatty essays to the front.

Outside, Egan's receding voice echoed up the stairs: "But, but, but, but . . ."

"I'll but you! Into the monastery!" shouted Brother Cox.

"Hail Mary full of grace, the Lord is . . ." continued Mr. Laverty as the lunchtime bell ground out its promise of temporary relief as soon as the praying was over.

In the ground floor Chemistry lab Mr. Barry thrust his hands deep into the pockets of his once-white lab coat and sighed heavily. He regarded the rows of confused first year faces in front of him and felt a hot, withering flush of despair at the thought that he would have to teach these dim-witted boys three times a week for the next nine months.

"We'll try it once again: energy can neither be created nor destroyed, it can only be changed from one form to another. You there with the greasy hair, repeat."

"Ehm, energy can either be created or . . ." struggled You There with the Greasy Hair.

"Destroyed . . ." prompted Mr. Barry impatiently.

"Destroyed . . ." repeated You There hopefully, and fell silent again.

"Enough!" sighed Mr. Barry. "Copy this down and write it out fifty times for homework. Let's see if some of it sticks in those empty heads of yours."

He turned to the two-tiered blackboard and rolled it to a blank spot. He had deliberately left some fifth year notes on photosynthesis there to show these puny first years what a wonderful, arcane, and difficult subject he was master of. Just as he put the chalk to the blackboard there was a heaving creak from the back of the class.

The wall supporting the huge periodic table gave way and the whole thing collapsed onto the workbench below. Mr. Barry spun around to watch glass fly all over the place as the wooden bars from the top and bottom of the chart smashed retorts, beakers, alembics, test tubes, and glass piping that had been sitting on the bench.

As suddenly as there had been noise there was silence again, and Mr. Barry looked at the crumpled mess of masonry, canvas, wood, and glass at the back of the lab. So many years of his career had been put into that periodic table and making the stupider boys polish the glassware instead of doing experiments. He remembered all the times he had climbed up with his red paint to add new elements to the table as they were discovered. It was what photo albums were to other people. This was the chart of his career and now it was a crumpled, seething heap being eaten away by the acids carelessly left sitting in the beakers. Heartlessly oblivious to the tragedy, the lunch bell rang. Mr. Barry hastily galloped through the Angelus and, deciding that there might be some harmful fumes from the concoction that had formed on the bench, he instructed the boys to leave quietly by the door that led into the monastery.

In the high-ceilinged refectory the Brothers sat around the long pine table, each in his appointed arse-shined chair. The paltry light that struggled through the high stained-glass windows cast an unhealthy green pall over the room.

"It's a miracle, that's what it is!" beamed Brother Tobin to wide indifference.

"It's those yahoos we let in from the flats, I tell you.

We should never have let the Department of Education foist them on us," whispered Brother Kennedy.

"They wouldn't dare!" hissed Brother Boland, appalled that anyone in the school would attempt such an outrage as sabotage.

"Well, the laboratory wall didn't collapse by itself. And what about the slates off the roof on the first day back? Answer me that!" countered Brother Kennedy.

Brother Boland opened his mouth to speak but allowed nothing more than a glottal stop to emerge when he saw Widower Frawley enter the refectory with the soup trolley. It was not right to speak of brotherly affairs in front of civilians.

Widower Frawley pushed the trolley around the long narrow table and ladled soup into the bowls whether there was anyone sitting in front of them or not. It wasn't for the likes of him to wonder whether particular Brothers were late or if they were not coming to lunch. If they didn't turn up he would just put it back in the pot, skin and all, and Mrs. McCurtin could use it as the base for the next day's soup.

When the squeaking of the trolley wheels and the clumsy scuffing of Widower Frawley's slippers receded into the kitchen, Brother Boland resumed. "It's not the boys. It's something else. Something other," he whispered darkly. He had no words for the tension he could sense in the walls, in the doorways. He could hear it in the creak of the stairs. He could almost smell it in the corridors. There was a tiredness, a sadness vibrating inside things. It was humming to him alone. He could not explain it to them. He shook his head in frustration, set his dentures on his side plate, and began slurping at his soup.

"Are you sure it isn't a miracle? Imagine! BLESSED

Saorseach O'Rahilly!" enthused Brother Tobin. He, like so many of the Brothers, yearned for a miracle to push O'Rahilly along the road to sainthood.

"Go away with you now, you and your miracles!" scoffed Brother Kennedy.

Brother Boland glanced nervously around the table. He noted with curiosity the empty places of Brothers Cox, Loughlin, and Mulligan. He did not know that they were otherwise engaged in trying to beat a vocation out of Brian Egan.

Brother Tobin gobbled down his stew, took a couple of mouthfuls of warm custard, and ran upstairs for a very hurried Grace After Meals.

"Calm down, child, can't you?" hissed Brother Loughlin, his voice choked to creepy strangeness by the attempt to sound concerned.

Still sobbing and trembling and on the edge of hyperventilation, Egan sat on the chair in front of the Brother's desk.

"You've had a fall, a bit of a fright," said Brother Cox softly.

"You pushed me!" choked Egan. "You tried to feel me balls!"

"I don't know what you think happened on the stairs, Mr. Egan, but I don't think that is the type of talk you want going around the school about you now, is it?" asked Brother Loughlin.

Egan looked up at him through his red eyes.

"And I certainly don't think you want to discuss this filthy talk with your mother and father, do you?"

"But . . . but . . ."

Sensing that he had Egan on the back foot, Brother

Loughlin pressed home: "And you know what the other boys will say, don't you? They'll say you were asking for it. They'll say you started it. They'll say that it was wishful thinking on your part. They'll say that it is you who are a little suspect. I think you would find things here very difficult if such rumours were to get out."

Egan half heard Brother Loughlin's words as if from the bottom of a dusty well shaft. Clearer to him were the images they conjured up: the sly comments in the toilets, the graffiti that would begin to appear in the bicycle sheds and the handball alleys and slowly creep through the whole school. The more he thought about it, the worse it got. Cox had a reputation and he was forever patting his favourites on the arse. But if anything got out about him and Cox in any way, it was sure that everyone would think the worst. He'd be branded.

"So why don't you take a little half day for yourself and we'll have no more of this silly talk?" coaxed Brother Loughlin. "I'll send someone for your bags and we'll have Brother Walsh drive you home."

"No!" shrieked Egan. He'd take the bus. He'd walk. Anything but have one of the Brothers drive him home. Even if no one was home, everyone on the street would see and they'd say something when his ma came in from work. Then he'd have to explain. "I'll get the bus."

"Very well then. Brothers, if I could have a word with Brian alone?" concluded Brother Loughlin.

Brothers Mulligan and Cox shuffled out and closed the door carefully behind them.

"Now, Brian, why don't you show me exactly what you think Brother Cox tried to do to you . . ."

9

After lunch Scully, Lynch, and McDonagh trudged up the stairs, Lynch pushing his way through a bunch of sixth years who had one look at him and thought the better of taking issue with it. That was the way with Lynch. Even as a first year he had been going around intimidating third years. It wasn't that he was particularly big or strong looking. He just had that crazed broken-glass glint in his eye of someone who really didn't give a shit. Few things are scarier than people who are so perfectly untouched by any sense of caution or consequence. One of the few reasons Lynch was in school at all was that it was a condition of his da's parole. It was not a great setup but it did keep his da off his back.

Mr. Murphy was already in the class pulling things from his bag when they arrived. Known to a lot of the boys as Spud, Mr. Murphy was one of the only soft places in the rocky barren landscape of the teaching staff. He was supposedly the History teacher, but even those who really liked him had to admit that he was a hopeless instructor in any conventional sense of getting the crap that you needed for exams into your head. He was, however, generally regarded as a good sort.

Spud had a mischievous twinkle of light in his eye and a ready smile that set him apart. The Brothers just about tolerated him, knowing from their last attempt that he kept a thorough diary and they could not fire him without some very solid pretext. The other lay teachers resented him and his easy way with the boys which they felt undermined their authority. He could not have cared less.

Spud closed the classroom door and the atmosphere was unlike anything Finbar had so far experienced. Gone was the boys' wary, watchful belligerence. Instead it felt like a bright airy space where laughter might erupt at any second. Everyone relaxed in the knowledge that you had to really piss Spud off before anything nasty would happen.

"Having a good return to school, genitalmen?" asked Spud.

"Are you?" called McDonagh.

Spud grinned. He had taught most of these boys since first year. Even though many had failed History in their Inter Cert, they would persist with it, knowing that under Spud's tutelage they would probably fail it in the Leaving Cert too. The important thing was to have three classes a week where they came in contact with someone who seemed to be from the same planet as them.

"Oh yeah, delighted to be back," he droned in a pained tone.

The boys laughed. Finbar was at first shocked by this sound, so alien to the school. It felt like he was temporarily inside some charmed circle.

"Well, anyway. It looks like I will have you lot in my nightmares for another two years then. Anyone new?" Spud peered around the class.

Finbar could feel himself going red again. Should he

put his hand up or just hope the question would go away? Smalley Mullen was having none of it. "Bogman is new!" he called out. Finbar reluctantly raised his hand.

"I assume that is not your real name."

"No sir. Finbar Sullivan, sir."

"And where did you come from, Finbar?"

"Eh, Cork City, sir."

There were a few giggles and echoes of Finbar's accent and Spud raised his eyebrows in tired admonishment. He nodded and, as he pulled another piece of paper from his bag, added: "That's nice. My mother was from Cork. Well, Finbar, welcome to the stately pleasure dome of Little Werburgh Street. They're not as bad as they seem. That's the boys, I mean. The staff are another kettle of different-coloured horses that you'll have to make up your own mind about."

A furtive mole-faced first year knocked at the door and Spud waved him in.

"Brother Loughlin sent . . ." He glanced at the note he clutched in his hand, then passed it to the teacher and bit his lip.

The note was in Irish and informed Spud that Brian Egan was indisposed and would be going home for the rest of the day, and that the bearer of the note was to be allowed to remove his things from class. Spud smiled wryly. For all the effort and beating that seemed to go into teaching the boys Irish, it was ironic that the Brothers still felt certain it was an impenetrable code for confidential messages.

"Where does Brian Egan sit?" he asked.

A chill silence fell over the class and Halloran, who sat beside Egan, raised his hand. Scully stared straight ahead of him into some unfocused distance that he wished was about four hours ago. Spud packed Egan's things into the large bag and gave it to the first year.

"Can you manage there?" asked Spud.

"Yes sir," squeaked the boy, and lurched out the door.

Spud closed the door behind him and turned to the class. "What kind of 'indisposed' was Brian Egan?" he asked levelly.

They all looked at him blankly.

"What happened to him?" Spud asked again.

"Brother Mulligan . . ."

"Vocations . . ."

"Put his name down . . ."

"Cox came . . ."

"Out in the corridor . . ."

"Lost the head . . ."

"Don't know . . ."

Spud shook his head sadly. "So what the hell happened? Brian put his name down for a vocation? Was he off his head?" He looked from face to evasive face. The boys avoided making eye contact and exuded silence like waves of heat off a road. "Oh no! Don't tell me! Did one of ye put his name down? Is that what happened?"

There was an involuntary tightening of the boys' silence.

"That's it, isn't it? One of ye put his bloody name down as a joke! Jesus wept! Have ye no sense? I mean lads, really, what were ye thinking?" He walked to the window and leaned his forehead against the glass.

Scully glanced up at the teacher and then back down at his desk. Bad sweat gathered in his armpits.

Spud pulled away from the window and sat down heavily on the radiator. "What did ye think would happen? Eh? Ye know what they're like, don't ye? Did ye really think it would be just a quick joke and then all over with?"

The fog of silence reluctantly admitted that was what

they thought would happen but should have known better.

"Did ye have it in for Brian? Did ye want to see them beat the lard out of him for some particular reason? Did he do something to ye? Or was it just plain stupid badness?"

Spud paused and walked to the centre of the class. He faced the boys and waited for his own silence to make them look up.

"All right, I know ye're not bad kids. I know ye like to mess around and have a laugh. There's no harm in that, but this sort of thing? This is stupid, thoughtless, and if ye think about it, sly and cowardly. If one of ye has something against Brian Egan or anyone else in the class, have it out with him, don't do this sort of crap. Look, lads, it's bad enough for ye without ye turning on one another like that and offering the Brothers easy targets. Just think before ye do things, can ye? Everything has consequences. Try to see them before ye act, will ye?"

The boys nodded reluctantly and Spud walked to the cupboard to retrieve and distribute *The Harbingers of the Age of Reason*, which would be their History textbook for the next two years.

When Spud left, Brother Walsh came in and launched straight into dictating his Geography notes from teacher-training college fifteen years before, which the boys had to copy down verbatim. After a double class of that, Larry Skelly arrived to give them their Civics lesson. Skelly had once been a French teacher, until a lot of expensive audio-visual equipment that the Department of Education had forced on the unwilling and suspicious Brothers had found its way into his car. Tenured, unfireable, and a cousin of the secretary of the Department of Education, Skelly was relegated to teaching Civics and giving career guidance.

He was not a bad sort and was fairly easygoing about his annual career assessment of the boys who came to his office one by one and told him they wanted to be brain surgeons, freelance astronauts, messenger boys for grocery shops, firemen, and gang lords. He knew and they knew that most of them would never get anywhere beyond the lowest levels of the Civil Service or the Electricity Supply Board or the rare Gaelic football prodigy who might get slid into a sinecure in the bank.

Skelly sat at his desk with a big tired sigh, dug out his Civics book, and started to read aloud. It was with great relief that the boys realised he was quite happy to let them put their heads on their desks while he did this.

Around the whole school the desultoriness of last class gasped its way toward the final bell.

"Ethanol is a colourless, tasteless liquid with a very low boiling point . . ." *Scribble, scribble, scribble*. "The common chemical formula for ethanol is . . ." *Scribble, scribble, scribble* . . .

"A, ab, absque, coram, de, palam, cum and ex, or e, sine, tenus, pro and prae, super, subter, sub and in, when rest not motion 'tis they mean. Now, these are the prepositions that take the ablative case. There is no other way to learn this except to learn it . . ."

"Now, the main fishing ports of Portugal are? . . . Aherne?"

"So taking x squared y and dividing across both sides we get the solution y=3x4 and from that we plot the curve. Any questions?"

"Ye're nothing but a pack of guttersnipes and I don't know why I even bother wasting my time trying to teach ye! I'd get better results from a pack of monkeys!"

It was twenty-five past three and there was only one fixed idea in everyone's mind: in five minutes the bell would ring and it would all be over for another day. That was what mattered. The fishing ports of Portugal and the properties of ethanol could go fuck themselves, along with the dative case in Irish, the poetry of Sebastian Cathach, Venn diagrams, the terrors of Hell reserved for those who touch themselves improperly, and all the other guff that was filling the air as the clock counted down. Two minutes before the bell the surreptitious packing up began. Scully was already completely packed and was sharing the Civics book with the reluctant Leake in the desk beside him.

Five, four, three, two, one . . . Nothing. The seconds began to crawl by. The boys grew edgy. This was not right. Valuable seconds of their misspendable youth were being stolen from them.

In the yard the clock above the main door sat silent, the seconds whirring away but no sound of release from the bell.

"Ignore question 3 and do questions 4, 5, and 8 on page 13 and also question 12 on page 15," called Mr. Pollock as he wrote the homework out on the board for his sixth year Geography class. He turned and flicked through his book looking for more questions.

"Sir . . ." said Molloy tentatively.

"Mr. Molloy?"

"Ehm, the bell didn't go."

"Correct, Mr. Molloy."

"Ehm, but it's twenty-five to four, sir."

"Question 11 on page 15 and question 14 on page 16," continued Mr. Pollock dismissively.

The boys sighed and glowered at Molloy. Now he'd made it worse.

While Mr. Pollock flicked through his book, a slow sound grew from two floors below on the ground floor where

Brother Mulligan was taking a free class. "OUT! OUT! OUT! OUT! OUT! OUT! OUT! OUT! OUT! OUT!" The chanting got louder and louder until it could not be ignored anymore. Then it stopped suddenly and was replaced by the cheering rush of boys into the yard. That was it. Someone had let a class out. There was no stopping the domino effect. Bell or no bell, they had to let them out.

Tired, dispirited, and almost numb from the tedium of writing down book lists, class rules, and special prayers to Venerable Saorseach O'Rahilly for help in each subject, Finbar stood at his front door and lazily rapped the knocker. Through the knobbed glass pane he saw his mother bustle down the narrow hall, wiping her hands on her apron as she came. She yanked the door open bursting with: "So? How did you get on? How many slaps did you get, pet?"

"Two," answered Finbar sullenly as he hung his blazer on the hallstand. He knew two was a good answer: neither low enough to arouse the suspicion of lying nor high enough to prompt further investigation.

"Sure, that's not bad. Were you talking? I know you're a terrible talker though I don't know where you get it from at all. You can't get a word out of your father and Declan is the same. Mind you, your Uncle Francie could talk the hind leg off a donkey. That must be where you get it from. Were the masters nice? That Brother Loughlin seems like a very holy man. I'm sure he'll look out for you. Was your uniform all right? I'm not certain those trousers are the right grey. Did anyone say anything to you about the trousers?"

Finbar drifted away through the flood of words. None of her questions really required answers. If she really wanted to know anything she would ask him again and again until he answered.

The bus stop incident had really pissed him off. Maybe it was the class with Spud Murphy that had made things worse. It had made him feel there was some warmth there. The way the others behaved with Spud showed they weren't all bad. When they saw him at the bus stop there was no need for them to throw his bag onto that passing bus. Why did they do that? He'd had to run after it for nearly a hundred yards before it hit a red light, and then he missed his own bus. What was the point of that? Why did they have to do that? He hated them. He really, really hated them.

10

After the evening rosary and the communal ice bath, Brother Tobin retired to his cell and his prayers to Saint Dearbhla of Armagh, to whom he felt a particular devotion. He pulled the book out from under his mattress. It had become harder since they took his public library card away and banned him from even entering the building. This one had taken a lot of work to get in. He had bribed one of the sixth years to bring it to him from England. It was still banned in the Republic as far as he knew. Invoking Saint Dearbhla, he set to work on *Where the Trade Winds Call Love*.

He had fallen behind lately so he was determined to do a bit at lunchtime every day this week. He removed the Saint Dearbhla bookmark and opened to page fifty-four. He read carefully and attentively, evaluating every nuance and innuendo he could capture. "Aha! There's one!"

Carefully he lifted his ruler from the table. He took the naked razor blade and deftly removed the word *corset*, leaving behind an inoffensive and uncorrupting empty rectangle on the page.

He picked up the sliver of vileness and, with another heartfelt invocation of Saint Dearbhla, popped it in his mouth and chewed it energetically. His eyes teared with pride as he caught sight of Saint Dearbhla on her little altar of already expurgated and purified books. She seemed to glow with approval of his labors.

* * *

Brother Loughlin sat back in his office chair and puffed nervously on a thin cigar. He picked up the phone and dialled.

"Noel? How in God's name are ye? How's the big fella? How's the County Council treating you? . . . Oh, it's Eamon, Eamon Loughlin at Little Werburgh Street . . . No, no, Greater Little Werburgh Street, *NORTH* . . . Yes, yes, fine, fine. I'm sorry to be disturbing you at home . . . Well, funny you should ask because, come here to me now, but I have a little favour to ask you. There's been some mix-up about a planning application that has the Brothers here in a bit of an uproar. You didn't see it in *The Way Forward*, did you? . . .

"Well, some go-boys by the names of Fionn and Patrick Sweeney put a planning application in the newspaper to build a warehouse on the site of the school here . . . Yes, yes, I know it sounds mad, but I have the paper here in front of me. I'm sure it's some mistake but I spent all morning on to the Department of Buildings and I could get no answer out of anyone so I was wondering if you could look into it . . . No, no, just to be sure it's a mistake . . . Sure, sure, that'd be great . . . Lovely then. Thanks very much, Noel, and give me best to Margaret and the boys. You must drop over and see us some time . . . Great. I'll look forward to hearing from you."

Brother Loughlin dropped the phone back in its cradle, sat back, and took a deep pull on his cigar. He was feeling very happy with himself. It was good to have friends in high places. That's why he was Head Brother and not some drone hammering away at Caesar's *Gallic Wars* all day. If he played his cards right, it wouldn't be long before he'd be able to insinuate himself into the running for the position on the Interdiocesan Presidium. Brother Butler was not going to last forever. In fact, he looked very shook at Brother Galligan's funeral in April. No, it wouldn't be long now.

Brother Loughlin switched off the desk light and sat in the dark smoking his cigar. Had he not been so engrossed in visions of his own grandeur, he might have noticed the squeaking of the gate that led from the monastery to the street. This gate was only ever used by visitors. It was never used at night except for the occasional passing drunk in need of a sheltered spot to relieve himself. Normally Brother Loughlin would have been at the window like a shot to vent his wrath on such a vagrant. But this was no vagrant he would have seen. Instead he would have spotted the porter-barrel shape of Brother Cox with the collar of his plastic raincoat pulled tight about his face sneaking out into the night.

Cox scurried as far as the corner and turned onto the West Circular Road with great relief. He stopped and pressed himself against the wall. His heart pounded in his ears and he listened beyond its clamour for any sound of pursuit or detection. When he was satisfied that he was safely and secretly out, he reached inside his raincoat and pulled off the red collar. He was now effectively wearing a black suit with a curiously red shirt but nothing that could really arouse suspicion.

The patrons of The Limping Gunman thought quite otherwise. In fact, they were already running a little book on what time Cox would arrive. A few of the less experienced had already lost by betting on him coming in on Friday night. Now all were sure he would not hold out for much longer. It had been four days since school began and Cox would have to crack soon.

When the Brother entered the bar he would never

have guessed that he himself had only seconds before been the subject of heated discussion for the whole room. He entered, placed himself at a small table, and patted himself on the back for his carefully cultivated anonymity.

He sat stiffly, tensing the muscles in his toes to try to keep still and look calm and casual. He would not go up to the bar. He didn't want to look like a desperate, thirsty man. He would wait until the barman came over. He could wait.

Already he could taste the warm tingling on the back of his throat. He could feel the golden current pulse through his veins. His forehead began to bead with little droplets of sweaty anticipation. He opened the top button of his plastic raincoat and ran his finger around the inside of his shirt collar, then raised his head and tried to catch the barman's eye.

The barman, Tom Stack, was pretending not to notice Cox. He wanted to see how long it would take the man to lose his composure. Finally realising that Cox was bloody-mindedly determined to sit there and sweat it out in the hope of looking casual, Stack relented and sauntered over to the table.

"What'll you have, pal?" he asked without a hint of ever having clapped eyes on Cox before.

"I'll have a large bottle of porter."

"Right you are," said Stack, and turned back toward the bar.

"Oh, and a ball of malt on the side. Actually, make it a large glass," added Cox as nonchalantly as possible, the eager thirst in his voice obvious to all ears but his.

"A large ball of malt it is," smiled Stack. He'd bet Riley ten bob it'd be a large ball of malt on the side. This was going to be a good night.

Cox stared at the small tabletop. He concentrated on the sticky rings and how they didn't reflect light the way the rest of the table did.

Sip, sip! Nice and slow. Sip, sip! he thought to himself. Only a few more minutes now. It seemed like years since he had been at his sister Bridie's in Dundalk. She never dared to say anything about his evening walks. It had been tough to get Brother Loughlin to agree to two weeks but he had finally conceded under Bridie's relentless promising to keep a good eye on him. Two whole lovely weeks. He glanced up and saw Stack pouring the large glass of whiskey. He rapidly clenched and unclenched his fists under the table. Any minute now he would be relishing the sour-sweetness of a mouthful of porter and a sip of Ballinasloe Red Label. He dug his fingernails into his palms; Stack seemed to be taking his time. Cox took out his purse and counted out the money. Nothing wrong with knowing exactly what a large bottle and a large glass came to. He stacked the change in a neat pile on the table and sat back just as Stack arrived with his drinks.

Sip! Sip! Sip! Cox chanted to himself. He poured the porter carefully down the side of the glass.

Stack took the money and returned to the bar. Now he had to time the man. He had two bob on with Matt Lynch that the ball of malt wouldn't last more than four minutes from the time it touched the table.

Brother Mulligan's size-fourteen carpet slippers flopped loudly through the silence of the monastery. He stood at the bottom of the stairs and paused for breath. He was annoyed at himself for missing the milk but was glad he had given himself the extra fifteen minutes of the hair shirt and the ashes in his mouth. He just hoped he'd put enough bromide in his milk. Widower Frawley usually did it and Brother Mulligan hoped he hadn't underdone it lest he be plagued by lustful thoughts through the night. He took a sip; it tasted like Widower Frawley's preparation through the residual taste of the ashes in his mouth so it should be sufficient to quell the animal within for twenty-four hours.

Carefully he mounted the stairs. Halfway up the first flight he heard the rattle of keys against the heavy oak door that led to the yard.

"Ah! Brother Mulligan!" called Brother Loughlin jovially as he shut the door behind him. "Forgot your milk again? Well, I have some good news! I just got off the phone with Noel Comiskey on the County Council and he's going to sort out this planning application business once and for all." Brother Loughlin had not intended telling anyone until the morning but his good spirits had gotten the better of him. "Well, good night now. See you bright and early," he concluded as he bundled up the stairs past Brother Mulligan.

Brother Mulligan muttered to himself and went back to concentrating on not spilling his milk while making his laborious way back upstairs. The overdose of bromide guaranteed that at least one Brother would be temptation-free for the night.

11

Go away out of that with you!" moaned thick-tongued Brother Cox at the bell for morning mass. He was not yet ready for another day. He still needed time to shake the dried-out inside of his head. He sat up slowly in his cot. Ah good, there was a time-saver anyway: he was still wearing his suit. He wondered to himself how he'd had the presence of mind to sleep in his suit, and then it came slinking back to him. He had gone out. He had gone to The Limping Gunman. He had shamed the Brotherhood, his family, his pledge of abstinence, himself. He was worthless. He was sinful. He was nothing more than a dirty wastrel drunkard.

He flopped out of bed and down on his knees, buried his face in the abrasive wool blanket, and murmured a tearful, throaty Act of Contrition. Then he got up and sat on the edge of the bed rubbing his hands together slowly and tightly. He slipped the belt out of his trousers and swung it viciously, buckle first, over his shoulder and into his back. He felt the biting sting on his skin through his jacket. He drew the belt back and swung again and again.

"I will not give in to the drink! I will not give in to the drink!"

When he had exhausted himself, he rocked gently like some whiskey-faced Humpty Dumpty in a black suit.

* * *

Father Flynn could just about make himself heard above the frantic rattling of Brother Boland's rosary beads. The man seemed to be praying for something very special indeed. Father Flynn was half-afraid that the little marble beads would turn to dust if Brother Boland pressed them together any harder.

The door at the back of the oratory creaked open and the tousle-haired Brother Cox slid in to the empty back pew. His face was dotted with tiny bloodied specks of toilet paper where he had cut himself shaving. He knelt forward and rested his head on his joined hands. Trancelike, he rolled his head slowly from side to side in time with Father Flynn's voice.

From the front pew Brother Loughlin pointedly cleared his throat and turned around. Brother Cox raised his head a little and his bloodshot eyes met Brother Loughlin's seething gaze. Brother Cox let his head drop back down and resumed his swaying.

"Finbar, love, it's ten to eight!" called Mrs. Sullivan from the stairs. Finbar reached under the bed and drew out his Boy Scout watch. Twenty-five past seven. Did she really think he was going to fall for that? He pulled the covers back over his head and dozed off again.

The pigeons cooed in the eaves outside the window. Drifting on the evocative sound, Finbar imagined himself in Na-Na Brogan's house in Kinsale where his mother was born. It was that endless summer of being four or five where every day seemed eternal and sun-filled. He had not been back to the house since Na-Na died last year.

"Finbar! It's nearly eight o'clock. You're going to be late!"

"I'm up!" he shouted, and closed his eyes again. *I'll*

get up in a minute, he thought heavily, and slipped back to sleep.

"Jesus, Mary, and Holy Saint Joseph!" Mrs. Sullivan cried.

Finbar jumped up in bed. "What? What? What? I'm up!"

His mother said nothing. He turned around and followed her gaze. Declan's bed was tossed and vacant. Finbar looked to his mother.

"Get dressed!" she snapped tonelessly, and opened the wardrobe door. The hangers rattled and jangled as she frantically searched inside the empty closet.

"God help us! What has he gone and done now?"

"What?" asked Finbar softly.

"What do you think? Declan's gone."

"Gone? Where?"

"How in God's name should I know?" Mrs. Sullivan fled downstairs.

Finbar heard his mother's voice in the hall, then his father's rang out: "For Christ sake! I can't stay home. There were twenty others looking for that job. I have to go! I'll come home as early as I can. This is all we need!"

The air in the yard was damp and stank of wet schoolboys and the bitter burnt hops blown down the river from Nesbitt's brewery. Conall McConnell shifted impatiently from foot to foot. Beside him stood Brother Loughlin anxiously staring up at the big electric clock over the school door.

"Watch, now," the Brother said solemnly.

McConnell pursed his lips and breathed out sharply through his nose.

The second hand glided toward 12 in imperceptible little jerks. As soon as it hit 12 the minute hand clicked into place and quivered for a moment. It was nine o'clock on the dot.

"There! See?" said Brother Loughlin triumphantly.

"Right, so the bell is broke," conceded McConnell.

"Well? Don't just stand there. Get your ladder and fix it!" Brother Loughlin strode away and began berating the boys. "Get into your classes!"

"But Brother, the bell didn't go!"

"I'll bell-didn't-go you! Now get into your classes!"

Suddenly, from the far side of the yard came a piercing clanging and Brother Boland's voice shrieking at the boys to hurry up.

Brother Loughlin only saw a blur of newly shined brass at the end of Boland's right hand, such was the fervour with which he was ringing the handbell.

"Bring out yer dead! Bring out yer dead!" called an anonymous voice from among the crowd in the shed.

Brother Loughlin watched approvingly as Brother Boland scurried toward the shed, the brassy blur of the bell in his right hand now complemented by the black blur of the leather in his left. From the shed the boys scattered toward their classes, so Brother Loughlin turned his attention back to the main door. There McConnell stood with his ladder leaning up against the wall, waiting for the stream of grey-clad boys to disappear up the stairs and out of his way.

"Put out that cigarette and get to work! This is not some seedy bookie's shop!" barked Brother Loughlin.

McConnell took one last drag on his cigarette and opened his ladder under the clock with deliberate, exasperating slowness.

"Well?" Brother Loughlin asked the back of McConnell's ankles once he had ascended the ladder.

"I haven't even opened the stupid thing yet. Hold yer horses."

"Come on! Come on, can't you?"

"Don't rush me. I shouldn't even be doing this. This is a job for a—"

There was a loud pop, a fizzle, and McConnell was flung backward in a cloud of cordite-scented smoke, knocking Brother Loughlin to the ground under him.

"Get off me!" Brother Loughlin was none too pleased to have broken McConnell's fall.

"I'm not touching that thing again. It's live so it is. You get yourself a proper electrician. There's something very wrong with that clock. It's not my job!" McConnell folded up his ladder and rushed off with uncharacteristic speed.

Brother Loughlin stood up and watched him go. "You'll be ringing the handbell for classes," he then said to the unmistakable sweaty smell of Brother Boland that had sidled up behind him.

"Very well," said Boland, and hurried off delightedly.

Brother Loughlin rubbed his hip where he had fallen and ruefully regarded the big clock now hanging by a few wires like some forlorn sea creature. "Bloody electricians! Licence to print money, that's all it is! Have the country ruined, so they do!"

Finbar bolted off the bus at the lights and sprinted down the West Circular Road, his schoolbag banging and rattling on his back. After his father's cross-examination to be sure he knew nothing about Declan's running away, he was really late. He glanced at his watch: a quarter past nine. Feck! Feck! Feck!

He dashed across the empty yard and up the stairs. His heart pounding, he slowed his pace to try to catch his breath. He could feel his wool vest sticking to his shoulders and the backs of his knees were sweating into the worsted wool trousers.

He paused at the top of the stairs and took one deep breath, then moved in front of the door to see Mr. Pollock writing furiously on the blackboard. After a moment's hesitation he knocked on the glass pane.

"Tar isteach!" called the teacher without looking across.

Finbar opened the door and walked into the classroom. Mr. Pollock continued to fill the blackboard and paid no attention to him. Finbar shifted his weight from foot to foot and stared at the teacher's desk. The leather was already out, sitting curled up on the roll book. Obviously there had been some disciplining done already.

Mr. Pollock finished writing with a wide flourish, tossed the remainder of the chalk into the bin in the corner, and whipped around on his heel to face Finbar. "An tUasal Ó Súilleabháin. Cén t-am é?"

Finbar glanced up at the clock on the wall. It was twenty past nine. "Fiche noiméad tar éis a naoi," he replied.

"Agus?"

The boy swallowed hard and launched into a reasonably fluent Gaelic explanation of the morning's events.

Mr. Pollock nodded and waved him to his desk. Finbar sat down relieved. The teacher seemed satisfied both with the explanation and the quality of the Gaelic. Finbar was not sure now which was worse, being leathered or being forced to carry on a conversation in Irish in front of the whole class.

He took out his books and glanced up at the board. "What's this?" he whispered to Smalley Mullen beside him.

Mullen made no sign that he had been addressed and continued to repeatedly write his name on the lid of the inkwell and then wipe it off with the ball of his thumb.

"Now, Master Egan, sor. Would you like to read what

is on the blackboard for us?" clipped Mr. Pollock as he surveyed his penmanship on the board.

There was no answer from Egan's empty seat.

"Tá sé slaughtered," offered McDonagh.

Pollock knew well that Egan wasn't in. He'd already called the roll. "I beg your pardon? Gabh mo leithscéal?"

"Tá sé as láthair, he's absent," said McDonagh calmly.

Mr. Pollock eyed him suspiciously. "Hmmm. Then you can read for us . . ." he circled his index finger in the air like some malevolent wizard, "Master Bradshaw."

12

By the time Mr. Pollock had made each boy read some of the extract from the Constitution in Irish and laboriously corrected accent and pronunciation, Brother Kennedy was already at the door waiting impatiently. Had it been any other lay teacher, he would have barged into the class, but Mr. Pollock was a little too close with Loughlin to bully.

For homework Mr. Pollock picked questions at random from the end of a lesson they had not even started yet and then overcourteously ushered Brother Kennedy in.

Without even glancing at Mr. Pollock, Brother Kennedy dropped his Latin books on the desk, went to the window, and blessed himself. The boys wearily stood up and waved their hands around in front of their faces.

"Ave Maria, gratia plena," intoned Brother Kennedy. He paused and turned to the boys to indicate that they should repeat. They shambled out something that sounded like "Have a Maria grassy airplaner."

"Dominus tecum."

"Dominoes take 'em."

"Benedicta tu in mulieribus."

"Benedict Twohey in the early bus."

"Et benedictus fructus ventris tui, Jesus."

"Ate Benny dicked us, fucked us, dangerous Twohey jaysus."

"Sancta Maria, mater Dei."

"Sank to Maria, matter day."

"Ora pro nobis peccatoribus."

"Oh, rat, provo bus peck a Tory bus."

"Nunc et in hora mortis nostrae."

"New kettle Nora, more tits no stray."

"Amen."

"Amen."

"In nomine Partii et filii et spiritus sancti."

"In ammonia Patrick ate filly ate spirits from Santy."

Brother Kennedy blessed himself and returned to the desk, oblivious to the blasphemy he had just occasioned. From among his books he took a small blue piece of paper. He viciously rubbed Mr. Pollock's work off the blackboard.

"Copy this down," he said, and began to write at the top left of the board. From experience, the boys guessed that they were in for a long bout of copying. "I doubt any of you baboons will recognise this but it is the translation text that was on your Inter Cert exam, which I am sure you all made a complete dog's dinner of." Brother Kennedy stopped when he had half filled the board. "I think that will be enough for the moment," he said derisively.

Cum dies hibernorum complures transissent frumentumque eo comportari iussisset, subito per exploratores certior factus est ex ea parte vici, quam Gallis concesserat, omnes noctu discessisse montesque qui impenderent a maxima multitudine Sedunorum et Veragrorum teneri. Id aliquot de causis acciderat, ut subito Galli belli renovandi legionisque opprimendae consilium caperent: primum, quod legionem neque eam plenissimam detractis cohortibus duabus et compluribus singillatim, qui commeatus petendi causa missi erant, absentibus propter paucitatem despiciebant; tum etiam, quod propter iniquitatem loci, cum ipsi ex montibus in vallem decurrerent et tela coicerent, ne primum quidem impetum suum posse sustineri existimabant stood incomprehensibly on the blackboard in front of the boys.

"Well?" inquired Brother Kennedy.

"Sir, sir, sir, sir, sir, sir, sir, sir, sir, sir, sir!" pleaded McDonagh, waving his hand frantically in the air.

"Yes, Mr. McDonagh?"

"It's Latin, Brother," beamed McDonagh.

It was hard to know exactly what motivated McDonagh sometimes. He knew Brother Kennedy was a psychotic bastard. If born in another place and time, McDonagh might have become a national hero, scaling unscalable mountains with a few bits of sash rope, a sturdy pair of sandals, and a good tweed jacket; or crossing the Atlantic single-handedly on an oversized Saint Bridget's Cross woven by blind monks. As things stood, however, he would be lucky to make it through fifth year alive for being so foolhardy.

"And?" asked Kennedy with a razor edge in his voice. "You will translate the first sentence as far as *transissent.*"

McDonagh peered at the board. Stalling desperately, he pointed at the top line: "Is that *comprures*?"

"Where, boy?"

"The fourth word, Brother."

"No, that is *complures*."

"Ah, right," mused McDonagh.

"Well? We don't have all day."

McDonagh peered at the board and the letters danced incomprehensibly in front of him. He thought hard and pointed at some words as if breaking down the phrase into the most translatable units. "Hibernian days came complaining—"

"Out to the line, you clown!" barked Brother Kennedy.

McDonagh put the most hurt expression imaginable on his face and walked, head down, out to the line.

"Mr., ehm, let me see, Mr. Lynch then."

Lynch stared at the blackboard as if it had just fallen flaming from the sky. "As the god of the Hibernians—"

"Out to the line, you ignorant guttersnipe!"

Lynch strode eagerly out to the line and stood at attention beside McDonagh.

"Mr., ehm, Sullivan."

Finbar stood up. He knew this; this was easy. He could still picture it on the page with the engraving of those mountains and Declan's stupid attempts at translation written in the margins. He knew the moment he stood up he was not going to put himself in the way of a beating just to keep company with McDonagh and Lynch. He could see already that Brother Kennedy was heading for bright purple boiling point. The rest of them already had him labelled as a sap, and getting himself leathered in PE hadn't done him any good.

"When several days had elapsed in winter quarters," he said slowly and confidently, then sat down.

Without comment Brother Kennedy scribbled the translation below the text. "Copy!" he shouted.

The boys copied down the translation. For all they knew, *complures* meant *winter*, but they at least had a translation.

"Continue, Mr., ehm, Ferrara."

Ferrara stood up and scratched his head.

"Come on, boy! The language of your forefathers," sneered Brother Kennedy.

Ferrara scratched his head more vigorously and began to blink repeatedly.

"Iussisset? What is it, Mr. Ferrara? It's like trying to get blood out of a turnip!"

"Jesus said?" hazarded Ferrara.

"God grant me strength! Out to the line, you uneducated

balooba!" Brother Kennedy's face was bright red and beads of sweat were beginning to twinkle on his scalp.

By the time Brother Kennedy got to *ex ea parte vici*, almost half of the class were out on the line and he himself was approaching apoplectic. Scully had saved himself by having actually recognised a couple of words, Mullen had taken Finbar's whispered prompt, and Bradshaw, who had repeated his Inter Cert three times, knew the translation by heart and took a good guess at which bit he should regurgitate.

When Brother Kennedy called on O'Connor, the boy stood up, looked at the board, and walked straight out to the line with a hopeless shrug of his shoulders.

The boredom of standing on the line was starting to take its toll on Lynch. "Go on, Macker, faint. Go on!" he whispered.

"Nah, it's too early," answered McDonagh.

Just in time, Brother Boland's bell rang out the end of class and morning break.

"You will all write out that passage ten times for punishment!" shouted Kennedy, and he leathered each boy once on his way out the door.

Finbar fled down the stairs with the throng. He reached the yard and watched all the boys break into little groups like spilled mercury. He moved to the edge of the small yard and looked across the big yard and noticed the seething cluster of bodies beside the grotto of Our Lady of Indefinite Duration.

In the granite wall beside the grotto there was a hatch two feet tall and three feet wide. It was so high off the ground that the smaller boys had to stand on their tiptoes just to get their eyes at the level of the countertop. Larger boys took hold of one of the metal bars that ran horizontally across the opening. Behind the bars Brother Boland was selling snacks.

Finbar watched as a bulky third year took stock of the line, stepped back, and then took a run at the hatch. He launched himself, rugby style, up and over the knot of bodies and grabbed on to the uppermost horizontal bar. Using that purchase he hauled himself through the knot to the counter's edge and began to shout: "Trigger bar and a packidge of salt 'n' vinegar, Brother! Trigger bar and a packidge of salt 'n' vinegar, Brother! Trigger bar and a packidge of salt 'n' vinegar, Brother!"

Finbar took a run and launched himself into the crowd. He grabbed the middle bar and pulled himself to the counter at the expense of three smaller boys, one of whom lost his tentative grip on the bar and fell backward on to the ground.

"Trigger bar and a packet of cheese 'n' onion, please, Brother! Trigger bar and a packet of cheese 'n' onion, please, Brother!" Finbar chanted, forcing his voice as much as he could into a resemblance of the Dublin accents around him. "Trigger bar and a packet of cheese 'n' onion, please, Brother! Trigger bar and a packet of cheese 'n' onion, please, Brother!" he shouted with increased vigour as he sensed his turn was coming.

Brother Boland acknowledged his order, turned, and grabbed the Trigger bar. Just as he was about to hand it over, he stopped suddenly and looked at his watch. He released the bar in the general direction of the box from which he had taken it, rang his handbell in the boys' faces, and then lurched forward with sinewy speed, his leather already magically in his other hand. He smacked the countertop and the bars rapidly to drive off the boys' hands and reached up. Finbar just got his hand away before the heavy wooden shutter slammed down. Instantly the knot of boys around the shop undid itself and drifted back toward the school.

Well that was just fecking great, thought Finbar bitterly, and sulked back to the yard.

Brother Boland fumbled in the darkness of the shop and switched on the light. Carefully he counted the takings, subtracted the float, and jotted the closing balance in the little black notebook that lived in the lid of the cash box. He locked it with the small key on his key ring and listened carefully at the door. When he was satisfied that the silence outside reflected an acceptable lack of menace, he carefully inserted the big key in the door and turned it as stealthily as he could.

He opened the door a crack and peered out. The yard was deserted. He turned off the light, poked his head out to give him a wider view, then slid through the door. He clutched the cash box under his arm while he locked the door again.

Glancing around him warily as he scurried across the big yard, he noticed a big truck parked at the side of the hall. As he stopped and watched, three men in overalls jumped out of the cab and looked around them in what struck Brother Boland as a very sinister, almost proprietary way. He tightened his grip on the cash box and increased his pace, finally breaking into the closest thing to a run he had achieved in almost twenty years.

Brother Mulligan, Brother Cox, and Brother Tobin were sitting at the big table in the refectory when Brother Boland burst in clutching the cash box as if someone had just tried to wrest it from him with unspeakable force.

"Men! Big truck! Lower yard! They're here already! Beginning of the end!" he croaked at them through his laboured breathing.

"What are you babbling about?" asked Brother Tobin sternly.

Brother Boland staggered to a chair and caught his breath in frantic gulps. "There are men in a big truck in the lower yard. Look like builders. It's them! They're here to start building the warehouse!"

Brother Tobin looked at Brother Cox who looked at Brother Mulligan who looked at Brother Boland who in turn continued to stare into Brother Tobin's face. A tiny web of tension wove itself around the four of them and the more they struggled against it, the more inextricably they became enmeshed in Brother Boland's contagious panic.

"Show us where!" the panic said as it forced its way out of Cox's mouth.

Brother Tobin helped Brother Boland up and the four of them shuffled at their combined top speed out of the refectory and down the parquet corridor, just managing to avoid Mrs. McCurtin who was on her hands and knees trying to remove a particularly stubborn stain.

When they reached the double doors that led to the yard, all four tried to go through at the same time and it was this mess of tangled limbs that Brother Loughlin came upon as he returned from his office to have words with Mrs. McCurtin about the rust on the statue of Venerable Saorseach O'Rahilly in his office.

"What in the name of God is going on here?" he bellowed.

"Men in the yard with a truck," explained Cox.

"This is how is starts," intoned Brother Boland in the ominous voice of some cavern-bound seer.

"Builders!" hissed Brother Mulligan.

"Builders?" guffawed Brother Loughlin. "Don't you think I would know if there were builders coming to the school?"

"It's them. The warehouse people," Brother Boland whispered fearfully.

"Well let's go see these 'builders' then, shall we?" announced Brother Loughlin condescendingly, and assumed a lead position as the rest of them extricated themselves from the doorway.

"Oh-oh. Here comes trouble," muttered Matt when he saw the group of Brothers approach, their cassocks flapping in the wind.

Lar and Con, his assistants, stood on either side of him and they waited for the Brothers to reach them.

"I bet the fat baldy one is the leader. You can always tell the leaders. They're fat but they don't move like fat people. I've noticed that," observed Lar.

"Now, there's a thing. Mussolini was a bit tubby all right but then Stalin was a skinny little fucker. Mind you, I never saw either of them walk so I couldn't really say," said Con.

Matt shook his head in despair. Every day he had this crap to put up with. Every day Con and Lar would muse on the vagaries of how baldness skips a generation or discuss the complexities of the messenger network used by the Incas. All sorts of stuff. He had no idea where they got it. Lunchtimes were the worst.

Brother Loughlin stopped about five feet from the trio of Matt, Con, and Lar. The other Brothers stood behind him and peered suspiciously.

"Is there something we can help you with?" asked Brother Loughlin haughtily.

"There was a load of old radiators and pipes we were supposed to pick up," answered Matt.

"Well, I'm afraid you are in the wrong place. There are no radiators here. Who sent you?"

"The depot. They said there was sixty radiators and eight hundred foot of pipe to be took away."

"Well, the depot made a mistake. Now, if you would please take yourselves and your vehicle off the premises before . . ." menaced Brother Loughlin, emboldened to a more high-handed approach by Matt's faulty grammar.

"Ah, but you see now, Brother, I'd love to oblige you but I have a docket. I can't leave until I get the scrap on the list and get the pickup signed for. Once a docket goes out of the depot the contents has to be picked up and signed for. Y'understand?" Matt held up the yellow form as incontrovertible proof that there were indeed radiators and pipes to be taken away. A docket could not lie.

Con and Lar nodded in solemn agreement with this sentiment. They were not fly-by-nights who went around grabbing stray bits of scrap. They were serious professionals who had a depot that issued dockets that had to be signed and put into files.

"May I see that?" Brother Loughlin held out his hand.

Matt handed over the docket. "You see, Brother, there it is in black and white."

Brother Loughlin looked carefully at the paper. *Brannigan Brothers, Purveyors of Fine Scrap Metals*, it declared across the top in bold print. Granted, the rest of it was all in a scrawl, but it was clear enough: sixty radiators and eight hundred feet of pipe to be removed for scrap from the Brothers School at Greater Little Werburgh Street, North.

"Wait one moment!" snapped Brother Loughlin suddenly. "This is the wrong date! This is dated next June!"

Matt snatched the docket back and glared at it. "I'll have to go back to the depot and get this looked into. This isn't right," he said glumly, and climbed back into the truck.

Con and Lar shrugged at one another and climbed up into the passenger side of the cab. The motor hawked and retched into life and the heavy truck lumbered away, leaving the Brothers staring after them in a cloud of filthy smoke.

Brother Loughlin watched the truck pass out the gate and turn up Greater Little Werburgh Street, North, with smug satisfaction. "I think that puts an end to that."

"But why were they here at all?" asked Brother Boland. "What depot did they come from? Who sent them?"

"Matter a damn! They're gone now and that's all there is to it! There's no big mystery in it," snapped Brother Loughlin impatiently. He strode away toward the yard.

"Maybe he's right," said Brother Tobin.

"Yes. Just a silly mistake," concurred Cox.

"No! No! No! They are part of it! Don't you see? Any outsiders could be part of it! How can we be safe?"

"I think you need a little lie-down, Brother," said Tobin, and glanced meaningfully at Cox and Mulligan.

"Yes, Brother. It's been a trying episode. You should take a little rest for yourself," the latter murmured, trying unsuccessfully to keep the condescension out of his voice.

"Blackguards! They're all blackguards! Good God! Where did I leave my cash box?" Brother Boland glanced around and then hurried off toward the monastery.

13

After tea, alone in the dark, Brother Boland listened carefully to the oratory. It breathed its silence into his own. It seemed to be waiting. It was ready for his prayers.

He rubbed the beads of his rosary together and opened and closed his lips rapidly. He was not entirely aware of what prayers he was reciting. They were coming more from his fingers and his lips than his mind. His mind was flinging unclear worry and anxiousness in the direction of the Lord in the hope of remedying whatever was lurking in the silence. It was indeed a great gesture of faith in the Creator's omniscience that Brother Boland expected Him to understand any of the inchoate rattle his mind was putting forth.

Brother Tobin sat on the edge of his cot and regarded Saint Dearbhla while he tried to move a stubborn piece of the word "breast" from between his teeth. On his knees lay *Where the Trade Winds Call Love*. He had already given himself heartburn by eating the buxom hussy draped shamelessly across the pirate captain on the cover. He vowed to burn covers in future and concentrate on eating only the words.

He had to get this sliver out of his teeth. That was what she wanted, all those shameful words consumed by the bile of his innards and shat out to the sewers where they belonged. It was at moments like this that Tobin wondered what had ever happened to the letter he'd sent to the Pope detailing his devotions to Saint Dearbhla and requesting permission to start his own Brotherhood, Holy Hoplites of Saint Dearbhla.

"Get away out of that and leave me alone!"

Brother Cox brushed another half-glimpsed imp off his shoulder. He shivered. He was cold, chilled to the marrow. That was it, he thought, ignoring as best he could the creature that seemed to be forming itself out of the shadows. All he needed was a little something to warm himself up. Then he'd be fine. He didn't necessarily *need* a drink; he just felt like one.

When the high-pitched squealing started, Brother Cox had no idea what to make of it. Then he started to wonder if it was coming from the thing in the corner. He looked to see that the shadowy homunculus was halfway up the wall, hanging on in an unnatural, sticky, viscous way that put a little catch of disgust at the back of his throat.

He wrenched his cell door open and hurried down the corridor, keeping his eyes firmly fixed on the redemptive point of light at the top of the stairs. He would not turn around and make eye contact with whatever was leering off the walls at him. Just down the stairs, out through the monastery, and a hot whiskey or two— and he'd be fine. Then he'd be able to sleep.

"Where the hell were you until this hour? We were worried sick! You could have been down a lane with a knife in your back for all we knew! Didn't you think we had enough to worry about with Declan running away like that?" shouted Mr. Sullivan. Finbar had barely closed the hall door behind him when his father had rushed out of the kitchen to grab him by the collar and shake him.

"I got lost," answered Finbar quietly.

"Got lost? How the hell did you get lost?"

"I walked back from games. I couldn't get a bus."

"Walked back from games? What games?"

"They have a games field away from the school near the power station."

"Are you gone soft in the head? What do you think we gave you the bus fare for? Is it simple you've gone on us? Did you even think for a second about what you were at? Did you? Did you?"

Finbar made no reply. Slowly his father's anger subsided and was tempered by the relief that Finbar was not in fact Down A Lane With A Knife In His Back.

"Your dinner's on the cooker," said Mr. Sullivan gruffly but not without affection.

Finbar put down his bags and hung his blazer on the hallstand. He walked carefully into the kitchen, braced for another barrage from his mother. There was no sign of her. He heard his father rustling the evening paper in the sitting room and decided it was best not to ask him anything. He could guess.

The stew was on low heat and showed all signs of having been there for about three hours. He put as much of it as looked remotely edible on a plate and sat at the table. The tablecloth was gone. He took a newspaper from the pile beside the door and put it under his plate. He knew the signals. His dinner could have been turned off and heated up when he got home. The tablecloth could have been left on the table until he'd had his dinner. But no, these ritual, guilt-inducing symbols, combined with his mother's withdrawal to the bedroom, were part of the slow punishment of disapproval, disappointment, and hurt that lasted so much longer and cut so much deeper than any beating or shouting. He took one mouthful of the burnt martyr–flavoured stew and threw the rest out into the backyard for the pigeons.

As he bolted the back door he sensed someone behind him. He turned to see his father standing against the sink. He looked incredibly tired. Finbar had never seen his father look this way before: tired, worried, and just a little bit lost.

"He took all the money out of the tea caddy," Mr. Sullivan said softly.

Finbar nodded.

"He could be anywhere."

Finbar nodded helplessly. He had no idea what to say to this. His father was generally a silent man of decision and action, not a man who asked for advice or help.

"Well, you lock up, like a good lad. I'm going to bed. I have to go to that stupid job at half past six. Don't stay up late, you have school in the morning," Mr. Sullivan murmured almost absently before drifting into the hall and up the stairs.

Finbar poured himself a glass of milk and stood at the sink. He shrugged at the pale stars that peeked out of the sliver of sky behind the coal shed. He noticed two new geraniums in pots outside on the windowsill, his father's latest attempt to brighten the cement-covered yard. He decided it was not the time to tell his parents that games day at his new school was a washout and consisted of picking stones off a newly dug field to refurbish the grotto of Our Lady of Indefinite Duration. But then there was never likely to be a good time to tell them that.

14

Hi! You there, me lad."

The burly man with the ladder stopped his slow progress across the yard and turned. He stared levelly at Brother Loughlin: "The name's Matthews, Matt Matthews."

"Oh! So you're the electrician?"

"That's what it says on the side of me van." Matt gestured to the gate where his two assistants were unloading toolboxes from a battered van bearing the sign *Brannigan Brothers, Electrical Contractors*.

Brother Loughlin peered at the two other men and furrowed his brow. There was something disconcertingly familiar about Matthews and the men. He turned to question Matt, who was already up on the ladder inspecting the clock.

"So? Can you fix it?" asked Brother Loughlin.

"I might if I could get a moment's peace to have a look at it."

Brother Loughlin bridled at the workman's sharp tone but bit his lip. Things had completely gone to the dogs. God be with the days when a tradesman would have been only too happy to come to his school to fix his bell. And would have kept a civil tongue in his head too! He was interrupted by two soft, wheedling voices behind him.

"There ye are now, Brother."

"Morning, Brother, soft day now, thank God."

Brother Loughlin turned and found himself being nodded to by Lar and Con. Each carried a small toolbox and tipped his tweed cap respectfully at him.

"You look very familiar. Don't I know you?" asked Brother Loughlin.

"Don't think so. You must have us confused with someone else."

"This clock has had it. It's all broke, completely banjaxed," declared Matt, and handed the big clock down to Lar.

"It takes three of you to change a clock?" asked Brother Loughlin archly.

"Oh no, Matt does all that. I'm here in case there's any socket work. Con here does meters and relays. From each according to his abilities; to each according to his needs," explained Lar.

"Where's the fuse box for this?" asked Matt.

"I don't know. You'll have to ask Mr. McConnell, the janitor."

"I'll find it meself, thanks all the same. I don't need to have any truck with some jumped-up janitor," said Matt as climbed down the ladder. He walked off in search of the fuse box leaving Brother Loughlin standing with Con and Lar.

"Is it fixed?" asked Brother Boland, suddenly appearing in the doorway.

"Not yet, Brother. You are still on bell duty until I tell you otherwise."

Brother Loughlin flinched a little when he saw the look of maniacal glee that momentarily possessed Boland's face, before it and its bearer disappeared back into the school.

Lar peered inside the discarded clock. "Looks like one of the differentiators fused," he said sagely.

"I don't think that model has a differentiator. It's a Volta 5-20, isn't it?" ventured Con.

"You know your models all right, but I think you'll find it has two differentiators."

"Ah no, the differentiators didn't come in until the 5-80."

"You might have a point there. Still, it's a Volta all right."

"Ah yeah, the Volta is yer only man for the regularity."

"You never said a truer word."

"Still and all, mind you, I always thought the Merrifield was a grand make of clock too."

"Them's the ones made in Sheffield, is it?"

"Oh yeah. Sheffield. The Toledo of the North."

"I never heard that one before."

"Oh yeah, famous for swords it used to be."

"Isn't that a gas thing now all the same?"

"Used to be the capital of Spain at one point."

"Sheffield? Are ye mad?"

"No, Toledo."

Brother Loughlin glanced from Lar to Con and back again as this tennis match of non-sequiturs started to make the ends of his nerves itch.

"Would you two just shut up!" snarled Matt as he returned. He shook his head despairingly and then fixed his attention on Brother Loughlin: "I'm surprised this place didn't all go up in flames years ago. The wiring is a caution, so it is. Jerry-built the whole bloody place! Eh, I think you can put the clock down there Larkin. It can't get any more broken than it already is."

"Right so." Lar rested the inert clock against the wall.

Back up the ladder Matt fiddled with the wires. "Would you go in there and screw the fuse back in? It's just in behind that door."

For a split second Brother Loughlin was actually on his way to do it. "I beg your pardon?!?"

"All right, I'll do it meself."

Matt set down his tools and strolled off into the school again.

Brother Loughlin was furious with this encounter. He took out a cigarette and lit it.

Matt soon returned and thrust a spent and blackened fuse into Con's hand before climbing back up the ladder. He fiddled some more with the wires and attached a small meter. "Right, we have a current."

Brother Loughlin cleared his throat impatiently and flicked his ash: "The new clock?"

"All right. All right. It's coming. Keep yer hair on. Conway, get me a 5-50 out of the van."

"A 5-50?" echoed Con, somewhat incredulously.

"Yeah. Is it deaf or just thick ye are?"

"Fair enough. I just thought—"

"Don't! Just get it!"

Brother Loughlin paced a little circle of impatience around the fallen ash from his cigarette until Con returned from the van bearing a brand-new clock. The Brother eyed the clock suspiciously: "And what is that going to set us back, might I ask?"

"The 5-50? Seventy pounds, but you'd pay at least a hundred for it in a shop," Matt replied.

"Get on with it," Brother Loughlin sighed. He watched carefully as Matt wired up the clock, set it for two minutes before nine, and hung it back in its place.

The four of them stood and watched the second hand sweep through its course and begin again.

"Time's a very quare thing all the same," mused Lar.

"Like as the waves hasten toward the pebbled shore,

so do our moments hasten to their end," intoned Con.

"Ah, the bard. Ye can't beat the bard."

"Indeed and you can't, Lar. Though there are some of Wyatt's lyrics I'm quite partial to. They have a Petrarchan quality to them. Very sophisticated for their time."

"I can't say as I've ever had much time for Wyatt."

"Will you two just shut up!" barked Matt.

The second hand inched toward ten.

"Eight, seven, six, five, four . . ." counted Lar and Con softly together. The clock struck nine o'clock and the bell pealed out.

"There ye are now!" smiled Matt. But his fleeting triumph was cut short by the unexpected slowing, stuttering, and stopping of the bell.

Brother Loughlin glowered at Matt and then at the clock. It was still running but he could see that the second hand was slowing down. Moments later it jerked slightly and then came to rest.

"What the . . . ?" Matt climbed back up and inspected the clock. "This is completely destroyed. Brand-new clock. Nothing wrong with the wires and there's nothing wrong with the bell. And now the whole thing is seized up. I don't know what's wrong with this at all. I'll have to take it back to the workshop and have one of the clock lads look it over. That's all I can do. Don't hook ANYTHING up to those wires."

"Horologists, they're called," noted Lar.

Matt hastily wrote the docket, shoved it into Brother Loughlin's unwilling hand, grabbed his tools, and walked back toward the truck.

"What about this?" called Brother Loughlin, holding up the first stricken clock.

"Ah no, afraid we don't do disposal," answered Con. "Good day to you now, Brother."

"Stay out of harm's way now, Brother."

Lar and Con stood side by side, smiled, and tipped their caps to Brother Loughlin before turning to follow Matt.

"Brother Boland! Brother Boland! Have McConnell get rid of that old clock immediately! You will still be ringing the handbell for classes!" Brother Loughlin shouted, then strode off to his office.

Brian Egan stood in front of Mr. Pollock, hopelessly trying to compose a Gaelic explanation of his lateness for two interminable, excruciating minutes before the teacher relented and told him to sit down.

Everyone looked but no one could make eye contact with Egan. He simply stared vacantly ahead.

Scully watched carefully. Something about Egan was making him uncomfortable: something menacingly missing about the boy stood over him, judge and jury, reminding him that he had set Egan up.

"Yeauw, Ego, how's it going?" whispered Scully at the first opportunity.

Egan did not move. No acknowledgment. This was not the same Egan who only a few days ago would have jumped with excitement at being spoken to by any of Scully's gang. Something had shifted here but Scully could not be sure what.

"Mr. McDonagh, Mr. Bradshaw, go to Brother Loughlin's office. As for the rest of you, listen carefully and you might learn something for a change. In the old days, the monks of Ireland would sit alone in stone huts and compose hundreds of staves of flawless mellifluous verse in their heads that they would then recite from memory. In honour of this great tradition you will now open your books at page one hundred and thirteen and learn by heart the first four verses of 'Caoineadh Art Uí Laoghaire.'"

Bradshaw and McDonagh shuffled out and the rest paged through their poetry books.

Mr. Pollock sat at the high desk and cleaned his fountain pen while the boys made half-hearted attempts to learn the verses. It did not help in the least that they had never before clapped eyes on said verses and they might as well have been trying to memorise a gangrene remedy in Old Norse. By the time Mr. Pollock had successfully overhauled his fountain pen, Brother Boland's bell rang and there was no time to examine the memorising.

"Write out the first four verses five times for your homework and I will examine you on them tomorrow."

Brother Loughlin pushed up the window and leaned his elbows on the outside sill. He cradled his hands against the wind, lit a cigarette, and looked down on the yard below with satisfaction. He listened behind him to the echoey dripping of leaky cisterns and the odd hissing of the troughlike urinal. From up here on the third floor he had a perfect view of the yard below. He farted loudly into the copious folds of his cassock and chuckled contentedly to himself.

Before he had even begun to leather them, he'd reduced them to the edge of tears. He knew these hard chaws. All you had to do with most of them was start in on how little their parents loved them and how they would be better off if there was another decent war where they could be of some use and die in the trenches. That would usually get the waterworks going. It was about pinpointing their vulnerable spots, and they all had them, even the hardest of the little bastards.

He watched the yard below patiently. As soon as he saw them appear round the corner straining under the weight of

Mr. Laverty's little bubble car, he reached down and took the copper megaphone from the floor. He leaned as far out the window as his girth allowed.

"All boys! All boys! This is Brother Loughlin! You will all take note of what is occurring in the yard below. All boys will form orderly viewing lines at the windows. Let this be an example to all of you who might consider blackguarding, and remember: my arm is long, my vengeance is total, and I will act when the time is meet!"

His voice echoed around the yard and heads began to appear at the windows. He smiled to himself and lit another cigarette off his first and drank in the spectacle below.

Slater, McDonagh, and Bradshaw struggled into the middle of the yard with Laverty's tiny three-wheeler and set it down. Wearing only their underpants, they shivered against the cold wind and walked gingerly on the concrete. McDonagh was the first one to notice all the faces at the windows. He cowered and shrank against the side of the car. The others followed his glance and saw the serried faces, some laughing, some blank, some sneering. Bradshaw attempted to pass it off as if he didn't care and Slater looked down at his grey-white underpants and pressed his knees together.

"Get the buckets, Mr. Bradshaw! And no dawdling!" bellowed Brother Loughlin.

Bradshaw ran toward the monastery and emerged carrying two metal buckets of water. Reluctantly the boys took the cloths from the buckets and painfully began to wash Laverty's car.

"Pay special attention to the windows and the door handle!" shouted Brother Loughlin.

Bradshaw felt the cold of the water bite into the leathered throbbing in his hands. Slater splashed some of the freezing water on his feet and tried hard not to flinch. McDonagh wrung as much of the water as he could out of his cloth and wiped the back of the car.

"More water, Mr. McDonagh, or I'll make you do it again!"

After fifteen minutes the car was clean and the boys soaked, cold, and humiliated.

"You may now recite at the top of your voices a heartfelt Act of Contrition, return the car to its place, and then go back to your classes!" cried Brother Loughlin triumphantly. "Let this be an example to the rest of you! Back to your studies!"

"I confess to Almighty God and to you, my brothers and sisters . . ." shouted McDonagh, Slater, and Bradshaw as they struggled out of the yard with the car, their hands barely able to keep hold of it. The faces gradually moved away from the windows. Brother Loughlin watched the boys stumble, shiver, and lurch and took heart. He could still do it. He could still take young boys and make them look small to themselves and their peers. He could still break the little bastards.

From the third year class where he was teaching, Laverty caught sight of Brother Loughlin's smug, self-satisfied face just before it disappeared back into the toilet in a cloud of cigarette smoke. He turned to see the stony faces of the class he now had to try to teach.

Before he knew it, he had opened his mouth and blurted out: "The bastard never asked me! This wasn't my idea!" The boys stared back at him in stunned admiration.

Brother Boland was in the refectory polishing his handbell when he felt it. It was like a sudden increase in atmospheric pressure. He fearfully laid the bell back on the table and set his polishing cloth over it. He closed his eyes and tuned his other senses to the frequency of the building. "It's getting worse!" he blurted out.

"What are you doing? Frightened the life out of me!" exclaimed Brother Cox as he spluttered tea all over himself.

"Have you lost your mind, Brother Boland?" asked Brother Walsh.

Brother Boland moved around the room feeling the walls and testing the windows as he spoke: "It's there! More present. It's tightening!"

"Will you calm down or I'll have to get Brother Loughlin. This is no way to behave," cautioned Brother Walsh.

"You'd want to watch these outbursts, Brother Boland. You know Brother Loughlin already thinks you might be a candidate for the attic," added Brother Cox.

Brother Boland stood rigidly and stared from Cox to Walsh. "Useless! Nothing but abuse!" he snapped, before rushing out and slamming the door behind him.

"Awake! Awake! Alarum! Éistigí! Éistigí! Alea iacta est! The time is upon us! There is a hosting!"

Brother Boland darted like some frantic butterfly along the top corridor of the monastery. This was where the moribund retired Brothers lived. It was a fearful place and Brother Boland could not even remember who lived up here. The elder Brothers were mostly bedridden or mad, and were not allowed to come to the refectory or to attend mass. They received communion every morning from Father Flynn who came after he celebrated mass for the other Brothers in the oratory. He and Widower Frawley, who brought them their food and changed their chamber pots, were the only ones who ever had regular contact with them.

The air of the place terrified Brother Boland. It smelt of

slow death. It was where they put the Brothers who were too far gone to do odd jobs like he did but were not yet dead enough to bury. Brother Boland dreaded ever coming up here, yet the insolent indifference of the younger Brothers had left him no alternative than to stir the ancients.

"Alarum! Alarum!" he shouted as he skittered along the corridor pounding on the cell doors. He reached the dead end of the corridor and leaned exhaustedly against the wall to catch his breath.

From behind the doors arose a doleful moaning.

"Right then, sit down all of you. I hope you have learnt something from that," barked Brother Kennedy, and started to take his Latin books out of his satchel.

He glanced down at the roll book. "Mr. Egan, you will clean the blackboard."

"He's outside talking to Mr. Murphy."

"He is, is he? Mr. Whitehall then."

Whitehall, who had based his whole school career thus far on never being noticed, went bright red and then green in the face. He walked wraithlike to the top of the class and clumsily cleaned the board.

"Take out your lines!"

Brother Kennedy started to work his way round the class inspecting the lines of Caesar's *Gallic Wars* he had set them. He cast his expert eye over each copybook, quickly counting the repetitions, looking for indications of pens being tied together, variances in handwriting that might indicate someone else's work, failure to follow the prescribed colour scheme for alternate words, or any other infraction that should merit a beating. Before moving on he scrawled his name across every page. He was wise to the practice of passing lines across the class to those who had not done them.

"Come on, boy! Get it out!"

He stood over Ferrara menacingly while the boy rummaged in his bag.

"Well, boy?"

"I can't find—"

Brother Kennedy grabbed him by the ear: "Out to the line!" He moved on down the row of desks, picked up Farrelly's copy, and scrutinised it. He could see that there was nothing wrong with it but he enjoyed seeing the little pup sweat.

Brother Loughlin tripped up the stairs with all the lightness that extreme self-satisfaction could possibly lend to his sinister bulk. Making the little brats wash the car had been a brainwave. After his leather had had such a strenuous morning, he'd decided to give it a good rub of the mink oil he kept in his cell.

"Easy! Easy! You'll kill me!"

"Who took me sandals?"

"The young lad here says there's trouble!"

"I'll trouble you!"

"Remember The Siege of Augh Na Breeeeeeeeeeeeee!"

What in God's name . . . ? wondered Brother Loughlin, but got no further before his thoughts were driven out by a crashing and bumping and then the appearance of some ancient figure in a bath chair bouncing down the stairs at him. In a bright green flash of pain, he found himself back at the bottom of the staircase with his left arm wedged between the spokes of one of the chair's wheels.

"What in the name of God is this?" shouted Brother Loughlin at the supine shape that lay motionless in the hallway after being flung from its chair.

Brother Loughlin wrested his arm out of the spokes and with great effort rose to his feet. The hem of his cassock was torn but otherwise he seemed to have escaped unscathed.

"It was young McGovern! I saw him. Deliberately let go of me chair!" murmured the shape on the ground.

"What are you talking about? What happened to you?"

The figure turned its face toward Brother Loughlin and gave him the full benefit of its ancientness. Brother Loughlin staggered back as though shoved by some spectral arm. A cadaverous skull loosely draped in a yellow parchment of skin stared at him with its one bloodshot eye. The toothless mouth opened slowly with no result other than the stretching of tiny lines of spittle between lips that seemed to be the only threads of life holding the head together.

"Who are you?" Brother Loughlin asked from the back of his suddenly dry throat.

"Brother Galvin. I think. And who the feck are you?"

Before Brother Loughlin could gather his wits, he heard a noise behind him on the stairs. He turned around to see Boland in front of a ragtag of more ancient wrecks.

"Brother Boland! What on earth do you think you are doing? Who are these people?"

"The, the, the elder Brothers, from the attic, Head Brother," stammered Boland.

"And what, might I ask, are they doing wandering about the monastery?"

"I was showing them."

"Showing them what?"

"Showing them the sabotage."

"Sabotage? Sabotage? What are you talking about? Have you completely lost your mind, Brother Boland?"

"They saw it! I showed them! I showed them the burnt-out bulbs. I showed them Venerable Saorseach O'Rahilly looking afraid on the stairs. I was going to show them the periodic table. I told them about the slates falling off the roof and the fear in the bell tower! I wanted them to hear the weeping in the walls. I told them! The young ones wouldn't listen!"

"You did, did you?" roared Brother Loughlin. "God give me strength! Fear in the bell tower? Weeping in the walls? What sort of raving is this? What do you think you are doing, disturbing these revered senior Brothers with your unhinged fantasies? Have you no respect for them or is it that you yourself have already slipped over the edge? Is that it? Are you ready for the top floor already? Eh?"

Brother Boland cowered and shook his head in denial. He was not gone yet. He was not ready to be banished to the world of bedsores, chamber pots, and yesterday's cold food. Not that. Not so soon.

"Well then, go get some help and get these Brothers back to their cells, and no more of this nonsense!" shouted Brother Loughlin, and barged through the knot of old wrecks and up the stairs to his cell to oil his leather.

Brother Boland shook and quaked and then tried to help Brother Galvin back into his bath chair.

"Take yer hands off me, ye Black and Tan bastard!" shrieked Galvin.

Brother Kennedy scrawled his signature all over Farrelly's lines and moved on. He was peering suspiciously at Doyle's lines when McDonagh and Bradshaw came in from the yard. He turned to the door and sneered at them: "Learnt your lesson, have you?"

"Yes, Brother," they muttered, their teeth chattering with the cold.

"Good! Then I expect you will both be more than happy

to show me your lines that I set you yesterday."

McDonagh and Bradshaw moved to their desks and pulled out their copybooks.

"Bring them up here!" called Brother Kennedy, and bustled back up to the top of the class.

Bradshaw and McDonagh shuffled toward him with their copybooks. A tense silence fell over the class.

"So, my little meneen, feeling proud of yourselves, are you?"

The two boys stood there shivering and said nothing. Wet patches were beginning to show through their trousers from their sodden underwear.

"Stand still when I'm talking to you!"

The silence in the class thickened.

"Hold up your copybooks!"

They held out their books in their shivering hands.

"Hold still! How do you expect me to correct this if you can't hold it still?"

McDonagh managed to steady his hands and Brother Kennedy flicked over the pages in his copybook. Bradshaw's copybook continued to twitch and jump in his shivering hands. Brother Kennedy's leather flashed through the air and slapped loudly down on Bradshaw's open copybook.

"Keep it still, damn you!"

Bradshaw looked up at the Brother. "I-I-I-I c-c-c-c-can't!"

"Can't or won't? Out to the line!"

Bradshaw walked to the line and leaned with relief against the warm radiator.

"Stand away from the wall, Mr. Bradshaw!" shouted Brother Kennedy, then turned back to McDonagh and flicked through the rest of his lines.

"What is this?" he asked in a low, suspicious voice, and

pointed at McDonagh's copybook.

"Ehm, a jam stain, Brother."

"A jam stain? A jam stain? How dare you ask me to correct this sloppy mess! Do you think I'm going to wade through the filthy leavings of your tea to correct your work? Do you?"

"No, Brother," McDonagh mumbled.

"Then do it again! And cleanly! Out to the line!"

McDonagh moved over to the line and stood there unsure if he wanted to curl up somewhere and cry or just launch himself at Brother Kennedy and kick him in the bollocks until he blacked out.

Brother Kennedy walked back to Doyle's desk and picked up his copybook again. He flicked over the pages and then held the copy in front of Doyle's face: "Where are the rest of them? There are pages missing!"

"Me little brother must've tore them out," explained Doyle matter-of-factly.

"Out to the line!"

"I left me copybook on the bus."

"Out to the line!"

"There was a power cut and me mother couldn't find the candles."

"Out to the line!"

Stealthily the message transmitted itself around the class. They were going for a blackout, as it was known when the whole class deliberately got themselves put out to the line. The boys carefully put away their copybooks and sat waiting for Brother Kennedy to approach.

Finbar noticed this and thought quickly. This was unfair. He had got the translation right and he still had to do the lines. He wasn't going to get a beating for not doing lines that he *had* done even though he shouldn't have had to do them in the first place, so there! He left his copybook sitting open on the desk in front of him and folded his arms.

"The cat ate it."

"Out to the line!"

"Me sister filled me pen with invisible ink and threw me pencil in the fire."

"Out to the line!"

"Me da took it to work by mistake."

"Out to the line!"

"I got the shit kicked out of me in the jakes of a pub."

By this stage Brother Kennedy was barely even listening.

"I wasn't in yesterday."

"Well, you're in today! Out to the line! And take that"—*whap!*—"for answering back!"

Finbar felt his palms sweat as Brother Kennedy progressed through the class. Everyone was getting sent out to the line. This was awful. Why should he stand up for Bradshaw and McDonagh like this? Would they stand up for him?

"Me house burnt down last night."

"Out to the line!"

"Me ma took me pen to bingo."

Brother Kennedy was more than halfway through the class and gathering speed. Soon he would be in sight of Finbar and then it would be too late for him to hide his copybook.

"The boys from the flats stole me bag."

"Out to the line!"

Brother Kennedy continued, dismissing ever more ridiculous excuses. It was getting very crowded in the corner and a perversely festive mood was starting to course through the boys. Smalley Mullen leaned over and gently closed Finbar's copybook and laid it on the floor. He looked levelly at Finbar and his face said it all. Unfair or not, this was something he could not stand out against on his own.

"I sprained me wrist."

"Out!"

"Me ma had a new baby last night."

"Out!"

"I did it in me science copy by mistake."

"Out!"

Finbar looked up at Brother Kennedy's interrogative face. "Me brother ran away to London and took me bag," he found himself saying.

"Out to the line!"

"And don't"—*whap!*—"you"—*whap!*—"ever"—*whap! whap!*—"answer"—*whap!*—"me"—*whap!*—"back"—*whap!*—"again"—*whap!*—"you"—*whap!*—"little"—*whap!*—"gurrier"—*whap! whap! whap!*

Thirteen! That was a lot to get into one sentence. Brother Kennedy was really out of control. You could see the veins pounding purple against the bright red of his bald skull. McDonagh was the last to be leathered and for some reason had decided to push the Brother just a little farther. All he had said was, "I don't know, Brother." Of course it did not help that the question had been: "Have you ever done your homework, McDonagh?" But McDonagh had an amazing talent for filling the most routine utterance with such a blend of wilful stupidity and insolence as could push the most even-tempered teacher over the edge. A firebrand like Brother Kennedy presented no challenge at all.

"Now sit down, ye insolent little pup!" yelled the Brother.

McDonagh walked stiffly back to his desk, and in the

yard below Brother Boland rang the bell for break. The boys ran for the door and left a purple-faced Brother Kennedy leaning against his desk trying desperately to catch his breath.

A ripple of excitement ran through the whole yard as the *bee-baw bee-baw* of the ambulance dopplered its way closer. Mr. Pollock met the ambulance at the gate and then cleared a path for it through the grey swarming of boys.

After what seemed like an age, the ambulance men emerged bearing Brother Kennedy on a stretcher. An unnatural groan of disappointment resulted when the boys saw that Brother Kennedy's face was not covered by the red blanket but by an oxygen mask. He was not dead yet.

"The good Lord must be waiting for Hell to get a bit hotter before he lets that one in," drawled Spud Murphy quietly from his vantage point at the staff room window.

Behind him Mr. Laverty chuckled with appreciation: "That's a good one all right. I like that."

Spud nodded neutrally at Laverty and went back to his chair. He had not yet made up his mind about the seemingly disdainful Laverty.

15

The third Thursday of November dawned as a feeble thinning of the darkness. It was already half past nine yet still dark enough that the streetlights were lit. For the last hundred years the Brothers had celebrated Venerable Saorseach O'Rahilly Day on this day, deemed by scholars to be the fourth Thursday after the first full moon following his death.

Not being prone to wanton acts of frivolity, the idea of giving the boys a day off school in observance of this special occasion had never even entered the Brothers' heads. This being a centenary, it promised more celebration than usual.

Conall McConnell's janitorial ill humour was of epic proportions for this Feast of Venerable Saorseach O'Rahilly. Since a quarter past six that morning he had been in the oratory under the supervision of Brother Boland. He was ready to strangle the man.

McConnell had to take the small terra-cotta statues of Venerable Saorseach O'Rahilly down from their niches in the walls of the oratory and transport them to the hall. The fact that there were five hundred of the little bastards was not a problem in itself. What was a problem, however, was Brother Boland's immovable insistence that they be brought down to the floor of the oratory one at a time.

Brother Loughlin had specifically picked Boland for

the Venerable Saorseach preparations to quell his stupid sabotage paranoia. Brother Boland had indeed become so engrossed in every little detail that he stopped noticing the so-called shudderings inside the school. Even the seemingly unfixable school clock had ceased to worry him.

Leg sore, hot, and dying for a smoke, McConnell stepped off the ladder and placed the last eight-inch-tall statue with the little army that had formed on the floor.

"Right then, that's the last of them," he said firmly, and began to load them into the velvet compartments of the custom-built crates. Each identical statue showed Venerable Saorseach O'Rahilly as a young man peering skyward while being moved by the spirit of the Holy Ghost. To McConnell they looked like figurines of a very drunk young man staring at the moon. "I'm going to move this lot over to the hall," he stated in a tone that left little room for contradiction.

"Be very careful!" implored Brother Boland.

"Just not good enough! It's inexcusable, that's what it is! A disgrace! A total disgrace!" Brother Loughlin snarled, and stomped back up to the corner of the West Circular Road for the tenth time. He looked up the main road. Still no sign of them. "A bloody disgrace, that's what it is!"

He pulled a cigarette from the top pocket of his cassock and leaned into the wall of the school to light up out of the biting wind. He took a drag and glanced up to see Father Flynn bustling up the West Circular Road toward him. *Late as usual*, thought Brother Loughlin.

"God save you, Brother Loughlin, but you're a hardier man than I. A bit cold for taking the air, I'd say," called Father Flynn amicably.

"Good morning, Father," replied Brother Loughlin, not

without taking a conspicuous glance at his watch.

"Sorry I'm a little late. We had a visit from the city manager this morning."

"You have building trouble in the chapel?"

"Oh no, no, no, just a social visit. Dropped in for breakfast. We went to school together at Southwell."

Brother Loughlin flinched at the mention of the Jesuit school. It always rankled him to think that the Jesuits were in the business of producing the bosses who would lord it over the drones he was in charge of turning out. It was not the inequality of the boys' fates that disturbed him. It was more about knowing that he would never have any link with that golden club of power and privilege. He bitterly consoled himself with the thought that Flynn had not made it into the Jesuits and was a mere diocesan priest.

"I see," he said flatly.

"So what has you out here in the cold?" asked Father Flynn.

"Waiting for the damn laundry van! They were supposed to be here at eight! The Brothers are waiting to get changed for the pageant and those eejits have our new underwear for the year and our gala cassocks off God knows where. Today of all days!"

"That'd be the Jezebel Laundry then?"

There was an undertone in Father Flynn's voice that Brother Loughlin did not entirely like. "Yes. The Brotherhood feels it is important to support such laudable institutions," he answered pompously. "Of course, we might get better service from a more businesslike laundry, but then who would take care of those poor fallen women?"

Father Flynn nodded noncommittally. He had heard the stories about the Jezebel Laundries and was not sure they were the noble institution they were made out to be. Stories of beatings and terrible punishments. Stories of family feuds that ended up in girls being put away in the laundries for no good reason. It was rumoured that the Bishop of Orris and Bargey had a young girl sent to a laundry because she refused his attentions and now he visited her weekly as her "personal confessor." Father Flynn had even brought it up with the parish priest but had been told that such rumours were the malicious gossip of atheists and socialists and if he wanted to join their ranks it would be on his own head. Since that admonition he had kept his own counsel on the subject.

Before either of them felt compelled to break the awkward silence that was growing, it was shattered by the metallic retching and hawking of the Jezebel Laundry van turning into Greater Little Werburgh Street, North.

"About bloody time!" Brother Loughlin shouted after it. He brushed past Father Flynn and hurried his bulk down to the yard to berate the laundry men.

"They're here! They're here!" cried Brother Tobin as he ran toward the bathhouse, or "balnearium" as Brother Loughlin insisted on calling it. The Brothers stood around the swimming pool-sized ice bath in their bathing cassocks, teeth chattering.

"Right Brothers, time to mortify the flesh that is our cross to bear!" cried Brother Loughlin as he entered. The Widower Frawley followed behind him with his arms full of new cassocks, underwear, and sandals. He set to hanging them in each Brother's cubicle. Loughlin checked the buttons on his bathing cassock and leapt into the pool. One by one the Brothers followed him into the pool with degrees of enthusiasm ranging from the gleefully masochistic to the condemned man.

Once all were in the pool, Brother Loughlin led a decade of the rosary for the intentions of the Brotherhood and the prompt beatification of Saorseach O'Rahilly, and then one by one the Brothers moved in front of him where he submerged their heads in the traditional symbolic rebaptism of Venerable Saorseach O'Rahilly Day.

"Venerable Saorseach O'Rahilly, bend me to your will," intoned Brother Loughlin as he dunked each one in turn before finally dunking himself.

The rebaptism completed, the Brothers went to their cubicles, removed their bathing cassocks, and dried off.

Brother Loughlin cleared his throat ceremoniously: "Venerable Saorseach O'Rahilly, shield me from the temptations of the flesh and all that is fleeting, corrupting, and tawdry in this life!"

With that, all the Brothers pulled on their brand-new tweed underpants and stepped out of their cubicles.

"Venerable Saorseach O'Rahilly, guard my heart from the lures that might distract me from the path of duty."

The Brothers donned their tweed undershirts which, like the underpants, were artfully designed for maximum discomfort and mortification of the flesh. Years of experience had perfected the nuns' design, and with wear they would become increasingly uncomfortable, bulking at the seams and growing ever itchier.

"Venerable Saorseach O'Rahilly, place my feet on the righteous path and keep them there, step after step in yours."

The Brothers put on the tweed socks with a lot of falling over and near disaster when Brother Cox, somewhat worse for wear from the naggin of gin he'd smuggled in the night before, bumped into Brother Tobin who almost fell headfirst into the pool.

"Now, armoured against the evils of the world, we don the sandals and outer garment that will proclaim to all our unswerving dedication to Venerable Saorseach O'Rahilly and the Brotherhood of Godly Coercion."

The black gala cassocks and birettas with their bright red trim and the new sandals completed the ritual. The Brothers marched out of the bathhouse scrubbed raw and ready to take the world by the scruff of the neck and teach it some manners.

Mr. Pollock sat at his desk and consulted the roll book. "Now then. In honour of the day that is in it, we will dispense with lessons as usual and instead prepare for the forthcoming celebrations by reacquainting ourselves with the life of Venerable Saorseach O'Rahilly, the esteemed founder of the Brothers of Godly Coercion." He blessed himself reverently as he uttered the honoured name.

"Mr. Sullivan, you will begin."

Mr. Pollock opened the slim hardback of *The Life of Venerable Saorseach O'Rahilly* by Marcus Madden, B.A., and held it out.

Finbar walked to the top of the class and took the book from the teacher. He did not look up. This was one of those very vulnerable situations where anyone with an aptitude for pulling faces would be out to make him laugh. He could already feel the others willing him to look up. He focused on the page and read slowly and expressionlessly the words he had heard so many times before.

"*Venerable Saorseach O'Rahilly was born at Dunbally in 1811, the first of two sons to Cathal and Brigid O'Rahilly. Cathal was a well-respected and successful grain merchant.*

"*The young Saorseach was educated at home by his mother, an unusually pious woman given to ecstatic visions. Despite her piousness, the evils of laudanum often tempted her, and whenever she gave in to these cravings, she would be plunged into bouts of anguished penance and self-mortification. On one occasion Cathal had to call the Bishop of Dervish and Ossory to the house to restrain her for fear she would cause herself fatal harm with a horsewhip. These instances made a strong impression on the young Saorseach."*

Finbar could barely keep himself awake as he read. Like all the boys, he had heard this story at least once a year since his first year of school in Cork. In primary school it had sometimes been accompanied by drawing and colouring scenes from O'Rahilly's life. Now there was no such levity. The whole thing induced in the boys a torporific waking coma, a viscous thickening of time that sapped all energy and light from them and their immediate surroundings.

"Mr. McDonagh, you will continue," crackled Mr. Pollock's voice through the leaden air.

McDonagh snapped out of his reverie and fumbled with the bottom of his sweater before standing up. He had to pull it down over the very evident erection prompted by daydreaming about Assumpta Cumberland who worked in the corner shop.

"Stand up straight and don't slouch like an apeman, McDonagh," sneered the teacher.

McDonagh reddened and straightened up. Mercifully his tumescence subsided as he took the book from Finbar and turned around to face the class. Assumpta Cumberland and her formidable breasts were replaced by the less stimulating minutiae of the life of Venerable Saorseach O'Rahilly.

"Saorseach's father Cathal was often away from home conducting his business in the distant thriving towns of Dunmoice and Rathaughram. When Saorseach was eighteen, his younger brother Bartholomew, perhaps deprived of his father's attentions, ran away to sea. Brigid

O'Rahilly went into a precipitous decline after this and spent much of her time roaming the gardens of the O'Rahilly demesne in search of the leprechauns whom she believed had taken her son. On these wanderings she carried with her a bag of gold sovereigns with which to ransom Bartholomew if she should come across the little people. Ultimately this would prove to be her undoing."

On and on it droned: Brigid having her head staved in by persons unknown and her bag of sovereigns stolen from her; the widowed Cathal first taking to the drink and then to ascetic religiousness; his conviction that the famine was a punishment from God on the locals who had killed his wife and his bloody-minded insistence on continuing to export grain to England while those around him wasted away; Saorseach's apprenticeship to a merchant in Dublin; his slide into dissolution and his eventual reformation. All of it washed over the boys like so much mind-numbing sludge. When finally it ended there was a huge sense of relief that even the decade of the rosary for the prompt beatification of Venerable Saorseach O'Rahilly could not entirely dampen.

"Aren't they lovely though, but?"

"What?"

"The statues. They're lovely, you know?"

Conall McConnell looked carefully at Ray McRae. He'd had a lot of apprentice janitors in his time and thought he'd seen everything, but this enthusiastic, wild-eyed, cheery outlook was a new one on him. He examined McRae's face but could find no trace of guile or sarcasm.

"Just get on with it," McConnell snapped, and disappeared out through the fire exit.

While his boss calmed himself with a smoke in the laneway, Ray McRae removed the statuettes of Venerable Saorseach O'Rahilly from their packing cases and placed one on each chair in the hall. He worked quickly and carefully and whistled happily to himself.

Soon he heard the fire exit open and close again. Without looking up he called out to McConnell: "They're like little works of art, you know what I mean? All the same, but each one a little bit different. Like this one. Looks a little sadder than the others. Even a little depressed. I knew a sculptor one time. Very depressed fellah. Did his sculptures, had a couple of pints in the local of an evening, but never really talked to anyone, you know what I mean? Next thing you know, he ups and cuts his throat with a safety razor. Funny, isn't it, that they call them safety razors and them such dangerous things?"

McRae fell silent and McConnell let out a sigh of relief. He was a man of few words himself and talkative people made him uncomfortable. He walked to the back of the hall and lifted another crate of statuettes. Swiftly he moved along the row of chairs and placed a statuette gently on each one.

"Ciúnas! Silence!"

When the desired silence fell on the hall, Brother Loughlin stepped to the front of the stage, looking, if anything, fatter than usual in his gala cassock; the red trim on the collar, cuffs, and hem lending him the appearance of a gigantic hot coal ready to burst into flames at any moment.

"Brother Boland will now demonstrate the correct and only way to handle the figures of Venerable Saorseach O'Rahilly. You will keep these with you at every moment from now until the end of the day when they will be returned to the oratory. Any damage or breakage will result in a hiding you will never forget and automatic transfer to an industrial school. These are holy statues. Is that clear?"

The boys nodded dumbly and Brother Boland stepped forward with his statuette. The base of it rested on the flat palm of his left hand and he held it reverently but firmly with his right hand clasped around the figure's chest.

"When we are in procession," Brother Loughlin resumed, "you will hold the figure above your head with both hands. The figure will at no moment be allowed to rest on the ground. You may hold the statue in one hand only, and I repeat only, when required to do so by a Brother or teacher who finds it necessary to use the strap on you. Right. Now walk slowly to your seats and CAREFULLY pick up the figure. They are all the same so it does not matter which one you get."

There was not exactly a stampede to get the best of the Venerable Saorseachs but there was a certain amount of competition for the chairs near the back of the hall. This was the impetuous rush of amateurs. Anyone so eager to be at the back was going to be picked off and moved up front where they could better be watched. Scully, Lynch, and McDonagh expertly restrained themselves and found themselves seats three rows from the back.

Lynch picked up his statue in the approved manner and set to whispering things of a very threatening and mostly anatomically impossible nature to it.

Brother Cox, who was going to narrate the pageant, took his place at the lectern, stage right. Over his gala cassock he wore a costume that was somewhere between Henry VIII and an Edwardian pimp. What it was supposed to evoke, other than mockery, was hard to tell.

"Before we begin, I would like to welcome Mr. Diarmaid DePaor of the Department of Education, who is our special guest here this morning," Cox began.

Mr. DePaor stood up and awkwardly acknowledged the

forced applause, squeezed from the boys by glowers and hissed warnings.

When DePaor sat down again Brother Cox took a deep portentous breath and continued: "*Venerable Saorseach O'Rahilly was born in Dunbally in 1811, the first of two sons to Cathal and Brigid O'Rahilly . . .*"

For the next hour and a half the boys would have to sit through the story they had already heard that day, this time being badly and reluctantly acted out in front of them. All round the hall right hands tightened around the chests of the terra-cotta figurines. To the accompaniment of this simulated strangulation, the pageant flapped its leaden wings on the first stage of its long flight toward lunchtime.

Finbar sat quietly two rows in front of Scully and the others and tried desperately to stay awake.

The cast for the Venerable Saorseach O'Rahilly pageant was mostly made up of conscripts. For three weeks they had been kept back after school for rehearsal. Among the most misguided pieces of press-ganged casting was Smalley Mullen in the role of Saorseach O'Rahilly's father, Cathal.

As did everyone, Smalley laboriously read his lines from pieces of cardboard that Brother Boland held up in the wings, but it was the boy's high-pitched voice that really topped it.

"Do not dare contradict me, boy! You will be taking over this business when I am gone so you must learn to shoulder the burden of responsibility!" he squeaked at Kelly, a gargantuan third year playing Saorseach, who towered over him.

"I want to be my own man! I want to see the world!" boomed Kelly, and stormed offstage and straight into the scenery for the forthcoming parish production of *An Bealach Solais*, or *The Way of Light*, a patriotic and devotional operetta in Irish composed by Michael Costigan, a local musician and patriot.

The high point of the life of Saorseach, if you really had to choose one, was the temptation scene. Consumed by despair and drink, the young dissolute Saorseach wandered the streets of Dublin to be assailed by drunken prostitutes. Had it been a less well-known scene the Brothers would gladly have cut it completely, but it was pivotal and had been cited often in the beatification process so it could not be left out.

The harlots, three third years dressed in Mrs. McCurtin's old kitchen clothes, would not have tempted even the most starved lothario.

"Get away from me, ye fallen women! Do not flaunt your shamelessness in my presence! Tempt me not with your sin!" bellowed Kelly, and flounced offstage, this time tripping and breaking the nose of Turlough Halpin, who was the only enthusiastic volunteer in the whole production and was playing the Pope.

Up and down the aisles the Brothers and lay teachers patrolled ceaselessly. No irreverence would be tolerated on this uplifting day.

The pageant ground on and on, and it was with a feeling of deep despair that Finbar opened his eyes to see that they were still only coming up to the stick fight scene. He watched lazily as the clandestine hurling match O'Rahilly had attended in Cahirdorras degenerated into a stick fight disputing a late foul that then amplified out to include some atavistic local land disputes.

In his drunken state (much played down in the Brothers' rendition), O'Rahilly wandered straight into the melee to be dealt a haymaker of a blow to the head.

The stick fight abated and the locals, not recognising

the unconscious O'Rahilly, left him for dead and headed off to the local public house to continue their disputations in a more sociable manner.

O'Rahilly lay there poleaxed while Brother Cox led the choir of first years whose balls had not yet dropped through a castrato chorus supposed to invoke imminent divine revelation. After the shrieking faded, nothing happened. When what might have been a pregnant pause clearly became an unbearable delay, Brother Cox hissed "Get up out of that, Kelly!" loud enough that it carried through the enforced silence of the hall.

Kelly melodramatically rose to his feet and stumbled around holding his head. From the wings came the squeaking of small wheels as Brother Tobin, implausibly dressed as God in a white sheet, was wheeled out on one of Mrs. McCurtin's tea trolleys.

"Saorseach, you must mend your ways! You have strayed from the path of righteousness!"

Saorseach fell on his knees before his precariously balanced God.

"What must I do, oh Lord? Show me the way."

"You must abjure your drunkenness and vice and dedicate yourself to steering the young boys of Ireland onto the path of goodness, devotion, Gaelic football, fluent mellifluous Gaelic, purity, chastity, and more Gaelic football."

In a puff of saltpetre far too small to fully cloak Brother Tobin's bulk, the tea trolley was wheeled back offstage and Saorseach was left to stand in wonder at the divine apparition that had just changed his life.

"He looks like someone just stuck a dead fish up his hole," whispered Lynch.

Scully elbowed him sharply in the ribs, almost knocking

his Saorseach O'Rahilly statue out of his hands.

"Ye bad bastard! I nearly dropped me holy Action Man!" hissed Lynch, somehow without moving his lips. Out of the corner of his eye he could see Pollock watching them suspiciously. Lynch knew full well that any sort of misbehaving carried extra severe punishment on Venerable Saorseach O'Rahilly Day.

The pageant dragged along, showing Saorseach O'Rahilly taking over the old mill in Dunbally and turning it into a school, chasing urchins off the streets and into the clutches of his staff; the formation of the Brotherhood; O'Rahilly's dementia and death from something that very much resembled syphilis but was referred to as a "fever"; the later miracle of the hurling triumph of Carlow over Cork which was ascribed to the intervention of O'Rahilly; and finally, the bloody-nosed Halpin as Pope granting permission for the limited veneration of Saorseach O'Rahilly on the basis of that miracle.

"We will now make our way, in an orderly fashion, to Saint Werburgh's Church for the celebratory mass."

Diarmaid DePaor was already on his feet and at the door, badly in need of the comforting isolation of the Department of Education. He would certainly not be attending any celebratory mass.

16

Giz a go of yer doll!" "Does yer sister know ye took that?" "Did ye forget to put on the dress?" "All ye need now is a little pram!" jeered the denizens of Markiewicz Mansions, the decrepit flats that had to be traversed to get to Saint Werburgh's Church.

Seething with shame and fury at the Brothers for this humiliation, the boys walked four abreast holding their little statuettes of Venerable Saorseach O'Rahilly above their heads.

Once inside the church of Saint Werburgh they were herded into pews and the form master of each class was posted on an outer aisle while the Brothers patrolled the centre aisle, leathers at the ready.

"What about me fuckin' lunch?" muttered Lynch to Scully as they sat down.

"This is it."

Father Flynn took the altar and cleared his throat into the hollow echoing silence. "In order to prepare ourselves to celebrate this mass in honour of the intentions of Venerable Saorseach O'Rahilly, let us all look into our hearts in preparation for a full and cleansing confession. We will also be offering up our prayers for the prompt recovery of Brother Kennedy." He bowed his head and peered deep into his soul. He vowed to try to be less judgmental of Brother Loughlin in future.

Suddenly, with military precision, a troop of hard-faced priests who had been drafted in from neighbouring parishes filed out of the sacristy and down the two side aisles, each one slipping into his confessional and slamming the door behind him.

Expertly the form masters ushered the boys into the confessionals from each pew and back to their places via the centre aisle, making a lovely little production line of confession, contrition, forgiveness, and penance.

"Bless me, Father, for I have sinned. It is two weeks since my last confession. I disobeyed my mother. I used bad words. I took the name of the Lord in vain. I told lies."

The priests absolved boy after boy of sins learned by rote at the time of first communion and unchanged since. The theological implications of someone like McDonagh claiming to have disobeyed a mother he did not have and then being absolved of this nonsin would have so addled the minds of any of the clergy present that it was best to not even think about it.

The standard three Hail Marys were doled out as penance for these standard sins. Once in a while there was a real one, though this was not the day for heartfelt confessions. None of the priests had the time for this and certainly not Father Fury, erstwhile chaplain to the school.

"Bless me, Father, for I have sinned. It is three months since my last confession."

"That is a long time, my son."

"Yes, Father."

"Good boy. Go on," said Fury, glad to have the token nod in the direction of thoroughness out of the way.

"I missed mass. I lied to me mother. I took the name of the Lord in vain and I let the parish priest put his mickey in my mouth."

The whole chapel turned around as Father Fury's door exploded open. He burst out and dragged the shocked Maher by the hair, up the aisle, and through the side door. Father Fury was further angered by the braces on Maher's legs that slowed him down.

Finbar watched the boy struggle up the aisle behind Father Fury and felt his stomach turn over. He could not take his eyes off the braces.

Maher was a quiet boy and a little simple. He had just opened a whole Pandora's box of trouble for himself. Father Fury was not the right one to be making these revelations to. He had received a call just that morning from the Bishop of Cloynes and Bardgey admonishing him for his somewhat indiscreet and excessive "fraternising" with the choristers of Saint Bodhrán's orphanage.

"Settle down now and get on with your confessions," bawled Brother Loughlin as he followed Father Fury outside.

When Loughlin came back fifteen minutes later and gestured to Brother Tobin to head outside, Lynch turned to Scully and whispered: "Get the body bag, Tobin!"

Scully turned and saw that Lynch was smiling wanly. He knew what Lynch meant. Maher would not be back that day, and it was unlikely they would ever see him again. Getting smacked around like that by a priest usually ended up with the boy disappearing off to the industrial school at Drumgloom or some other institution of retribution and betterment.

From outside the church the desultory praying sounded like a large group of people sighing out their woes for the world to hear.

The locals from Markiewicz Mansions, long tired of being chased away from snooping around the church doors by Brother Boland, were delighted to see this new development. The Black Maria had arrived. This was deadly. They hadn't seen one in about a week. It was always entertaining when the law came to take someone away.

The Black Maria pulled up outside the sacristy and two guards hopped out. The sacristy door opened and Father Fury emerged with Maher's collar grasped in his thick ruddy fist. Maher's nose was bleeding and his face was stained with tears.

"Little animal has lost his mind. Raving he is. Tried to bite me on the neck. Obviously no parental control at all. He should be locked up. I'd say Drumgloom is the place for him."

"Right you are, Father. Isn't it fierce all the same, Father," chirped one of the guards as he grabbed Maher and bundled him into the back of the vehicle.

"You won't be getting any more trouble from this one, Father. He'll be locked up before the day is out, and not a minute too soon by the sounds of him," said the driver over the sounds of Maher banging and screaming in the back. The guard handed Father Fury the committal papers to sign.

"Louth man is it you are?" asked Father Fury.

"Oh be gob, yes, Father, Louth be name and loud be nature, wha'?" replied the guard ingratiatingly.

"Good one! I'll just get these witnessed and I'll be back to you in a minute," laughed Fury hollowly, and disappeared back inside the sacristy.

As the two altar boys carried up the bread and wine to be consecrated into the flesh-and-blood sacrifice of Christ on the cross, Father Fury sidled in beside Brother Loughlin and handed him the committal papers to countersign.

"Are ye finished dusting them nooks yet? They'll be back soon."

Ray McRae turned around on the ladder and beamed down into the gloom of the oratory at Conall McConnell. "Nearly there. Just have to do the ones over this window."

"Well hurry up. I don't want them back on top of us and the nooks not done."

"No problem," beamed McRae, and went back to work.

McConnell turned to go and had his hand on the door handle when McRae's wheedling voice brought him up short.

"Do you know what I'm going to ask you though, but?"

"What up with ye now?"

"Was that crack in the ceiling always there? It's only that I didn't notice it before earlier."

"Fucked if I know. Just do them nooks and get it over with," McConnell snapped, then left.

From the landing he watched the tired grey line of boys that snaked across the yard, their arms straining to keep the statues of O'Rahilly above their heads. The line wound into the monastery and up to the oratory door.

Mr. Pollock strode up the stairs three at a time flailing with his leather to keep the boys in single file. At the oratory door he stood and waited for the bustle to die down. Beaming with centennial pride, the Brothers filed past him into the oratory and took their places in the pews.

"Keep those statues over your heads!" barked Mr. Pollock, and then motioned the first boy on the line to move into the oratory.

The puzzled and exhausted first year stumbled into the room and was stopped by the pudgy hand of Brother Cox.

Brother Cox took the statue from the boy, kissed its feet, and passed it to Brother Boland, who did the same and then passed it to Brother Loughlin, who did the same and then passed it to Father Flynn, who blessed it and passed it to Conall McConnell, who passed it immediately on to Ray McRae on the ladder, who put it in a nook.

"Now go back to your class and wait there until you are told to go home. The roll will be called so no monkey business," called Mr. Pollock when each boy came out, dashing any hopes that Venerable Saorseach O'Rahilly Day had finally come to an end.

"I'm going to smash mine and get expelled. At least that way I can go home now," whispered Scully.

"Deadly idea," agreed Lynch.

Neither of them moved, and when the line in front of them inched up the stairs they reluctantly inched after it.

17

Finbar felt under the doormat and found nothing. He lifted it completely and confirmed the total absence of key. Maybe his mother hadn't gone into town, though she had sounded very certain that morning.

He lifted the knocker on the letter box and let it drop. He heard feet coming down the stairs and the door was pulled open.

"What the fuck? When did you come back?" he gasped.

"There ye are, ye little shite! Lovely uniform!" jeered Declan.

Finbar gaped at his brother's beaming face.

Declan turned and walked down the hall, leaving Finbar standing on the doorstep, stunned. "Mam?" he called.

"She's not here. She went into town," answered Declan from the kitchen.

Finbar closed the hall door behind him, dropped his bag and blazer in the hall, and went into the scullery where his brother was just taking two slices of bread from under the grill. He looked at the empty breadboard on the table.

"Is that all the bread?" asked Finbar pointedly.

"Looks like it."

"I'm starving! They didn't let us have lunch today."

Declan proceeded to use up the last of the butter on his toast and sat munching at the table while Finbar stared angrily at him.

"Aren't ye going to ask me where I was?" asked Declan with his mouth full.

"Up yer hole for all I care," snapped Finbar, and rummaged in the cupboard for the biscuit tin. There were two rubbery stale custard creams. He stuffed them into his mouth, more to make sure that Declan didn't get them than any real desire to eat stale custard creams.

"There's no milk," remarked Declan carelessly.

"You finished that too?" yelled Finbar in exasperated disbelief. The stale biscuits were waking the hunger that he had managed to almost ignore through Venerable Saorseach O'Rahilly Day.

"I was hungry, so shut up!"

"You're in for it when they get home." Finbar could think of nothing else to say or do and soon found himself outside the front door looking up and down the street for somewhere to go. With sudden decision he strode off toward the park beside the railway.

The moon was poking through the clouds high above the rooftops when Finbar returned home.

"Where the hell were you until now?" shouted Mr. Sullivan as he yanked the hall door open.

"Out," replied Finbar.

"Out where?"

"Walking."

"Walking? Walking? Have you any idea what time it is? Is it mad you are? You don't even know where you are, for God sake! You could have been down a lane with a knife in your back for all we knew!"

From the table Declan grinned at his brother. Finbar couldn't help noticing that they'd had liver and bacon, Declan's favourite, for tea.

"But what about him? He's been missing for weeks!" yelled Finbar.

"Declan said he's sorry and I think he learnt his lesson," said Mrs. Sullivan softly.

"And don't you raise your voice like that in this house again," cautioned Mr. Sullivan.

Finbar stared sullenly at the floor.

"So, where the hell were you?" repeated Mr. Sullivan.

"Walking. The park. Nowhere."

"The park? What park?"

"Don't know. One with big pillars and statues. Over there." He gestured vaguely in the direction of the back of the scullery.

"What do you think you're doing wandering around parks in the dark? This isn't Cork, you know."

"I know. Wish it was."

"Ah, sit down and eat your tea before I lose patience with you," snapped Mr. Sullivan, and headed out the low door that led to the backyard. Through the steamed-up window of the scullery, Finbar saw the unmistakable flare of a match and the tiny red glow of a cigarette. When had his father started smoking again? He sat down and his mother put his dried-out tea in front of him.

Finbar poked at the liver with his fork. He hated liver. Sitting in a low oven for two hours with a saucepan lid over it did not help either. His mother knew he hated liver. Why did his tea have to be horrible just because Declan liked liver? That wasn't fair. None of it was fair.

"How come I only got two bits of fried potato?"

"Because you were late, and anyway, poor Declan was starving," answered his mother.

"Oh yeah, poor Declan was starving! Poor Declan stole a hundred quid and fecked off God knows where and now that he's back we all have to lick his arse for him!" exploded Finbar.

Mr. Sullivan almost took the scullery door off its hinges as he shot in from the yard. Already he was drawing his belt out of the loops of his trousers.

"Don't speak to your mother like that! Get up those stairs in front of me! I'll put manners on you!" He whipped the belt at the back of Finbar's legs and the boy dashed up the stairs.

Mr. Sullivan stopped and heard the bedroom door slam. He rested his head heavily on the banister rail and sighed, taking a deep breath as if to summon up one last burst of energy. From the living room doorway Mrs. Sullivan watched as he seemed to slump and then shouted up the stairs after Finbar: "And don't come down again until you've learnt some manners!"

Mr. Sullivan walked into the unlit parlour. He stared out the window at the narrow street and wondered how they had come to this. This was not what he had hoped for: a pokey little house in Dublin, an annoying job in the Customs House overseeing the incineration of stupid imports that no one would pay the duty on, and now his family slowly drifting away from one another into their own private silences. He squeezed the bridge of his nose with his thumb and forefinger and shook his head sadly.

"Finbar! Come back down and finish your tea!" he called up the stairs.

The rest of the tea things had already been cleared away and Finbar's tea sat alone on the table.

"Will I make a fresh pot?" asked Mrs. Sullivan, already up to her elbows in the sinkful of washing up.

"It's all right. I'll have milk."

"There's only just enough for the breakfast. That stupid milkman never comes until well after eight."

"The tea in the pot is fine."

Finbar poured himself a cup of dark, stewed tea. He sipped it and then added three spoons of sugar to mask its bitterness. His fried eggs were like rubber from being kept warm in the oven. Nonetheless, hunger got the better of him. He cut off a piece of liver and spiked a slice of fried potato. He chewed determinedly.

"Do you still have homework to do?" called his mother from the scullery.

"A bit."

"Well don't dawdle over your tea. It's getting late."

"Where's dad?"

"He went out for a walk. Declan's in the parlour. He's writing away for a job that was in the paper. You can do your homework at the table here when you've finished your tea."

"I can do it on the bed. It's only a bit of Geography and some Latin verbs.

"All right so. Just be sure to get straight to it. No daydreaming."

Finbar gobbled down the last bits of crispy rasher and fried bread, then drained his teacup and shuddered a little at the strong tannic bite of it. He picked up his dishes and carried them out to the scullery.

"Just drop them in the sink, pet. I have to boil the kettle. The hot water's on the blink again. Go on now and finish your homework like a good boy."

Finbar peeked in the half-open parlour door as he passed down the hall. Declan was sitting on the vinyl sofa with a writing pad on his knees and the Help Wanted pages of the evening *Way Forward* on the cushion beside him. He wrote furiously, stopped, ripped the page out of the writing pad, and crumpled it up into a little ball. He glanced up expressionlessly at Finbar and then, without a word, dropped the ball of paper on the floor, lowered his head, and again started his letter.

Finbar took his schoolbag from beside the hallstand and quietly went up the stairs two at a time. He paused at the top and listened. The only sounds were the soft, warm chuckling of the tea dishes in the soapy water from the scullery and a short tearing of paper followed by a quietly hissed "Fuck!" from Declan.

Finbar propped his pillow up against the headboard and sat back. He pulled out his Latin copybook and his Geography book. On Declan's bed sat his duffel bag, still waiting to be unpacked.

Amabo, Amabas, Amabat, Amabamus, Amabatis, Amabant. I used to love, You used to love, He/She/It used to love, We you used to love, You used to love, They used to love, Finbar wrote for the tenth and last time.

All he had to do now was the pluperfect ten times and learn off the fishing ports of Ireland counterclockwise starting with Howth.

"Don't disturb Finbar, he's doing his homework," he heard his mother's voice call out from the scullery.

"I won't!" replied Declan from the landing.

The bedroom door opened. Declan came in and closed the door softly behind him. Without looking at Finbar, he dropped the newspaper, writing pad, and pen on his bed and set to emptying out his duffel bag.

Keeping his head still, Finbar moved his eyes to watch. Declan dug into the bag and pulled out a pair of trousers that looked like they had been tied up in knots and left out in the middle of the road for trucks to run over.

Piece by piece Declan removed his clothes from the bag and threw them into a pile at the foot of his bed. Then he stopped suddenly and picked them all up. He unrolled them and started folding them as neatly as he could, setting them in a pile on the bed. He went to the wardrobe, opened the door, looked inside, and closed the door again. "Fuck sake," he whispered to himself. He turned and glanced toward Finbar.

Amareram, Amareras, Amarerat, Amareramus, Amareratis, Amarerant, I had loved, You had loved, He/She/It had loved, We had loved, You had loved, They had loved, he wrote, and then added above the two neat columns, *Pluperfect Tense Active*. He drew a line and started two more columns, this time writing the English first for variety's sake.

"What're you doing?" asked Declan quietly.

"Latin."

"Hated Latin," said Declan.

Finbar simply continued to write.

Declan sat down on the edge of his bed and faced his brother. Finbar pretended to be engrossed in the pluperfect tense and ignored him.

"I was in London," said Declan suddenly, as if he were answering a question.

Amareramus, Amareratis, Amarerant, wrote Finbar without looking up.

"I met this fellah on the mail boat over. Ambrose, his name was. From Dundalk. Said he had a cousin in London. Said I could stay with them until I found me feet. Said he could set me up with a job on the buildings. So we get the train to London and when we arrive we go to this pub somewhere to meet his cousin. The cousin seems all pissed off that Ambrose said I could stay."

Declan paused. Out of the corner of his eye Finbar

could see that his brother was watching him, waiting for some reaction. He couldn't help feeling somehow pleased by Declan's discomfort. Finbar could sense this story was going nowhere nice. He knew Declan had made a mess of running away to London; he could hear it in his voice.

"Fin, it was poxy. The cousin got me a job bricklaying. It was fucking awful. I had to get up at five in the morning. Then the cousin says I have to start paying rent and he and Ambrose have this big fight and the cousin kicks me out."

Finbar put down his pen and for the first time looked straight at Declan. He intended saying something smartarsed but when he saw his brother's face—tired, defeated, pitiful—he just shook his head lightly.

"Did you make any money?" asked Finbar.

Declan shook his head.

"Then why did you go? I had to put up with them while you were away all full of *could be down a laneway somewhere with a knife in his back* and all that."

"Yeah. Look. I'm sorry. I wanted to get out. I needed to . . . I wanted to . . ."

"What?"

"I just needed to get away and I fucked it up and now I'm back like an eejit without a penny and I have to listen to them again. Fuck sake! They want me to apply for this stupid job at the gas company."

"So? They let you back."

"Ah fuck, Fin, it's just miserable. I miss Cork. I miss . . ."

"What?"

"Nothing. It's just . . . Remember when Sheila dumped me?" Declan stared down at his fists in his lap as he spoke. "Well. She didn't really dump me. She was knocked up."

"Fuck sake!"

"Don't you start too. They took her away. One of those

fucking laundries in the middle of nowhere."

"Jaysus, Dec, that's shite. I didn't know."

"Yeah, Fin. It is the worst shite. I don't know what to do. It's like I'm trying to do everything with the wrong hand. I fuck everything up. I'm really fucked off—"

Declan stopped abruptly, gathered up all his dirty clothes, and went downstairs. Finbar picked up Declan's writing pad from his bed:

Dear Sir,

I want to apply for the job of Accounts Clerk, Third Class, Grade IV. Give me the job or I'll break your head, ye fucker!

Declan had scribbled all over the page after writing the words.

Stupid sap, thought Finbar, but smiled a little. He picked up the pad and wrote:

Dear Sir,

I wish to apply for the position of Accounts Clerk, Second Class, Grade IV, as advertised in this evening's Way Forward. I am hard-working, thorough, and reliable. I can be available for interview at any time and I look forward to hearing from you.

He wrote *Try this, Dec* at the top of the page, threw the pad back on his brother's bed, and returned to his homework.

18

From the outside it looked just like any of the other squalid mill and warehouse buildings that huddled together on the Limerick Road just beyond Dullow. The only indications that it was a Jezebel Laundry were the bricked-up windows facing the road and the small brass crucifix affixed to the padlocked metal gates. Above the crucifix sat a small brass plate that bore the inscription: *Purgatorio Per Ardua: Purgatory Through Drudgery.*

"Fifty-seven! Put your back into it or I'll tan your hide for you, you ignorant slattern!" Sister Delia's voice cut its way through the hot damp air of the washing room.

Standing on her tall stool over the vat of dirty steaming water, Maureen Heffernan punched and twisted the unwieldy washing peggy into the heavy sodden clothes again. Her arms ached and throbbed. All she had eaten that day was one slice of dry toast for breakfast. Her dinner had been fed to the dogs as punishment for her slowness in the ironing room. She felt weak and the sweat soaked through her black dress in large itchy patches.

Sister Delia watched Maureen with satisfaction. She recalled the fiery young girl who had been brought to the laundry only a year before, shouting, kicking, and spitting.

Sister Delia passed out of the room, stopping near the door to grab Agnes Kerrigan by what was left of her unevenly hacked hair. "Cured of your vanity and back answers now, are you, thirty-eight?" she barked into the girl's face.

Agnes crouched and twisted with the force of Sister Delia's grasp and found herself kneeling on one knee in front of the nun. The stench from her habit made Agnes's throat contract. "Yes, Sister," she sobbed, only too aware that hacking off her hair with a bread knife in front of the whole laundry was a trifle compared to what Sister Delia was capable of.

"Good! Get back to work!" Sister Delia released her roughly and strode on. In the lye room she stood silently against the wall and watched the scene in front of her. Sheila Barry, the new girl, coughed and spluttered in the cloud of fine ash that rose up to envelop her. She could just about keep hold of the huge kettle of water she was pouring into the lye dropper. As the water saturated the applewood ashes that filled the large box, the ash died down and the kettle grew lighter. Sheila set the kettle next to her feet and wiped her face with the sleeve of her coarse black dress.

"Eighty-two! Fill the other box with ashes and then collect the lye out of the bottom of this one!"

Sheila had not seen Sister Delia standing there but was exhausted beyond the point of fright. She nodded heavily and picked up the kettle. "I have to go out to the pump for more water," she said heavily.

"Well be quick about it! And make sure that fire doesn't die down. Get some wood while you're at it!" Sister Delia was feeling very pleased with herself. It had taken some work convincing Father Higgins to return to the lye. He had voiced concern at the antiquated nature of the process and pointed out the easy availability of commercial soaps. Sister Delia recalled the thrill that had run through her as she made her case. It was the angels speaking through her. She had explained that what these fallen sinful girls needed most was hard work and discipline. Of course the nuns could buy the soap, but what would the girls learn from that? Where was the mortification of the flesh in unwrapping a bar of soap?

"And don't let me catch you idling or I'll be taking a knife to that fine hair of yours too!" she called after the figure of Sheila Barry as it disappeared through the door to the courtyard.

Sister Delia left the lye room and moved along the corridor past the scapular-making room. She made a mental note to herself that they needed to order more leather thongs from the boys' reformatory in Dromlane.

"Ah, go ask me arse, ye twisted old bitch," muttered Sheila as the door closed behind her. For a few brief seconds the cold of the courtyard came as a relief after the heat of the lye room. Sheila stood and relished the fleeting sensation of being neither too cold nor too hot. But the moment quickly passed and she felt the wind biting into her wet chapped hands. She held the kettle close, her arms barely meeting around its huge belly, and hurried to the pump in the opposite corner of the courtyard.

Sheila dropped the kettle at the foot of the pump and lined it up under the spigot, then blew on her hands and rubbed them together. She grabbed the cold handle of the pump, pulled it up, pushed it down, and it spat reluctantly into the kettle. Again she cranked the stiff handle and coaxed another paltry splutter.

"What you need, little Miss 82, is a nice ice bath to chill the cravings of your weak, corrupted flesh!" she whispered, mimicking Sister Delia for her own amusement.

The pump spat and sprayed her feet with icy water.

"Fuck it!" she hissed. The water soaked through the thin canvas shoes the nuns had given her. "Probably sold me boots too, the fucking dried-up bitches."

Sheila cranked the pump viciously as she remembered how Sister Delia had set on her from the very first day. She had been crying all the way from Cork in the bus after they had taken her little girl from her and told her to pack her things and leave the Sisters of Forbearance Fallen Mother and Child Home. No explanation. No news of her family and not a word from Declan. The nuns told her Declan had been sent away to the army and that the Sullivans had left Cork for good.

"The devil put an itch in yer knickers, did he? Well, we'll soon knock that out of ye!" was the first thing Sister Delia had said to her. Sheila had never heard a nun speak like that before. When her breast milk had seeped through her dress, Sister Delia stood her up in front of the whole refectory and pointed it out: "Were you not a filthy slut, that milk would be to feed your infant. But instead it is a reminder of harlotry. Take that dress off!"

And she had made her do it. Sheila took off her dress and stood there shivering in her greying underwear while Sister Delia circled, pointing at the milk stains on her bodice and shouting about lust and sin and all the time slapping at the girl's arms and legs with her big brown belt.

"Eighty-two! Hurry up! Don't make me come over there or you'll be sorry!" Sister Delia's voice now echoed around the courtyard. She was standing there in the doorway of the lye room.

Fucking dried-up old fucking bitch! May she die roaring! Sheila thought to herself and started again with the pump.

19

The stairs creaked deep into the surrounding silence as Brother Boland made his way to the oratory. As was his custom, he would go alone to the dark oratory and recite a decade of the rosary for the repose of his mother's soul. Not that Brother Boland had any idea who his mother was, but it made her feel real to him. For the week since the centenary he had been saying an extra decade for Venerable Saorseach O'Rahilly.

Alone in the oratory he whispered the prayers through his trembling lips. He knew that the Virgin Mary would be able to make out what he was saying. Lost in the prayerful lip smack and clatter of his dentures, he did not hear the straining that softly, casually played and stretched itself in the rafters above him.

"Haymery fur grey lorbeweeiu dib, dib, dib . . ."

Slowly Brother Boland became aware of something approaching out of the distance behind his words. It was like an onrush down a long tunnel. There was a gathering, clenching tension that was suddenly all around him.

A soft cloud of sawdust and plaster flakes tickled his scalp just moments before the enormous light fixture fell from the ceiling and crashed heavily two pews behind where he was sitting.

"Dib, dib, dib, Mother of dib, dib, dib, God!"

Brother Boland dived for cover under the pew. There he

cowered and listened to the soft crackle of plaster falling like snowflakes on the pews and floor around him. He looked at the gaping hole in the ceiling that the chandelier had left and then peered accusingly at the chandelier itself where it sprawled across two pews like some grotesque wrought-iron spider.

In the aftershock silence Brother Boland waited. Nothing more, it seemed, was going to happen. He untangled himself, got out from under the pew, and stood up stiffly. Just as he was having another look around the oratory, there was a tired wheezing sound and parts of the ceiling and the back wall came thundering down, showering him with wood, plaster, and a couple dozen Venerable Saorseach O'Rahilly miniatures.

Brother Boland fell to the floor and curled his arms over his head. Over his long life of misfortunes and clumsy accidents, this had become a vital reflex.

In the darkness of his mind, the Brother prayed to Venerable Saorseach O'Rahilly. The general gist of his prayer was: *I know the hymn says bend me to Your will but I hope me being killed by a falling ceiling is not part of Your will and that You help me survive this.*

In seeming answer to his prayers the noise stopped. Brother Boland opened his eyes slowly and tentatively for fear that any sudden movement would cause further destruction. On the floor around him lay fragments of plaster, pieces of electrical wiring, hunks of rotten wooden beams, and, scattered among the detritus, pieces of Venerable Saorseach O'Rahilly. Brother Boland stared in horror at the tragically disfigured effigies of the Brothers' founder. A wave of awe and terror rolled up from his stomach and pressed against the base of his throat. He looked sadly from one shard of O'Rahilly to the next as if commiserating with each of them.

Out of the corner of his eye he saw something glisten. He lurched toward it and stared aghast. On the floor in front of him was the severed trunk of one of the O'Rahilly miniatures. It was like all the others except that this one was bleeding copiously where it had been broken. Brother Boland looked heavenward in awe and glimpsed a few more flakes of paint drifting down from the ceiling. As they floated and turned, he saw them transform into perfect miniature communion hosts. A lightning flash of spiritual revelation engulfed him and before he knew what was happening he was standing at the head of the stairs, clutching the shattered figurine, his voice echoing shrilly through the quietness of the monastery: "It's a miracle! It's a miracle! It's a miracle! The second miracle of Venerable Saorseach O'Rahilly!"

From the common room below he could hear the muted sounds of the ten o'clock news on the radio. Its quotidian normality clashed horribly with the laden silence oozing out of the oratory. Gathering up the hem of his cassock in his empty left hand, he propelled himself down the stairs with a clattering of slippers on the polished steps.

"It's a miracle! It's a miracle! It's a miracle!"

20

Father Martin Mulvey, S.J., paused in his reading and closed his eyes. The Adagietto of Mahler's Fifth gripped him and he surrendered himself to its slow, tragic swelling. It brought to his mind's eye the paintings of El Greco he had seen when he travelled to Toledo after his ordination almost thirty years before. The strings soared and glided and he felt his eyes strain upward in their sockets as they followed the music. Behind the rich fabric of sound emerged a distant, insistent discordance, at first barely there, but once noticed, more evident and disruptive with each passing second.

"Bloody phone!" huffed Father Mulvey, and stood up suddenly. *The Maltese Falcon* fell out of his lap onto the floor as he hurried out to the hall.

"2402," he said gruffly into the receiver. "Ah yes, good evening, Father Sheehan," he continued, his voice gliding into a more respectful lilt.

He listened intently and his face darkened, not with fear but with the soot of determination accrued from the almost forgotten flame of passion that now flared up anew within him. This was what he had been waiting for all his life. This was it. This had to be it.

After twenty years of being dragged out to the middle of nowhere in the small hours of the morning to look at two-headed calves; afternoons drinking stewed tea while he listened to old women tell him how they had lost their keys only to find them in their sleeve or handbag after praying to Saint Anthony; numerous tortuous examinations and cross-examinations of eye witnesses to apparitions who would turn out to have been on a poteen binge for the best part of a week before the supposed apparition, this finally sounded like a real chance. No more sitting in drafty country churches waiting for statues to weep. No more perfunctory investigations of supposed Immaculate Conceptions before mother and child were bundled off to the nearest Jezebel Laundry and Herod's Orphanage respectively. This was the one. This was the one that would pluck him out of obscurity and take him to Rome to form part of the beatification process of Venerable Saorseach O'Rahilly. Father Mulvey did not hold the Brothers of Godly Coercion in great esteem but a miracle was a miracle, no matter where it came from.

"I'll be over there in a flash, Father," he told Sheehan, and dashed upstairs to get his boots. He bounded down the stairs and flailed around in the hallstand drawer looking for his bicycle clips. Despairing of finding them, he tucked his trousers into his socks as best he could and ran out the front door, cramming his hat onto his head as he went.

"Father Mulvey, S.J., Diocesan Investigator," announced Mulvey portentously as he held open his wallet with his identification.

"Ah, Father, wasn't it very good of you to come all the way over here on this cold night now," said Brother Loughlin as he ushered Mulvey into his office.

"When the Bishop calls Father Sheehan and I get the call, there's no time to waste."

"Sit down, won't you, Father."

"You know what, Brother, to be honest, I think I'd like

to get right to work. If I could see the scene of the, uhm, happening and the, uhm, subject or witness?"

"Of course, Father, how silly of me to be thinking you'd be having time for a ball of malt."

Father Mulvey arched his eyebrows. "Maybe later," he said without conviction, noting both the obvious relish with which Brother Loughlin talked of the ball of malt and the gold total abstinence Pioneer pin that glinted prominently in his lapel.

Brother Loughlin stood awkwardly for a few moments. He did not at all like the way this Jesuit had refused to have a drink with him, as if it somehow put Mulvey at a moral advantage.

"Shall we go then, Brother? It was, after all, you who called me in. It is not my miracle," said Father Mulvey sternly.

"Very well," replied Brother Loughlin, and held the door of the office open with overstated ceremony and politeness. Father Mulvey ignored this display of childishness.

"The more time that elapses between the happening and the investigation, the more the subject's impressions are likely to fade. You wouldn't want that to happen, would you now, Brother?"

Loughlin took this mix of hint and threat and used it to power up his legs. He waddled down the corridor at top speed in front of Father Mulvey.

Inside the door of the monastery they were met by a knot of Brothers who all set upon the investigator like a pack of starving dogs.

"How long do you think it will take, Father?"

"Have you told the Holy Father yet?"

"Don't be stupid, it's already after bedtime in Rome!"

"Is the Bishop here?"

"Don't call me stupid!"

"I have more miracles I can show you! Do you remember I wrote to you about the time Venerable Saorseach gave me the name of that horse when I didn't have enough money for me sister's birthday present?"

"Will we be able to get Saorseach miraculous medals when he's made Blessed?"

"Have you ever seen a statue bleed before?"

"Brothers! Please leave Father Mulvey in peace to conduct his work," shouted Brother Loughlin above the din. "You will know anything that happens as soon as we do. Now stay down here out of the way."

He opened a path through the babbling Brothers and ushered Father Mulvey through.

"It's just up the stairs on your left, Father," Brother Loughlin explained, then turned on the Brothers in a menacing undertone: "That is the last time you uncultured goms are going to disgrace me in front of someone like that! Do you hear?"

The oratory smelt like a long-abandoned house. The mix of damp plaster and rotten wood tickled the back of Father Mulvey's throat. He stood on the threshold and surveyed the scene carefully.

"It was just over here that . . ." started Brother Loughlin as he stepped into the room before feeling Father Mulvey's restraining arm across his chest.

"Please, Brother, do me a favour, don't go in there. I don't want anything disturbed," rapped Mulvey.

Brother Loughlin stood still, surprised as much by the authority in the priest's voice as by the unexpected strength of his wiry arm.

"Let's just keep the scene as intact as we can, okay?" Father Mulvey pulled on his surgical gloves and moved carefully into the oratory. From his raincoat pocket he withdrew his bicycle lamp and shone it up into the hole in the ceiling. Even with all the lights in the oratory except the fallen one still working, this remarkable bicycle lamp threw great illumination on the joists and wires exposed by the collapse. Brother Loughlin wondered whether such lamps were special issue to all Jesuits or just to Diocesan Investigators.

"Looks like a nice clean job," observed Father Mulvey.

"What do you mean by *clean job*? Are you insinuating that someone did this deliberately?" spluttered Brother Loughlin.

"No, no. That's a term we use in the trade for a scene that doesn't show any outside tampering. What I think you have here, Brother, is a pretty genuine ceiling collapse. Bona fide. That's always good. It gets hard to pin anything on the Lord if there are hammers and crowbars lying around the scene.

"Okay, let's take a look at these guys then," continued Father Mulvey, and bent down to inspect the shards of terra-cotta statuettes. Did any of these little guys make it?"

"Well, all the ones in the nooks at the far end seem to be undamaged."

That was not so good, thought Mulvey, but he could probably work with it. He continued to peer at all the shards on the floor while Brother Loughlin looked on in exasperated impatience.

"Any other witnesses?" asked Father Mulvey without looking up.

"I'm afraid not," said Brother Loughlin sadly.

"Okay, let's go see what Brother Boland has to say for himself," said Mulvey, and abruptly slipped out of the oratory past Loughlin.

* * *

Brother Boland's cell was dark except for the tired moonlight that came through the small window.

Father Mulvey turned to Brother Loughlin and brusquely motioned him to stay quiet.

As their eyes became accustomed to the dim light they saw Boland sitting on the edge of his cot. He was rocking to and fro and crooning to the small figure he held in his hands.

"Brother Boland, there's a man from the Bishop here to see you," announced Brother Loughlin.

Boland's crooning took on a more urgent tone and his rocking grew faster.

Father Mulvey turned on Brother Loughlin. "Let me do the talking here, Brother," he hissed, then waited for the sound Boland was making to return to a less urgent pitch. He felt an excitement grow inside him. This looked good. This looked very promising. This could really be it. This could be the one that would put him on the miracle map. Then there'd be no stopping him: seminars, lecture tours, maybe even a post in the Curia. Yep, this could be Martin Mulvey's Momentous Miraculous Mother Lode. He took a deep breath to calm himself.

"Brother Boland? It's okay," he began softly. "You don't have to talk right now. I'm Father Mulvey. My friends call me Martin. I'd like you to call me Martin. I'm here to be your friend. I'm here to help you. What do you think of that, Brother Boland?"

Boland made no reply though his crooning did stop for a moment to indicate he had at least heard what had been said to him.

"Good, Brother Boland. That's very good," purred Father Mulvey soothingly.

"Ah, for God Sake! Enough of this fecking around! Let the dog see the rabbit and get on with it!" cried Brother Loughlin, and turned on the light.

The crooning turned into a high-pitched shrieking and Boland curled himself up into a ball on the bed. Father Mulvey spun round and with one continuous motion turned off the light, opened the door, and pushed Brother Loughlin out into the corridor.

"Brother, I asked you not to interfere. Now I'm telling you! Don't interfere with the vidente miraculus. I think you should just wait out here until I need you. Agreed?"

Brother Loughlin found himself in the corridor with the door closed in his face, surrounded by the Brothers.

"I thought I told you all to stay downstairs!" he barked at them, suddenly very conscious that he did not want Father Mulvey to come out and tell him to be quiet. "It's got more official now. Father Mulvey needs me to wait here outside while he interviews the vidente miraculus."

The Brothers murmured among themselves at this; slowly there emerged more concrete phrases.

"More official, is it?"

"Vidente miraculus, did you hear that?"

"That means it is a miracle."

"Let them try to build a warehouse here now and the Pope himself will be down on the lot of them like a ton of bricks."

"Holy ground."

"Very important site."

"Could be pilgrimages."

"Tour buses even."

Slowly the knot of Brothers was winding and tightening itself like some dynamic force. It was only a matter of time before this energy had to be released, and it would only take the tiniest spark, if it was the right one. Brother Loughlin watched in amazement as this group-hysteria event unfolded in front of him.

"Pope's visit."

"We'll be on the news!"

"People from all over the world."

There was a slight pause as the group trembled and teetered on the brink of explosion. Then it came.

"Relics!"

It was like a burning rag in a gasometer. The knot of Brothers tore apart and became a roiling fracas trying to get downstairs to the oratory as quickly as possible. Brother Loughlin watched them and smiled in the knowledge that *he* would have the profits generated from any relics and not those hapless drones.

"Are you okay there, Brother Boland? Can I get you anything? A cup of tea?"

The Brother's crooning and humming continued but there was just the barely perceptible shaking of the head.

"Well, if you change your mind, just let me know, okay?"

Boland nodded slightly and continued to hum and croon.

Father Mulvey listened patiently to the tones and nuances. After a few minutes the crooning stabilised.

"A nice moon tonight. Funny how it clears up sometimes at night when it's been cloudy all day. A bit frosty though. I cycled over here. It was already getting icy but I thought you might want to have a chat after what you saw."

Brother Boland's sounds momentarily caught in his throat and slowly took on the tones of being ready to speak.

"Do you think Venerable Saorseach is all right?" asked Father Mulvey gently.

"I don't know," whispered Brother Boland.

"Do you think I could see?"

"Mmm-hmm," assented Boland hesitantly.

"I'm going to turn on the light, Brother Boland, okay? I can't see Venerable Saorseach without the light. Is that okay?"

"Yes," wheezed Boland.

Father Mulvey moved slowly to the door and turned the light on. Brother Boland flinched a little and brought his arms more tightly around the piece of statue he cradled.

Mulvey sat down on the bed about a foot from Boland. It was risky but it was time to move things along.

"You know I'm here to help, Brother. Can I see Venerable Saorseach, do you think?"

Boland looked up for the first time, then glanced around the cell as if it were some vast hall. He seemed to be searching inside and behind every floorboard and brick to make sure there were no malevolent presences in the room. He glared suspiciously at the door and then turned and stared at the priest. Mulvey had been expecting this and had composed his face into its most sympathetic and trustworthy configuration.

Brother Boland slowly lowered his eyes toward his lap where he gently opened his arms to reveal the half figurine cradled in his upturned hands.

Mulvey could see the blood on the broken edges of the statuette and had to exercise great self-restraint not to reach out for it. "Now, Brother, you know that if we are going to call this a miracle there will have to be an investigation. You understand that, don't you, Brother?"

"I do," said Boland confidently, and continued to stare lovingly at the statuette.

"So you have to trust me. You know I'm your friend,

don't you, Brother? And we trust our friends, don't we?"

After a short pause Brother Boland nodded in agreement.

"Can I touch the statue?"

Boland looked up and stared hard at Father Mulvey.

"If we are going to get recognition for Venerable Saorseach, a lot of people are going to have to look at it. It may even have to go to Rome to the Holy Father himself," said Father Mulvey gently while holding Boland's gaze in his.

The Brother nodded again and slowly, almost painfully, moved his cradled hands toward Father Mulvey. As he lifted it gently out of Brother Boland's hands, Mulvey caught sight of the long gash on the back of the Brother's right hand. It took all his discipline and experience not to react to it. He focused his attention on the statue and inspected it while his mind raced. He had to hold on to this one. This was make or break. One false move here and the whole miracle was gone.

"Did you cut your hand there, Brother?" asked Father Mulvey softly.

Brother Boland glanced down, noticing for the first time the cut just below his wrist.

"Oh yes. I suppose I must have. Yes, cut my hand, I did." Each word came out more hesitantly than the last as it took Boland closer to the same realisation as was running through Father Mulvey's mind.

In a flash the priest made up his mind: "Well, these things are bound to happen with so many broken pieces lying around the floor. But let's have a good look at this, shall we? This is the important thing at the minute." As if to reinforce his unadversarial stance, Father Mulvey set to examining the statuette with renewed interest.

"Now, Brother, can you remember if Venerable Saorseach

O'Rahilly spoke to you at all while you were in the oratory?"

"No, no, I don't believe he did. No, no, he didn't."

"Are you sure now, Brother? It might have been very difficult to hear him with all the noise in there, what with everything falling and breaking like that."

"No, I can't say I heard anything. But there were communion hosts!"

"Right. But you heard nothing?" asked Father Mulvey softly and with benign incredulity. "There was nothing at all, not even a little voice in the silence after all the noise?"

"I don't know. Maybe there was but I couldn't hear it. What about the communion hosts I saw?"

"We'll get to those in time. But there could have been a voice, couldn't there?"

"Could have been. I don't know."

"All right, all right, Brother. No need to get yourself worked up now. It's all fine. We're all on your side here." Mulvey glanced down at the statue. He bit his lip. He needed time to think about this. "Here you are, Brother, why don't you take Venerable Saorseach back. I'll close the light and leave you alone for a little while and maybe you might find Venerable Saorseach has something to say to you. What do you think about that?"

Brother Boland's eyes lit up at the prospect of getting the statuette back and he held out his hands imploringly, almost greedily.

Mulvey turned off the light and gently opened the door as little as possible and stepped out into the corridor. He looked Brother Loughlin in the eye and then mustered a slight conciliatory smile.

"I think I might take you up on that offer of a ball of malt now, Brother."

21

"Ahhhhhh! That's a fine drop of whiskey, Brother," mused Father Mulvey as the mouthful of first-shot from the unmarked bottle teased and warmed him with its spicy fire.

"It is indeed. You wouldn't get the like of it anywhere in the city, I can tell you. I have an old friend gets it for me at the distillery in Listowel."

"Ah, it is a good thing to have friends in the right places."

"It is, Father, it is."

The pleasantries over, Father Mulvey leaned forward in his chair and rested his elbows on his knees. He stared deep into the glass of whiskey in his right hand. Loughlin tried hard to maintain a veneer of indifference.

"A holy man, your Brother Boland, would you say, Brother?" asked Father Mulvey carefully.

"I would have to say so, yes. He's a pious man, a great devotion to Our Lady of Indefinite Duration and, of course, to Venerable Saorseach O'Rahilly."

"That is very commendable, very commendable indeed. But tell me this, would there be anything in Brother Boland's character that might, how could I put this, be used to discredit him if, for example, he were to be investigated by the Regional Subcommittee of the Congregation for the Causes of Saints?"

Brother Loughlin peered at Father Mulvey. He knew

these Jesuits and their tricky rhetorical ways. He was not going to be outflanked or hoodwinked. "I'm not entirely sure I understand what you're driving at, Father."

"Let me put it this way. Every year the Subcommittee investigates about a hundred alleged miracles or apparitions. They keep as balanced a view as possible but they must play devil's advocate to each case. My question is whether Brother Boland would stand up to the rigours of such an investigation?"

"How rigourous an investigation are we talking about?"

Father Mulvey took a long draught from his glass and allowed Brother Loughlin to refill it. He sat back in his chair and observed the Brother as if from a great distance. "The most rigourous. Here's the thing, Brother: to a man on a galloping horse it all looks like a first-class miracle, but to an unfriendly eye there might appear certain facts that might seriously weaken our case." On the word *our*, Father Mulvey again leaned forward in his seat.

Brother Loughlin sat forward in his too, placed his glass on the desk, and put his right hand gently over his left in a gesture of undivided attention. "And what might these unhelpful facts be?"

"Well, I couldn't help noticing that Brother Boland had quite a cut on the back of his right hand. Now, the first thing an investigator would do—and don't get me wrong here, he would be only doing his job—would be to check if the blood on the statuette was Brother Boland's. If it turned out to be the same type then there would certainly be a temptation to take the blood on the statuette, the cut in Brother Boland's hand, put them together, and *poof!* No more miracle." Father Mulvey raised his left hand and spread his fingers wide in a gesture of evaporating dreams of beatification, fame, pilgrimages, papal visits, souvenir shops, and renown for the Brothers of Greater Little Werburgh Street, North.

"I see your point," replied Brother Loughlin levelly.

"Now, of course, if the blood on the statue did not match Brother Boland's, then we would have a much stronger case for a miracle. So, if you were to go and get the statuette and bring it here to me, then I could initiate the investigation, hopefully happy in the knowledge that the blood on it was not Brother Boland's. And you know what, Brother? If Brother Boland could possibly remember anything that Venerable Saorseach said to him during the miracle, it would be all the better for us."

"I see your point, Father."

"Call me Martin."

"Why don't you help yourself to another dram of whiskey there, Martin, while I get the statue and have a little chat with Brother Boland."

Father Mulvey smiled back winningly and poured himself another generous measure of Brother Loughlin's whiskey.

In fifteen minutes Brother Loughlin returned to the office with a broken statuette. It did not require much in the line of acuity to see that it was a completely different statuette, but it was generously edged with fresh blood. Father Mulvey took it, looked at it, and then at Brother Loughlin. He nodded meaningfully.

"Good work, Brother. Brother Boland didn't mention anything that Venerable Saorseach had said to him by any chance, did he?"

"Ah, no, he didn't. He didn't say a whole lot. He was very reluctant to give up the statue."

"Not to worry. There'll be plenty of time for that."

"I see."

"Well, I'll take this over to the Bishop's Palace first thing in the morning and we'll get the ball rolling," said Father Mulvey, suddenly standing up.

"You'll, uhm . . ."

"I'll be in touch." Father Mulvey transferred the statue to a plastic bag and held out his hand to Loughlin. "In the meantime, keep everyone out of the oratory. I'll have a man over first thing in the morning to take some measurements and photographs and then you can start fixing things up."

The Brother took the priest's outstretched hand and shook it. Mulvey pressed firmly and Loughlin couldn't help thinking he was doing it deliberately to increase the soreness of the fresh cut in his forearm.

"Very nice work, Brother," said Father Mulvey mischievously. He released Loughlin's hand and pulled the door open. "Sleep well," he called, and let himself out the front door, which he pulled shut behind him with a cavalier flourish.

Brother Loughlin stood and stared at the door. In his pocket he fingered bits of the freshly broken statuette along with the one he had wrested from Brother Boland. He had a sudden thought.

"Feck! Relics!" he shouted, and bolted out of his office.

22

"Ah, would you look at that for a mess. Isn't it disgraceful? Ah, God help us, but that's a terrible sight and all them little statues too. Most of them destroyed. Broken to bits. That's a shame that is. Terrible sad it is."

From the bottom of the stairs Conall McConnell could hear Ray McRae's lamenting voice. "Christ on a crutch!" he muttered to himself, and stomped heavily up the stairs.

"Ah, there you are now! Would you take a look at this?" lamented McRae when McConnell reached the landing.

McConnell ignored his apprentice and looked past him into the oratory. The floor and pews were littered with plaster and bits of wood, and the gaping hole in the ceiling gave the place a look of war-torn desolation.

"Brother Loughlin said not to touch anything," added McRae

"I know. I saw him on my way in. Why don't you go and do the toilets?" growled McConnell.

"Ah, I don't think they need to be done. I gave them a good going over on Wednesday so I'd say they'll be fine. Used that new stuff with the extra ammonia I did. It's a power for the germs, so it is. You see, they didn't even know germs existed until—"

"Look! Just go and do them. You can talk to yourself all you like while you're at it!"

"Take it easy. Don't go giving yourself a heart attack. I'll go do the toilets if that's what you want. You should make yourself a cup of tea and calm down," McRae said.

McConnell stared viciously at him.

McRae thought the better of saying anything more and scampered off down the stairs to get his mop and bucket. McConnell put his foot up on the pew that Brother Loughlin had hastily pulled across the doorway and whistled softly at the mess.

"So, can you fix that up, Mr. McConnell?"

McConnell spun around to find Brother Loughlin standing behind him. He hated when they snuck up on him like that. Brother Loughlin was baggy-eyed and unshaven.

"Me?"

"Yes. Of course Mr., uhm, uhm, McWhatsisname could help."

"McRae. Eh, I don't think so, Brother. That's a job for proper tradesmen. You need a joiner to replace those joists and a plasterer to do the ceiling."

"Mmmm, that presents a slight problem," mused Brother Loughlin.

"What sort of problem?"

"Well, after our little incident last night, the Brothers feel that it would be wisest to, how shall we say, keep all strangers off the premises. There will be no outside workmen allowed into the school while the miracle is being investigated. You will be taking care of things for a while."

McConnell looked from Brother Loughlin's face to the hole in the oratory ceiling and back to the Brother's face. "You must be joking," he stumbled.

"Not in the least," replied Brother Loughlin. "I'd better get back downstairs. I'm expecting someone. You have a think about fixing the ceiling and let me know what materials you'll be needing. You could take another look at that roof while you're at it."

McConnell stared open-mouthed after the seemingly possessed figure of Brother Loughlin that bounded down the stairs toward the yard. Staying up almost all night getting the Brothers to return the relics they had pillaged from the oratory so they could be photographed and logged seemed to have given him extraordinary energy.

Mrs. Broderick knocked gently on Brother Loughlin's office door.

"Come in!" roared the Brother imperiously.

"There are two men here to see you. They say they are from the Diocesan Investigator's office," said Mrs. Broderick as she poked her head in the door, her acid tone implying that the two gentlemen looked like total gangsters from some made-up office.

"Ah, good! Show them in!"

Mrs. Broderick offered a fierce frown of disapproval and turned to the men. "You can go in now," she told them reluctantly.

When Brother Loughlin and the two visitors emerged from the office ten minutes later, the men had opened their coats to reveal that they were not just from the Diocesan Investigator's office but they were also men of the cloth. It had to be conceded in Mrs. Broderick's defence that in their overcoats and fedoras they still looked a little like gangsters.

Brother Loughlin ushered the two priests out in front of him. "I'll be in the oratory with Father Cronin and Father Mulcahy if anyone is looking for me, Mrs. Broderick."

Mrs. Broderick snorted bad-humouredly and pursed her lips. "And if no one is looking for you, where will you be?" she muttered derisively, taking tiny pedantic revenge on Brother Loughlin's suspect grammar. Such were the little moments that kept her going.

Spud Murphy sat in the staff room correcting his History tests. What were the three main causes of the collapse of the feudal system? *No football, rats, the First World War.* What were the guilds? *What the ancient fish breathed through.* Who were at the bottom of the Feudal Pyramid? *The pyramid builders.*

"Ah, for Christ sake!" Spud couldn't help smiling a little. He knew they weren't stupid boys. They just didn't want to learn. Somewhere in their heads, learning had become inextricably tied up with what the Brothers wanted to force them to do, and as such it had to be resisted. At least they paid him the courtesy of making up amusing answers for his tests.

"Five D?" asked Laverty from the windowsill where he sat reading the paper.

"Yeah."

"Bunch of baboons!"

"Don't be such a harsh bastard. They're all right. It's just hard to go in after the gestapo and expect them to want to learn anything."

"I suppose you're right," conceded Laverty sheepishly. "But they could make an effort. I mean, you know what I'm saying. If they don't get some kind of a decent Leaving Cert, they're always going to be working for ignorant bastards not much better than the Brothers."

"I know and you know, but have you tried to explain that? Would you have listened when you were their age?"

"Nah. I mean, I don't know, but, you know, they're only damaging themselves."

"Yeah, but I think they see it as trying to avoid damage."

"But it doesn't work. Look at that stupid eejit Maher.

What did he think he was at, messing at confession like that? He'll be locked up in a loony bin or something."

"He's not the kind of kid to mess like that. I'd love to know what he said though. Fury threw a fit."

"Oh, I'm sure 'Broader' Loughlin will tell us all about it."

Spud smiled wanly. "Oh yeah, right. Just before Hell freezes over and the flying pigs learn to ice skate." Considering how much he had disliked Laverty when he first arrived, the man was now the closest thing to human company he had at the school. The rest of the lay teachers were just short of blessing themselves every time they passed a Brother in the hall, and as for Mr. Pollock, he was so thick with the Brothers that it was almost unholy.

Spud turned back to his tests. "Ah, for God sake, would you listen to this. What was the Hanseatic League? *An old version of the World Cup*. You have to laugh, I suppose."

"Well, it's that or turn out like the rest of them," sighed Laverty, as he stared out the window where Mr. Hourican and Mr. Pollock were having a confab in the yard.

"Now there's a horrible thought," shuddered Spud.

"And now with that stupid ceiling falling in and locking the gates and their miracle investigation, they've gone completely mad. I had to park down on Danegild Street. There'll be nothing left of me car when I get back."

"I know. It's worse this place is getting."

The bell for small break rang out and Spud stuffed the tests into his bag. "Can't wait to get back to them," he joked.

"Are you on yard duty this week?"

"Yeah."

"Take it easy."

"I'll try. Thank God it's Christmas next week."

Spud stashed his bag in his cubbyhole and headed out into the yard.

23

In the IRA shop Finbar stood back and let a couple of third years go in front of him. He had to make sure how this was done. He had to look like he'd been doing it for years. He did not want to end up appearing foolish. He wanted to have the exact change in his hand like he knew exactly what he was doing. Ideally he would have liked the shop to be empty, but that was not going to happen at this hour of the morning.

He hadn't smoked again since Christmas Eve when he'd stolen one of Uncle Francie's and smoked it out the bathroom window. He'd only inhaled a couple of drags and had somewhat enjoyed the light-headedness. But since the miserable Christmas Day he'd been dreaming of another one. His mother had insisted on badgering Declan about getting a job all through dinner and his father had got snarlingly drunk after the meal and argued with Francie, who'd driven straight back to Cork that afternoon even though he was supposed to stay for a week. Later that night he'd heard Declan and his father talking in low angry voices in the parlour—something about Sheila Barry, but he couldn't make it out.

Finbar was also convinced that the tiny microscope his parents had given him was a complete last-minute purchase. Never in his life had he expressed the slightest interest in science. He directed all his anger at them into this defiant act of buying cigarettes on this, the first day back at school after the break.

"Two loosies and two matches," muttered the ragged third year.

"Are ye sure ye can do it with two matches? It's a windy day out there. Five for a penny?"

Malachy was on a marketing drive. He had been told to up profitability. The dream of Irish reunification could not be realised if he kept selling only one match per loose cigarette.

Malachy turned and suddenly it was Finbar's turn. He took a deep breath and let it out as casually and confidently as he could: "Two loosies and two matches, please."

Malachy flipped the loose cigarettes onto the counter and two matches on top of them. Finbar dropped four pennies into the expectant palm. Malachy raised his eyebrows in derision: "What d'you think? Matches grow on trees?"

Finbar handed over another ha'penny. Malachy's hand snapped shut like a trap and he fired the change into the little drawer under the counter. The boy stuffed his smokes and matches into the top pocket of his shirt and bolted for the door.

"It's all right. You can light up in here before you go out," called Malachy.

Finbar ignored him. He was not going to attempt to light a cigarette in full view of anyone.

"Now, before you all go running at this thing like a bull at a gate, take a couple of minutes to make sure you have everything. Each group. . . Ah, good morning, Mr. Sullivan, nice of you to finally join us. Sit down there with Scully and Ferrara. Each group should have a beaker, a pipette, copper oxide crystals, a piece of turnip, and some blotting paper," explained Mr. Devlin, the Biology teacher.

Finbar squeezed in at the bench beside Ferrara. Beads of now cold sweat sat on his forehead. He was chilled and his face felt like it was pulled too tight across his skull. Notwithstanding, it was a vast improvement on how he had felt five minutes before as he threw his guts up in the lane behind Baker's Pride with the smell of fresh-baked bread mocking his upheaving stomach. He tried to not even think of the second cigarette that still nestled in his shirt pocket, filled with the promise of new experiences of nausea, dizziness, and puking.

"Sir! Sir!"

"Yes, Mr. McDonagh?"

"We don't have a pipette."

Mr. Devlin walked down to the bench where McDonagh was sitting. He picked up the pipette that was lying on the bench and held it up: "And what do you think this is? Blotting paper?"

"No sir," muttered McDonagh. He was not going to admit that he thought a pipette was one of those really sharp little knives.

The boys watched bemused as Mr. Devlin demonstrated the experiment. He put some copper sulfate crystals in the bottom of a beaker, added some water using the pipette, then laid the slice of turnip on the solution and placed the blotting paper on top. The experiment would show how the turnip would conduct the solution up into itself; the blotting paper would then turn bright blue. It was a boring experiment and Mr. Devlin knew it.

"Now, each group should repeat the experiment a second time to verify, but be very sure that you only get eighty millilitres of water in the pipette; no more, no less." *That should slow them down*, he thought with satisfaction.

There was a momentary lull as the boys tried to figure out exactly what to do. Then there was a slight shift in the silence. To a more experienced ear than Mr. Devlin's it would have signalled danger, but he noticed nothing. It was that crystalline moment when the boys understood, intuitively as a unit, that Devlin did not know what he was doing and had not really prepared the class. Lack of total control was like a gasoline smell in the air and the boys could sense it almost immediately. They were on.

It was only a matter of time before Mr. Devlin dozed off. He had done it before and all the signs were there. There were the red eyes, the one day's worth of stubble shading his cheeks, and the general hungover delicacy with which he moved. All they had to do was wait.

Finbar was surprised by the care with which the boys conducted themselves. He would have expected any hungover teacher to get the noisy treatment: the squeaking of boots on the floor, the crashing geometry sets. It was not until Devlin actually dozed off and began to snore softly that Finbar understood: they were in a science lab with unlocked cupboards.

The first to go was McDonagh. All the others seemed to know what to do. They huddled over their experiments looking like they were working while McDonagh got on his hands and knees and made his way to the back of the lab. Lynch was the alarm giver and sniffed twice in quick succession when Devlin appeared to be waking. When the danger passed, Lynch gave one long sniff and the sounds of creeping among the workbenches resumed. Finbar watched one of the cupboards open as if by remote control and then McDonagh's hand reached inside. There was a short fumble and then the boy's arm withdrew, the cupboard door closed, and he crept back to his place. He put something inside his jacket and resumed his part in the tableau vivant of Young Boys at Science Experiment.

Scully got up next and slid down to the floor. He waited for Lynch's all-clear sniff and then crawled silently toward the back of the lab. Finbar glanced round the class to see the intentness with which the boys were all cooperating. It was something he had not witnessed since he'd come to the school.

Again the cupboard door opened, but this time Scully emerged from behind the last workbench. He took a careful look at Devlin, then turned to look inside. When he shifted back he had his hands carefully cupped; instead of crawling, he tiptoed silently back.

As the boy slid onto the stool, Finbar could see the shiny liquid in his palm. Scully rested his hands on his knees and carefully cradled his precious cargo of mercury.

After that Egan went and seemed to take ages searching in a second cupboard before returning with a test tube filled with clear liquid. Then Lynch himself went while McDonagh kept watch. Finally, with five minutes to go before the end of class, all activity ceased and the boys waited patiently over their bogus unfinished experiments.

Devlin woke with a start when the bell rang and was foolishly reassured to see the boys all bent studiously over their experiments.

"Okay, that's enough, we'll write up the results on Thursday. Mr. Scully, you can clean the blackboard."

"Fuck!" breathed Scully under his breath. "Take it," he hissed to Finbar, and poured the mercury into his helpless hands. "Don't drop it or you're dead," Scully added, and went to clean the blackboard.

Finbar sat uneasily with the heavy shiny liquid in his

palms. He had heard mercury was poisonous but reckoned it was still safer to hold on to it than drop it.

"I need three volunteers to help me tidy up," announced Mr. Devlin. It was a cursory, almost ironic nod toward encouraging participation that he knew would elicit no response. "Right then: Bradshaw, Clark, Hennessy, you're all volunteered. The rest of you can go."

"I'll cover you," said Ferrara to Finbar, and picked up Finbar's bag.

With no time or inclination to argue, Finbar followed slightly behind the other boy and left the lab. Behind him he heard Scully's low voice: "Slow down when you get to the door."

At the door leading out of the lab and into the yard, Finbar slowed down. In front of him he saw the boys pause when they passed the first window. As he got closer he saw McDonagh lean toward a massive bowl sitting on the windowsill. He dropped what looked to Finbar like a piece of phosphorous into the bowl. McDonagh quickened his pace and moved on into the yard. Without slowing down much, Egan emptied the contents of his test tube into the bowl. "A colourless, odourless, tasteless liquid," he intoned mirthlessly.

Jesus! If that's acid . . . thought Finbar, and would have stopped in his tracks had it not been for Scully right behind him who pushed him gently along.

"Into the custard," said Scully.

Not knowing what else to do, Finbar deftly turned his hand over and watched the silvery globules of mercury sink into the bowl of cooling custard.

With a strange sense of exhilaration he walked on into the yard and was surprised when he stopped and found Scully was still beside him.

"Stupid bastards always have custard on Mondays," said Scully without further preamble, "and they always leave it sitting out on the windowsill to cool. Don't know how they're not all dead with the shite that goes into it."

"What did Egan put in?"

"Don't know. Looked like acid. Wouldn't be surprised what Egan would do these days. Gone in the head he is now. Coming for a smoke?"

Finbar gave a passably casual *why not?* shrug to disguise the soaring he felt, and he and Scully walked out of the small yard toward the smoking hideaway behind the hall.

Oh God! Oh God! Let me die now! thought Finbar as he retched once more into the toilet bowl. Nothing came up except vile acidic spittle. His determination to persist with the task at hand—that of making himself sick again so he'd eventually get used to smoking cigarettes—would have been admirable had it been applied to something that wouldn't leave him in an emphysema ward later in life. As women forget the pains of childbirth to ensure the continuance of mankind, so did schoolboys forget the misery of being sick from cigarettes to ensure the continuance of retailers of loose cigarettes such as the IRA shop.

Finbar blew some more burning snot out of his nose, spat again, and leaned back against the wall of the cubicle. He felt better now. He glanced up at the cistern above him in relief, greatly comforted by the cold-sounding gurgle of water inside it. It was the next best thing to a fresh breeze. As he looked at the wall above the cistern, it let out a creak and surrendered a chunk of plaster, which fell into the toilet bowl with a crack and a plop. Finbar stared at it, feeling, in his post-vomiting relief, a sense of heightened lucidity and appreciation of the smaller things. He looked on as little crumbs broke from the main piece settling in the bottom of the toilet bowl. Slowly the big chunk started to absorb the water and changed its colour from institutional green to a slightly warmer olive shade, before finally sinking. Finbar watched in wonder as the reverse fresco of decay enacted itself in the toilet among his bile and spit.

"Hey, Bogman, the bell is gone. Better move or you'll get a hiding," called Scully from outside the cubicle.

"You all right now?" he asked when Finbar emerged.

"Yeah. Thanks."

"It's no big deal." Scully turned to walk away.

"How do you do it?" called Finbar after him.

"Do what?"

"Smoke and drink and all that. Don't you get sick?"

"Oh yeah, the first few times. After that you get used to it. Most of the time. So? You okay now?"

"Yeah, I think so, but come here to me," said Finbar.

"What?"

"I think there's something weird about this place."

"So? What do you want, a rubber medal?"

"No, I mean something creepy. Like when I was sent over to the monastery that day to get the spare leather. I saw Boland on the stairs. It was like he was listening to the walls and whispering to them. He was touching the walls like you'd pet a dog or something."

Scully looked hard at Finbar. "You know they're all gone in the head, don't you?"

"Yeah, but this was different. I can't explain. If you saw it you'd know what I mean. He was talking to the walls, humming to them. He was nearly crying."

"So? Everyone knows he's completely mental. They're all mental. Welcome to Werburgh Street!"

Finbar couldn't help but smile. This felt like something.

It was a thawing feeling inside, a feeling that at least Scully was starting to see him.

"What the fuck are you laughing at?"

"Nothing."

"Come on before we get snared for being late."

24

Finbar stood in the small shed with Scully, Lynch, and McDonagh. They all shivered against the April wind.

"Did you see Mulligan in the yard this morning trying to stop the pigeons shitting on the railings?" asked Scully.

"Yeah, that was gas," said Finbar

"Come here, did you hear what happened to Maher after they took him away?" asked Lynch suddenly.

"Attracta Maher told Imelda the law came to the house with a priest and a court order and told Mrs. Maher he was sent to Drumgloom for attacking that priest at the O'Rahilly mass," said Scully. "Imelda is me sister," he explained to Finbar.

"She's a beaut!" beamed McDonagh.

"Shut up! She wouldn't touch you with a barge pole," said Scully.

"Maher never touched that priest!" said Finbar.

"That's what you say. You're not Father Fury and Brother Loughlin, are you? It's what those fuckers say that counts," muttered Scully.

"Drumgloom. Fuck!" said Lynch quietly. "They'll eat him alive."

"What's Drumgloom?" asked Finbar.

"Industrial school in Navan. The worst. Like a reformatory only worse," McDonagh informed him. "Some young fellah from Drimnagh hung himself there the year before last. Anto Rourke, who was in first year with us, got five years there for mitching off school. The Brothers there are real bastards. Much worse than these fuckers here. Most of them get transferred there out of schools like this for being too vicious. If Kennedy wasn't still so sick, he'd probably be there by now."

"Jaysus!" Finbar did not know Drumgloom but the words *industrial school* chilled him to the marrow. Boys in Cork had been sent away to the Oblates of the Impervious Heart of Herod for years just for throwing muckballs at the railway bridge.

"Yeah," concurred McDonagh in a momentary slide into seriousness.

A cold silence descended on the boys and through it came the distant sound of the bell announcing the end of small break.

"Deadly! Latin next. Free class," declared McDonagh gleefully.

"Gift!" added Lynch, his mind already racing with new ideas of what to do with the hinge he had removed from the lid of his desk.

"Yayyyy!" cheered McDonagh when Brother Mulligan shuffled in and closed the door. So far the coverage for Brother Kennedy while he recuperated from his heart attack had been numerous talks on the evils of drink from Father Flynn; Brother Loughlin repeatedly setting them bits of long division to do while he smoked and farted out in the corridor and periodically came in to leather someone at random; and endless classes of Larry Skelly telling them they should all become bread-van drivers and letting them do their homework while he read the horse-racing page of the *Morning Herald*. This promised to be another easy doss.

A free class with Brother Mulligan was always a bit of a giggle. First, he made everyone copy down the old Gaelic alphabet from the blackboard. The delicate curves of the Gaelic scribe were never designed to be reproduced using two-penny nib pens that dug and bit the coarse paper like rakes on wet grass. That invariably led to the amusing spectacle of Brother Mulligan correcting the copies and trying to hurt people with his leathering.

When the calligraphic tutoring had run its course, Brother Mulligan would perform his favourite party trick. He would pick up a piece of chalk in his shaky hand, hold it over the blackboard for a few seconds while he tensed and braced himself, and then, with a superhuman effort, he would channel all his shakes and quivers into one sudden flourish and leave behind on the blackboard a perfect circle. This ability genuinely impressed the boys, though there were rumours abroad that being able to draw a perfect freehand circle like that was a sign of complete madness.

Once the entertainment was over, Brother Mulligan would launch into what he saw as the vital lesson for survival in an ever-changing and puzzling world, one that could never be repeated too often: "What are the three things we must always be on the watch for if we are to keep clear of Protestants? How do we spot them?"

The boys had been through this dozens of times but none of them could be bothered to volunteer an answer. It was more enjoyable to watch Brother Mulligan wind himself up into a sweat of frustration.

"Ah, ye are useless. Ye remember nothing! If they came in the night and swapped yer parents for Protestant doppelgängers ye'd never even notice. Ye need to be on yer guard against them. They'll sneak up on you and before you know it, you'll be keeping all your old twine neatly bundled up and taking unnecessary pride in shining your shoes.

"What do we look for? What are the three key signs?"

The boys remained silent and did a passable show of appearing interested in the answer, though the main preoccupation was that there was only one more class after this until lunchtime.

"The yellah skin, the eyes too close together, and the quarter-past-nine feet. What are they?"

"The yellah skin, the eyes too close together, and the quarter-past-nine feet," droned the boys in mimicking chorus. Finbar joined in leadenly, recognising here some firmly held precepts of his mother's.

"Good! Now what do we do when we see a Protestant?"

Again the boys remained impassive and silent.

"I'd have an easier time training chickens to ride bicycles! What we do when we see a Protestant coming is we cross the street and turn the back part of our scapulars to them. Are you all wearing your scapulars?"

"Yes, Brother," they lied. No one but the most over-mothered wore them. They scratched and got caught in your navel and the string would burn your neck if you had to walk fast or run. Finbar had thrown his into the back of his wardrobe after the first week of school. Anyway, no one believed that a medallion of the Blessed Virgin Mary hanging down your back and a leather pouch with a picture of Venerable Saorseach O'Rahilly hanging down your front could really afford much protection against the type of things they most needed protection from, such as the gangs in Markiewicz Mansions and the Brothers themselves. People with sallow skin, close-set eyes, and splayed feet in clean shoes who kept old twine and did not venerate the Blessed Virgin were not really that much of a threat when it came down to it.

Just as Brother Mulligan was about to launch into how to tell a souper (one who came from a family that had betrayed their true faith and converted to Protestantism in order to get charity soup during the famine and thus doubly suspect) from a Protestant of older stock, there was a sharp knocking at the door.

"Good morning, Brother Mulligan. We have come to relieve you. This is Brother Moody," clipped Mr. Pollock as he entered.

"Now, you boys," said Mr. Pollock, abruptly turning his attention from Mulligan to the class, "this is Brother Moody. He has been seconded to us from Drumgloom Industrial School to replace Brother Kennedy who will be resting for the remainder of the school year, and I can tell you that Brother Moody will be standing for no nonsense."

Mr. Pollock had no need to point that out to them. They had spotted it from the very first moment. Moody was young, far younger than any of the Brothers in the school. He couldn't have been more than thirty and he had that look. Finbar had seen it before on the younger Brothers in Cork. It was that blue shave, that raw, overly close shaved look to the face that lasted all day and bespoke a vicious temper and an indefatigable capacity for punishment. They could not do a blackout on him. They could not tire him out by having him beat them. He came from Drumgloom, a name that sent a shudder through even Lynch.

"Well, Brother Moody, we'll leave you to take over," grinned Mr. Pollock evilly, and ushered the puzzled Brother Mulligan out the door in front of him.

Brother Moody accompanied them to the door and bid them goodbye with a smile that died into absolute menace when he turned to face the boys.

* * *

"Don't dare answer me back again, you little brat!"

Finbar sat down stunned. He'd barely managed to stand up before Brother Moody had smacked him across the face with the leather strap. All Finbar had said was that there was a glare and he couldn't see the part of the blackboard where Brother Moody had written.

"Any other blind boys who need a waking up?" asked Brother Moody.

No one moved. No one made a sound.

Brother Moody smiled in satisfaction. He inhaled deeply. Yes, there it was, that beautiful, unmistakable, invigorating odour: ungovernable little brats stewing in their own fear.

The Brother proceeded to call the roll, fixed each boy with a stare when he answered his name, and made little knowing nods of his head to show that he had been filled in on exactly who to watch out for.

The rest of the class was spent conjugating verbs and declining nouns in chorus, and copying down sentences to translate that night for homework.

"Ye know nothing now but I'll learn ye Latin if it kills ye," concluded Brother Moody, and strode out as Brother Boland's bell echoed up from the yard.

25

In the quiet of the empty hall, disturbed only by the muffled sounds of the boys going home from the yard outside, the untunable school piano became host to a jolt of unease that ran through its dusty frame.

Warped, battered, and now condemned to having occasional hymns and the so-called tunes of alleged musicals pounded out on it between the long periods of neglect, it languished. In its heyday it had been used in the at-homes of Mrs. Dorothy Nesbitt-Blenner (née Beckett), an affluent Rathmines widow, much given to acts of philanthropy and founder-member of the Providential Ladies Choir. In her well-appointed drawing room it had accompanied no less than Count John McCormack himself as he rendered a memorable "Sliabh Na mBan" and a perfectly serviceable "Madre, non dormi?" from *Il Trovatore*.

A brief tremulous residue of that glory day rippled through the piano's woodwork. Its hammers shuddered minutely against the rusted strings and a tiny shiver of warm recollection ran along its stained ivory keys just before the wall above it softened and buckled and the climbing ropes and frame, together with one of the large metal window frames, came crashing down on it to forever put it out of its misery. One sad, regretful discord shimmered through the crushed wood and severed strings before silence again settled on the hall.

* * *

"That Moody is a complete fucking bollix!" shouted Scully as they ran for the light.

"I would've kicked him in the head!" spat Lynch.

"Yeah. Dead right," concurred Finbar.

The bus narrowly missed them as they ran across the busy junction at Breen Street. They were not in a hurry. They were just playing chicken with the buses as usual, their liberation from Moody giving them more wilful, mad energy than normal. Finbar felt almost giddy; infected by Lynch's reckless verve.

"Come on! Quick!" yelled Lynch, and ran into the traffic behind a large truck. He grabbed onto one of the door handles on the back and put his feet on the crash bar. Just as the vehicle started to pull off, Scully jumped up beside him. Finbar stood rooted to the spot; he had not bargained for this.

"Come on, Bogman!" urged Lynch.

Finbar broke into a trot and managed to clamber on to the truck before it moved into second gear. His breath came in short catches and the sweat gathered under his arms. This was such a bad idea.

"I know!" shouted Lynch.

"What?" called Scully above the noise of the truck.

"L&N!"

The L&N was Aladdin's Cave. It was El Dorado. It was the mother lode. It was a dingy little shop on the West Circular Road full of sweets and ragged secondhand comics and was so apparently unprofitable that everyone assumed it was just another front for the IRA.

The truck began to pick up speed and Lynch cheered loudly. Scully never thoroughly enjoyed scutting: he thought it was tough but a bit scary and did not completely share

Lynch's total disregard for his own safety that at times seemed to border on a death wish. Finbar held on and tried to keep his eyes open, praying that this would soon be over and vowing never to do it again. The driver of the car behind them blew his horn and shook his fist at them. They could slip at any moment and end up under his front wheels. Lynch turned around and gave the driver two fingers with slow balletic elaborateness. The driver swore at them and shook his fist more vigorously.

The truck soon slowed and came to a full stop. They were stuck at the lights. The driver behind them began to grin evilly. He leaned out his window and shouted, "I'm going to give ye the hidin' of yer lives, ye little shites!"

An icy, dangerous smile flickered across Lynch's face and he dropped off the truck. Scully and Finbar watched amazed as he ran to the driver's door and started taunting him. The man flung his door open and began to get out. In that split second, when the driver was off balance and had only one foot outside on the road, Lynch viciously kicked the door shut on the protruding leg. It made a sickening dull sort of crack and the man screamed in pain.

"Run for it!" Lynch shouted at Scully and Finbar, who were still clinging to the truck, numb and disbelieving. The vehicle began to move and the two boys dropped off and belted after Lynch down a narrow street of single-storey houses.

"Lynch! You're fuckin' mad!" Scully yelled hysterically. He could not believe that even Lynch could do something so senselessly violent. Finbar fixed his eyes on the ground and ran with every ounce of fearful energy he possessed.

Lynch was about ten yards in front of them when he turned around. "Ah, bollix!" he shouted, and began to run even faster. Scully glanced over his shoulder to see the ominous and unmistakable dark blue hulk of a squad car coming down the street after them.

"Oh Jesus!" cried Finbar when he spotted it. He turned around again just in time to see Lynch and then Scully turn sharply down a laneway. He dashed after them, reciting the "Oh God, oh God, oh God, oh God, oh God" mantra of one who knows he is suddenly in deeper than imagined.

The lane was damp and treacherous with moss and rubbish. Scully slipped and went flat on his face and Finbar fell over him. They picked themselves up, ignored the hot stinging coming from knees and elbows, and scrambled after Lynch. Some instinct guided Lynch through the unfamiliar maze of lanes and he led them to a deserted part of the canal where they lay panting in the lee of one of the old locks.

Scully's heart was in his mouth and he expected to be grabbed by a big culchie cop hand any second, but Lynch was exhilarated. Finbar sat shaking and avoided looking at his companions. He could feel fear settle in his stomach like a cobblestone. He could hear his father's voice: *Run with the wrong crowd and before you know it, you'll be swearing and smoking and hanging around street corners. Short step from there to reform school and your life is ruined. End up in the gutter.* His father was given to such vatic pronouncements of doom whenever Declan got into trouble, and now Finbar felt himself assaulted by panic. He would soon be arrested and sent to Drumgloom and his father would disown him and—

"That was fuckin' deadly!" whooshed Lynch.

"Yeah," whispered Scully, as he furtively glanced around for signs of arriving cops.

"Stupid fucker was askin' for it," said Lynch solemnly.

"Oh yeah. Stupid shitebag," agreed Scully automatically.

"Come on."

"Where?" asked Finbar cautiously.

"L&N."

"What!?!" gasped Scully.

"Yeah! It'll be grand."

It took Scully two seconds to weigh up looking chicken versus the imprudence of returning to the scene of the crime: "Okay. Deadly. Let's go."

Finbar sat on the grass staring at them.

"You staying there, Bogman?"

The only thing worse than going with them was staying there alone and waiting to be hauled home in a squad car. He got up heavily and followed them.

Finbar was frantic as they reached the main road again. He furtively watched for prowling cop cars and tried to keep calm. Barely concealing his relief, he stepped into the L&N after Lynch and Scully and closed the door behind them.

At the sound of the little bell that hung on the back of the door, L&N—the only name anyone had ever given the proprietor—came out of the back room to check. He scowled darkly at them, tugged at the buttons on his dark blue nylon housecoat, and returned to whatever he was at.

The L&N was a treasure trove of old comics, books, sweets that were probably illegal in a lot of the developed world, and, of course, loose cigarettes. The boys stood for a few moments waiting for the gloom to teach their eyes to see right. Ragged piles of comics and paperback books lined the walls. The glass counter was full of toffee bars and unnaturally coloured boiled sweets. On the high shelves behind the counter there were faded boxes of breakfast cereals and washing powders no longer generally available.

As soon as his eyes adjusted, Finbar dived into the box of two-penny superhero comics. The L&N was one of the few places left where you could still rent comics. Of course, L&N deemed that the value of the comics depreciated greatly with each reading, so every comic you rented cost two pennies; on return L&N would give you back one.

While Scully rummaged through the war comics, Lynch slipped behind the counter and silently pulled open the drawer of *Naughty Night Nurse Confessions* and *Tittler*, with their promise of almost naked large-breasted women and stories about English women who had sex because they liked it. Had Lynch been aware of L&N's special stash of Scandinavian "marital guides" in the back room, he would have been back late at night with a crowbar and a wheelbarrow.

"Scully, look at this ride," he hissed, holding up an enormously breasted cover girl.

"Deadly," cooed Scully.

Finbar barely caught a glance of full-colour flesh before Lynch pocketed the magazine and grabbed another one.

"Get out from behind that counter before I come out there and split ye!" shouted L&N from the back room.

Casually Lynch put the *Tittler* in his jacket and ostentatiously stomped out from behind the counter. Scully had already picked out three pocket-sized war comics full of stealthy sentry knifings, intrepid allied heroes, and swift deaths of fiendish enemies. Finbar had two *Dan Dare*s, one *Commando*, and one *Superman* that he had not read before.

"I'm taking these!" called out Scully, waving his fistful of fictional wartime fury in the direction of the back room. No answer was forthcoming. Calmly he walked to the curtain that separated the back from the rest of the shop. Finbar followed him with his comics in one hand and eight pennies in the other. There, hunched over a low table sitting on beer crates, were L&N and Taft, the English teacher from Southwell, immersed in a game of checkers.

"I'm taking these," repeated Scully.

"I have four," said Finbar.

Taft did not even seem to notice the intrusion and L&N barely glanced up. "Sixp'nce and eightp'nce," he muttered, and held out his hand. He didn't look as the boys dropped the coins into his palm. Instead he made his move and Taft pounced delightedly, capturing four pieces. The expression of maniacal glee on Taft's face was enough to send the boys scurrying out onto the street.

"Fuckin' weirdoes," said Lynch.

"Fuckin' madser, Taft," laughed Scully.

"Who's he?" asked Finbar.

"English teacher at Southwell. He's mental," said Scully a little fearfully. "Seen him at football game last time we played Southwell. He was wearing a top hat." He had, in a perverse way, a certain respect for the lunatic unease Taft exuded.

From under his jacket Lynch produced the *Tittler* and handed it to Scully. He showed the *Naughty Night Nurse Confessions* to Finbar and said: "You can borrow this when I'm finished."

"Right, yeah," answered Finbar drily, promising himself that he would not ask for it if Lynch forgot.

26

Martin Mulvey, S.J., Diocesan Investigator, pedalled along the Howth Road with all his might. The driving wind whipped the sea spray against his face. "Blast!" he shouted, and stopped abruptly. He let his bicycle fall roughly against the pavement and strode back to retrieve his hat. He crumpled it up and stuffed it into the pocket of his plastic raincoat. "Damn and blast!" he cursed again as the first tiny drops of rain started to patter on his coat.

Furiously he mounted his bicycle and resumed pedaling into the wind. Through the misting rain he could make out the hulk of Howth Head away to his right across the grey waters of the bay.

What could have possessed him to cycle all the way out to Howth on a day like this? He could have taken the train or telephoned and arranged for Marcus Madden to visit him in the comfort of his office. Oh no, he had to get on his bicycle and drag all the way out to Howth Head!

Still, Father Sheehan had decided that the revision of *The Life of Venerable Saorseach O'Rahilly* should be done as speedily as possible, and Father Mulvey was not in the habit of arguing with his superior, particularly when he was showing a lot more enthusiasm for this case than any of Mulvey's previous investigations.

After twenty yards of stiff ascent up Howth Head,

Mulvey gave up and dismounted. He peered up the long winding road and began to push his bike. He noted with irony that the wind had died down now that he was no longer cycling. The rain fell in a gentle yet drenching mizzle. He consoled himself with the sweet smell of gorse that came to him from the gardens of the nearby houses.

He stopped outside a small ramshackle cottage distinguished from its tidy neighbours by its overgrown garden and rusted gate. He consulted his notebook: this was it. He pushed open the protesting gate and leaned his bicycle against the inside wall. Scraping his boots on the flagstone in front of the house, he knocked authoritatively yet respectfully on the low wooden door, a trick only Jesuits and a handful of Holy Ghost Fathers could pull off.

After a prolonged silence, Father Mulvey knocked on the door again, this time imbuing it with holy urgency, a feat beyond even the most gifted of Holy Ghost Fathers. He jiggled his keys and waited.

Next he moved to the small window in the front of the cottage and peered through its dirty glass. Inside he saw a small dining table covered in opened cans, dirty plates, and empty stout bottles, but no other signs of life. He pushed his way past the rambling rose that grew wild around the front and side of the cottage and peeked through another window. Now he saw a smaller room. The filthy desk was covered by more empty cans and the shards of a broken whiskey bottle. Opposite the window Mulvey could make out the fireplace, and in it a pile of ashes on which sat a couple of half-burned books and charred papers.

"Hopeless!" muttered Mulvey to himself, and stomped back to the front of the cottage.

"You'll be there all night."

Mulvey jumped at the harsh guttural voice and looked

around. Above him, in the branches of the gnarled apple tree, sat a young boy. He looked no older than eight. Mulvey found it hard to believe that such a docker's voice had emanated from this tiny frame, but so it seemed to be. The boy was calmly picking his nose and watching Mulvey with a mix of mild interest and barely concealed disdain. He left his nose alone and moved on to scratching at his scalp through his close-shorn red hair.

Reaching the conclusion that Mulvey was either hard of hearing or just plain thick, the boy restated his assessment of the situation: "I said you'll be there all night. You're looking for Madser Madden, right?"

Mulvey saw the boy speak and heard the voice but still could not get over the incongruity of the two. He drew himself up to his full height and put on his best imperious face: "And what precisely do you mean by that, young man?"

"Won't be home for hours."

"Is that so?"

"Down the boozer by now."

"That is no way to speak of your elders, young man. You should show more respect before I take you down out of that tree and put manners on you!"

The boy fixed Mulvey in a sneering gaze as if defying him to make the first move. "I'm just saying it's dole day and you'll be here all night or you can go down to The Wharf and get him there. If and you wait it'll be closing time and he'll be footless when he gets home and he might shoot ye. It's no skin off my nose."

With that the boy scampered through the branches and dropped down on the other side of the wall and was off.

"Come back here, you young scamp!" shouted Mulvey hopelessly.

"Up yer arse!" countered the boy as he disappeared

through the bushes toward the warren of lanes behind the cottages.

How bad can it be? thought Father Mulvey to himself as he freewheeled down the hill toward the port. *I've been in public houses before.*

By the time he found The Wharf, he was beginning to have second thoughts. While he was leaning his bicycle against a lamppost, the sudden exit of one of the clients, horizontally and at great speed through the air, made him even more apprehensive. He locked his bike.

Mulvey stepped over the stunned customer where he had landed, took a deep breath, and pushed open the door. A wall of unhealthy heat hit him. His eyes smarted immediately under the assault of tobacco smoke. The air was thin and used, thanks to the gaslights that begrudgingly lit the bar. An odour of stale beer, smoke, and wet overcoats presided over the place. The dismal murmur of conversation faded into a suspicious silence. Mulvey nodded to a couple of the patrons who were staring at him and moved toward the nearest empty spot at the bar. The patrons ignored his greeting and went back to nursing the pints of stout on the counter in front of them.

Behind the bar Tony Loftus casually slapped a length of lead pipe down on the counter with a loud whack. "Any more of that carry on and you're out on yer ear too, Maher! I can see you."

In the corner beside the rings board where Maher was threatening Tommy Grogan with a broken glass, it was as if the barman had suddenly frozen time. Maher took one look at Loftus and through the haze of his drunken rage he recognised real trouble when he saw it. He set down the broken glass and hugged Grogan warmly. "Ah, sure, I was only having a bit of fun here with Tommy, wasn't I?" Grogan, glad to be relieved of a broken glass to the face, was only too happy to concur with this fabrication.

"Just watch your step, right?" barked Loftus, and replaced the pipe in easy reach under the bar. He took a cursory glance along the bar: all of the patrons who were still conscious had drinks in front of them.

"A small port, please," said Mulvey to Loftus's face when it turned to him.

The barman exhibited no reaction beyond making a big deal of taking a very dusty bottle of port down from a high shelf and searching under the bar for a suitable glass. He eyed Mulvey carefully. The last time a priest had set foot in The Wharf, it had been a temperance raid by the Redemptorist Fathers who were having a retreat in the town.

Father Mulvey carefully glanced from side to side along the length of the bar. Could that scruffy urchin be telling him the truth? Could Marcus Madden, B.A., official biographer of the Venerable Saorseach O'Rahilly, really be in here among these broken, defeated men?

Loftus carefully placed the port on the counter and took the money Mulvey had left. When he returned with the change Mulvey caught his eye and smiled winningly.

"I wonder if you could help me out. I'm looking for an old pal of mine."

Loftus nodded solemnly.

"I'm looking for a chap by the name of Marcus Madden, B.A. Do you know him at all?"

Loftus's face creased into an ugly chuckle: "If B.A. stands for Bullshit Artist, I know your man."

Before Mulvey could react to this unexpected piece of vulgarity, there was a burst of shouting and glass-breaking from the back room.

"Get out to fuck, Madden! You've never bought me a drink in yer life, ye stingy bastard!" A beer-soaked Marcus Madden, B.A., was propelled backward into the bar by some unseen fist. He stood reeling in the middle of the room, oblivious to the blood that was running freely from his nose. His eyes darted around the room and eventually came to rest on the unfamiliar Mulvey, who was staring in disbelief at this dishevelled wreck of a man who seemed to be Marcus Madden, B.A.

"Ah, be gob, a man of the cloth. Sure aren't the clergy of Holy Mother Ireland awful charitable. Would ye stand me a drink there now, Father?"

"Mr. Madden? Marcus Madden?" inquired Mulvey timidly.

"Who's asking?"

"Martin Mulvey, S.J., Dio—" Mulvey stopped himself short and decided that the term "Diocesan Investigator" was unlikely go down too well in these surroundings.

"Oh yeah?" said Madden defensively, licking distractedly at the blood on his top lip.

"Why don't you pull up a stool here and I'll buy you a drink," suggested Mulvey in his most soothing tone.

Madden underwent a miraculous change of disposition and lurched toward the barstool beside Mulvey. He leaned over the bar: "A large bottle and a glass of Crested Ten and whatever the good Father is having," he commanded, as if he were suddenly the one buying.

"You might want . . . You seem to have, uhm, a cut on your nose there," said Mulvey, proffering his handkerchief.

Madden gallantly waved away the pristine cotton and rubbed his sleeve roughly over his mouth. "Be gob, would you look at that now! Isn't that the strangest thing?" he remarked casually as he inspected the mass of blood and snot on his sleeve.

Loftus sullenly served the drinks and moved as far down the bar as he could. He did not like the feeling of Madden lording it over him under the auspices of some strange Jesuit priest, but was not entirely sure what he could do about it: taking a length of lead pipe to a man of the cloth, even one who drank port, did not present itself as an appropriate course of action.

Madden poured his stout down the side of the glass with great concentration. While it settled he took the large glass of whiskey and held it up to the gaslight appraisingly. "Good luck, Father," he said brightly, and emptied the whiskey down his throat in one voracious gulp. He held the empty glass up to Mulvey and winked knowingly.

"Another whiskey for Mr. Madden, please, barman, when you have a moment," called Mulvey resignedly.

"So what is it I can do you for?" asked Madden lightly, his humour buoyed by the warming fire of the whiskey hitting his stomach. He picked up the fresh whiskey from the bar and eyed it lovingly. Then he topped off his stout and took a long slow drink, the hops smouldering deliciously in his mouth with the peaty aftertaste of the whiskey.

"Well, Mr. Madden, I know you are a scholar of some renown and I have a little work I thought you might be able to help us with." Mulvey listened carefully to his own voice, almost stunned by the multilevel incongruity of the conversation he was trying to conduct, the surroundings in which he was doing it, and his unlikely looking companion. "I am sure we could pay you a not unrespectable fee," he found himself adding.

"Is that so? Now this is very interesting, I have to say, Father." Madden wiped his mouth and smoothed his hair.

"Yes, I have been empowered to commission you to

revise your biography of Venerable Saorseach O'—"

Madden recoiled violently. He stood up and jumped from foot to foot like a man scalded. "Don't mention that name to me! Isn't it enough to have that infernal book ruin my life once without having you come in here to dig it up again? What did I do to deserve this? Is there no end to that fucking book haunting me?"

Mulvey blanched under this violent tirade and was at a momentary loss for words. He lifted his glass of port and emptied it while signaling to Loftus for another round.

"A whiskey as well?" shouted Loftus from the other end of the bar.

Mulvey nodded and turned his attention back to Madden, who was running his hands agitatedly through his matted hair.

"I could have been someone! I could have had my picture on the back of a hundred books by now! I could be off in London sipping gin-and-tonics with the best of them! I could be running me hands all over gorgeous women in the backseats of Daimlers. But no! I had to go and write that stupid fucking book! Do you know how much they paid me? Do you? Do you? Go on! Guess! Just guess! Five pounds, eight and sixpence! Five pounds, eight and sixpence for a life! Ruined! They fucking ruined me! I'm marked for life. They damn near tried to make a saint out of me for writing that fucking book! Ruined my fucking life! Look! Take a look at that!"

Madden drew a crumpled page from his pocket and thrust it at Mulvey, who opened the sheet and read:

Dear Mr. Madden,

Thank you for sending us your manuscript of "The Glencullen Gang Take Stock." Unfortunately, this work does not meet our current editorial needs. We regretfully return your manuscript and wish you every success in your literary endeavours. We trust you understand that ours is but one subjective opinion and that you will persist in your search for a suitable publisher. On a personal note, I would just like to add that despite being a devout Anglican, I was greatly moved by your 'Life of Saorseach O'Rahilly.'

Kindest regards,
D.W. Thompson-Greene

"See? See? See what they did to me? The manuscript wasn't even opened. I glued pages eleven and twelve together at the corners and they were still glued. The bastards! That O'Rahilly shite is the only thing anyone takes me seriously for. I have hundreds of letters like that. Not any of the Glencullen Gang books. Fifteen of them I've written. Not a single one published! When I submitted *Gold of Antrim*, they suggested that I should take up teaching! They even sent back *Muiris Fogarty and the Jungle of Fear*. Because of that fucking Saorseach O'fucking Rahilly, I live in a pigsty and the world will never know Stephen Brennan, Private Eye, or how Patsy Nugent helped the Blackfoot Indians at the Battle of Two-Rock Canyon, or *Tom Miley and the Martian Menace*! Nothing! I can publish nothing! I can never escape that bastarding book! Ruined me, it did!"

Madden paused for breath, leaned over, and, with surprising adroitness, grabbed the letter from Mulvey, downed his whiskey, and tucked the bottle of stout into his coat pocket before reeling toward the door in a flurry of shouts and incomprehensible curses.

Mulvey stood up and hastily exited after him just in time to see two urchins, one suspiciously like the boy he had encountered earlier and the other smaller and stockier, making off with his handlebars, pedals, and both wheels. Beside the naked frame of his bicycle lay the barely conscious figure of Madden, who was now drooling copiously onto the cobblestones beside his face.

Mulvey shook his head sadly and walked down the hill to the village. He turned the corner just in time to see the train pull out of the station. A soft rain began and just as suddenly intensified.

"I'll write the fecking thing myself if I have to," he muttered, and stomped toward the station to wait for the next Dublin train. He could get off at Denmark Street Station and walk up to Werburgh Street from there. He smiled as this new plan began to take shape in his head.

"I know it is very late, but I do need to ask you some more questions," said Father Mulvey softly. "You see, I was on the telephone with the Bishop of Spokes and Duggery and he had a few questions he needed answered before he spoke to Cardinal Russell."

Brother Boland nodded sadly as if wishing none of this had ever happened.

"So, can you remember the night you found the statuette of Venerable Saorseach?"

Brother Boland nodded slowly.

"The bleeding one?"

Boland nodded again, barely aware of what Mulvey was saying to him. Inside his head, a distracting clamour swirled through his brain. The something wrong was out there again, inside him, all around him, growing wronger. Mulvey was not making it any better. Venerable Saorseach O'Rahilly was not making it any better.

"Can you recall hearing anything? A voice? Music?

Anything out of the ordinary?"

"I have to go," said the Brother hoarsely.

Father Mulvey watched in shock as the man's frail frame seemed to tighten and brace before scuttling to the door. Mulvey ran to the door after him and saw him move up the stairs. Ever the intrepid Diocesan Investigator, he followed.

Mulvey had seriously underestimated Brother Boland's speed, and by the time he got to the first landing, the man was out of sight.

Several lucky deductive leaps and one false start of bursting into the empty toilets on the second floor were required before Mulvey found his way to the top landing. From there it was easy. Brother Boland had no thoughts of concealing his trail. His only purpose was haste.

Mulvey cautiously passed through the open doorway and looked upward. He saw the spiral stairs and could hear Boland's laboured movement above him. He started cautiously up.

When he came to the ladder he saw the Brother at the top of it keening softly to himself and stroking the big bell as though it had been hurt. Concluding that the ladder could not support both of them, Mulvey prudently waited at the bottom and watched Boland soothe the bell and run his hands over the walls of the bell tower like some shamanic medicine man.

Gradually the Brother's movements slowed and finally stopped. Exhausted, he crept carefully down the ladder and sat on the bottom rung. He was breathing heavily and sweat was running down his face. When he looked up, he did not seem the least bit surprised to see Father Mulvey standing there.

"Are you all right there, Brother?" asked Mulvey.

Brother Boland nodded.

"Is there something wrong?"

"I don't know. There is something. Around us. Inside. Something cracking. A sundering. Shards."

"Is it Venerable Saorseach?"

Brother Boland shook his head, then stopped and peered sadly at Mulvey: "I don't know. I don't know."

"Well, let's say it is Venerable Saorseach. What do you think he is trying to tell you?"

"I don't know."

"Do you think maybe he thinks the country is on a downward spiral of moral decay and needs to renew its dedication to piety?"

"I don't know."

"And Gaelic football?"

"I don't know."

"And the Irish language?"

"I don't know."

It was only then Boland noticed that Mulvey was writing everything down in his little red notebook.

"I don't know, I tell you! I don't know!" he snapped, and abruptly left.

Father Mulvey sat on the ladder and finished his notes. He closed his notebook, wrapped the rubber band around it, and tapped it thoughtfully on his chin. Yes, he should be able to write this up into a convincing draft for Father Sheehan. If he used *implied*, *demonstrated*, and *intimated*, instead of *said*, he should be fine.

27

Van! Men! In the yard! Again! In the yard! I saw them drive in. The janitor opened the gate for them."

Brother Loughlin looked up from his desk to see Brother Boland hopping up and down with agitation in the doorway. "Contain yourself, Brother Boland. I will deal with this."

Calmly Loughlin got up from his desk and walked down the corridor past the first year classes and out into the yard.

"There! See?" Boland pointed at the rickety van in the middle of the yard. *Brannigan Brothers Roofing Contractors*, read the legend on the side of the van. Two men were unloading timber and tools while a third looked on.

"You can't park there! You have to leave!" barked Brother Loughlin.

Matt, the overseer, looked up and acknowledged Loughlin with a desultory but friendly wave of his hand.

"I said you'll have to leave. Move that van," repeated Loughlin as he walked toward the man.

"No bother, Brother. The lads'll just load up our stuff and we'll be on our way. Lar, Con, hurry up, we have to load up again."

"It's all very well that you're here at nine in the morning, but you were supposed to be here months ago. The janitor should not have let you in. We're not allowing any outsiders into the school," Loughlin continued.

"Game ball. That's up to you," said Matt indifferently.

"Your face rings a bell. I can't place you. Have you done work here before?" asked Loughlin. He eyed Matt carefully.

"The radiators! The radiators! They were here about the radiators! And the clock! I remember now!" rambled Brother Boland.

"Ah, no, that would be the scrap metal division and the electrical division. They're completely separate from us," explained Matt.

Brother Loughlin continued to eye him suspiciously. "What's your name?"

"Matt. Matt Matthews."

"All done," announced Lar as he approached.

"We're all set," concurred Con.

Again Loughlin found himself assailed by a sense of familiarity. He looked from Lar to Con and back again. "Are you sure you haven't been here before?"

"Maybe in a previous life, Brother, but not as far as I know," replied Lar cheerfully.

"Metempsychosis, that is," Con added with a smile.

"Don't you two start," cautioned Matt. "I'm sorry, Brother, they're forever going on like that. I blame night school."

"Indeed. Here's Mr. McConnell now. He'll open the gate to let you out."

"Game ball, Brother," said Matt.

Loughlin shook his head and pulled Boland, who was staring open-mouthed at the three men, after him.

"Stop that carry on, Brother Boland, or I'll have you locked in your cell!"

"But it's them! It's them! They're part of it all. I'm sure of it."

"Part of all what? Stop your nonsense or you'll end up

raving and covered in your own spit in the attic like Brother Garvey. Go sweep out your tuck shop. I'm sure it's filthy."

"Part of the sadness in the walls."

"I'll give you sadness in the walls! Go sweep out your shop!"

"What time is it?" shouted McDonagh above the buzz of voices.

"Nearly half ten."

"Deadly!"

"Betcha he was out drinking again."

There was no sign of Mr. Devlin and the intoxicating smell of double free class wafted through the air. The Biology lab was the best place for a free class. It was tucked into a disused part of the monastery and apart from the rest of the classrooms.

By eleven o'clock they were fully convinced Devlin was not going to show up. McDonagh put his head down on the workbench and went to sleep. Lynch dug the stolen *Naughty Night Nurse Confessions* out of his bag and flicked through the pictures of near naked women with an intensity of purpose unusual for him. Scully looked around him for something to do. Finbar started to doodle aimlessly in his copy while furtively staring at the women in Lynch's magazine. Egan calmly walked to the back of the lab and started to go through the cupboards, occasionally returning to secrete something in his bag.

"Yeaw! Ego! Bringing home yer homework?" called McDonagh. Egan looked at him blankly and went back to the cupboard.

Suddenly bored, Lynch handed the *Naughty Night Nurse Confessions* to Ferrara and walked to the teacher's desk.

"Now, this morning we're going to perform an

experiment of picking our holes and doing nothing until lunch time," began Lynch in a near perfect imitation of Mr. Devlin, "cos I was out last night getting locked and woke up under a car and have a head like a balloon on me this morning. While I fall asleep, I want yiz all to pick yer holes and keep quiet. When yiz are done yiz can write a fourteen-page essay about it. When—"

"Sketch!" hissed McDonagh, who could see out into the corridor through the partially open door.

Lynch calmly stepped away from the desk and feigned dropping something in the wastepaper basket.

"It's okay. It was only Frawley," said McDonagh after a moment.

Lynch resumed his teaching post: "If yiz have any questions, yiz can ask me hole."

The mood of a free class could change from one of somnolent laziness to one of giddy messing in a flash, and taking off the teachers was almost guaranteed to make it happen.

Gradually, almost organically, the noise level increased as more and more boys had a go. The scene reached a fever pitch when Lynch as Mr. Devlin was threatening to vomit all over McDonagh as Mr. Pollock, while Scully as Brother Boland gibbered, shook, and drooled all over the floor and Ferrara did a passable parody of Father Flynn trying to calm them all down. So carried away did they get that they lost track of who was keeping watch and it took a couple of seconds for it to dawn on them that the "What in the name of God is the meaning of this outrage?" actually came from the real Brother Kennedy.

Lynch, McDonagh, Scully, and Ferrara were caught. There was no pretending to be looking for a pen or putting something in the bin. Brother Kennedy grabbed them roughly by the arms and put them out to the line by the door.

"The rest of you can write this out fifty times while I deal with these baloobas. Take out your copybooks!" he shouted, and wrote on the board:

> *If I had given the slightest bit of thought to my fortunate position as a pupil in this school, I would have taken advantage of the opportunity to repay the time and effort that has gone into making me a better person by applying myself to my books instead of howling and carrying on like an ill-bred corner boy. I am a worthless bowsie only good for cannon-fodder and do not deserve the effort expended on my education by my betters.*

Brother Kennedy turned on his four victims: "Oh no, you couldn't just show a little respect. You couldn't use a free class for some useful purpose. You had to start acting the blackguard and draw attention to yourselves, didn't you? I'm still supposed to be resting, you know. I'll learn you manners!"

He leathered each of them twice on each hand and sent them back to their places.

"Copy that fifty times before the end of this class and no messing! If you're not finished, you will stay back after school to finish."

Brother Kennedy started pacing round the lab. He stopped behind Brian Egan and stared over his shoulder. The boy sensed Kennedy behind him and shrank down into his shoulders. He continued to write nervously under the scrutiny.

"Perhaps you can tell me what that is supposed to be," he said, pointing at Egan's copybook.

"*Fortunate,*" answered Egan, his voice hesitant against

the coagulating resentful silence that was emanating from the rest of the class.

"Spell it."

"F-O-R-T-U-N-E-A-T-E."

"Is that so? Look at the board! How many E's in *fortunate*?"

"One, Brother."

"Yes. *One, Brother*. For God sake, you can't even copy down from the board! What sort of eejit are you?" Brother Kennedy leathered Egan twice on his writing hand.

From the other side of the lab there came the sudden metallic crash of a geometry set hitting the floor.

"What clumsy fool did that?" barked Brother Kennedy.

"I did," called Scully, much to the relief of Shorthall, whose geometry set he had just deliberately pushed onto the floor.

"Get out to the line!"

"Which line?" asked Scully.

"Over there by the door!" snarled Brother Kennedy.

Scully nodded solemnly to himself and bounded out to the line, satisfied that Kennedy's fuse was now lit. Picking on Egan like that was not on. There was something broken inside Egan that made Scully weirdly protective.

"You expect me to correct that tiny handwriting, do you, Mr. Sullivan?"

Finbar froze in his seat. He'd read Scully's signal. Was there a perfect wrong answer to this question? He could feel Mullen tense beside him as if waiting for the blow. He was trapped. Now that he actually wanted to annoy Brother Kennedy, he couldn't think of the right wrong thing to say.

"Brother, can I bring me lines out to the line?" bellowed Scully suddenly.

Kennedy spun around and stared carefully at Scully, checking for any sign of disrespect or slyness. Finding none, he gruffly nodded his assent and returned to baiting Finbar.

"Start that one again! Make it legible!"

Scully grabbed his jotter and returned to the line. There he made an awkward show of trying to lean on the windowsill and write, the exaggerated eagerness of his movements conveying its message to the rest. They were going out of their way to provoke Kennedy. This was another blackout.

The Brother stood over Finbar and watched carefully as he rewrote the line in unnaturally large letters. Kennedy gently tapped his leather against his cassock in anticipation of the slightest mistake. Finbar let the pen take over and suddenly there it was in large block letters: *IF I HAD GIVEN THE SHITEST BIT OF THOUGHT—*

"Out to the line!" rasped Brother Kennedy, and snapped his knuckles hard across the back of Finbar's head.

"An bhfuil cead agam dul go dtí an leabharlann?" (May I go to the library?)

Brother Kennedy turned and saw McDonagh standing at the end of the workbench.

"What?" asked Brother Kennedy, bewildered.

"An bhfuil cead agam dul go dtí an leabharlann?" repeated McDonagh more urgently.

Kennedy continued to stare at him.

McDonagh started to make little jigging movements and tried again: "An bhfuil cead agam dul go dtí an liathróid?" he tried hopefully. (May I go to the ball?)

In time, with Brother Kennedy's gradual understanding that the word McDonagh was grasping for was in fact *leithreas* (toilet), McDonagh's I'm-about-to-piss-myself dance became more vigorous.

"Have you learnt nothing at all ever? *Leithreas* is the

word. Get out to the line!"

"But Brother, I'm bursting!"

"Out to the line before I—"

Kennedy was interrupted by a long rasping fart from the other side of the lab. He turned to pinpoint the source and McDonagh took his opportunity to get out to the line while the getting was good. Egan, despite his already precarious position, could not help himself and started to rock with suppressed laughter.

"Who did that? Who was that animal?" yelled Brother Kennedy. There was a short silence ended by a higher-pitched aftershock of a fart. Egan could not help it; the tears were streaming down his face.

"Do you think that is funny, you insolent little pup?" shouted Brother Kennedy as he turned and grabbed Egan's hand.

He was just about to deliver the second blow to Egan when he was interrupted by Rutledge: "An bhfuil cead agam dul go dtí an leathlá?" (May I go to the half day?)

Brother Kennedy stared at him in disbelief: "*Leathlá? Leathlá?* What are you talking about?

"The jakes, Brother. I have to go to the jakes."

"*Jakes? Jakes?* I'll *jakes* you! Out to the line, you ignorant pup!" He moved across the room and delivered four stinging blows on each hand to everyone on the line. The sweat poured down his glowing face. He had just finished when Brother Boland's handbell rang out from the yard. It was noon and time for the Angelus.

Brother Kennedy pocketed his leather, turned to face the ever-suffering Christ on his cross perched above the blackboard, and blessed himself. Reluctantly the boys stood up. A lot of indifferent and inaccurate blessing ensued, and they were off.

"The Angel of the Lord declared unto Mary," wheezed Brother Kennedy.

"And she conceived of the Holy Ghost," murmured the boys, dragging each syllable out for all its leaden weight.

"Hail Mary, full of grace, the Lord is with thee / Blessed art thou amongst women / And blessed is the fruit of thy womb, Jesus," struggled Brother Kennedy, bowing his head deeply.

"Holy Mary, mother of God / Pray for us sinners, now / And at the hour of our death, Amen," chanted the boys.

"Behold the handmaid of the Lord," intoned Brother Kennedy.

"Be it done unto me according to thy word / Hail Mary, full of grace, the Lord is with thee / Blessed art thou amongst women . . ."

"And blessed—" Brother Kennedy stopped abruptly and seemed to go rigid. "Is the fruit," he croaked, and clutched his chest. A weird choking, collapsing sound came from the back of his throat and he buckled against the door. The boys could see his face going from red to purple as he gasped for breath. Kennedy flailed and gurgled, then stumbled and grabbed onto the top of Lynch's desk.

"Is the fruit of thy womb, Jesus," came Egan's voice from the back of the class.

Slowly, reluctantly, Egan's intention made itself clear. At first it was only Scully, Lynch, and a couple of others, but gradually more voices joined in: "Holy Mary, mother of God, pray for us sinners now, and at the hour of our DEATH, Amen."

"And the word was made flesh," blurted Egan, trying to keep his voice as steady as possible, suddenly coming to the full realisation of what he had just set in motion. Brother Kennedy slumped to the floor.

"And dwelt amongst us," answered the rest, Lynch's voice now towering above the others.

Finbar's guts sang. The back of his neck ran with sweat. His mind flooded with fire and the sound of heavy metal doors. This was so wrong. His breathing tightened. He closed his eyes and willed it all to stop. He knew it would not. This was real; the most real and terrifying thing he had ever been caught up in.

"Hail Mary, full of grace, the Lord is with thee," continued Egan, speeding up a little. Brother Kennedy had gone very pale and his lips were turning blue. His hand slipped from Lynch's desk and fell limply to the floor. Egan hesitated.

"BLESSED ART THOU AMONGST WOMEN!" prompted Lynch.

"And blessed is the fruit of thy womb, Jesus," concluded Egan.

In the silence before the response there was a worse one, the no-sound-at-all from Brother Kennedy.

The moment froze and hung in the air like the screeching, rending second before a thunderclap. Kennedy retched and choked and his right hand flailed in the air.

"What's that, Brother? You'll have to speak up, you miserable bastard," said Egan, and stood up. This was not just badness. Egan had gone somewhere beyond reach. He wanted only vengeance. "Are ye all right there, Brother? Can we get ye anything? A kick in the head maybe?" Egan's voice carried through the unbreathing silence around him like a scream.

Brother Kennedy struggled to speak and turned purple. The spittle rolled from his lips and down his chin.

"Are ye dead yet, ye bastard?" asked Egan. He was oblivious to the others who now watched in open-mouthed horror.

Brother Kennedy choked and gasped in a twitching heap on the floor. He stopped moving and then shuddered once more and was still.

A new layer of silence fell over the class. It was momentous, irreversible, and frightening. Boys moved forward to look at the inert heap of the Brother on the floor. He was done.

"Fucking bastard," said Egan quietly.

Steeled by this response, the others sat back down in their places. Egan moved to the door, then turned and faced the rest of the class, his eyes two stony points of purpose that glinted with unholy energy in his weirdly calm face. His was the dreadful energy of someone with nothing left to lose. He started rubbing Kennedy's lines off the blackboard and addressed the rest of them.

"Mr. Devlin didn't come in. We were waiting for him when Brother Kennedy came in," he began, his voice catching with invented upset and shock. "He was asking us questions about photosynthesis and suddenly he started coughing. We didn't know what was happening. Then he started choking." Egan's voice was taut with emotion. He moved to the workbench and casually filled a beaker with water. "Brother Kennedy asked me to give him some water but before I gave it to him he just kind of collapsed." The boy calmly poured a little water on the floor in demonstration and dropped the beaker beside Kennedy's inert shape. His voice was now strained with suppressed hysteria and tears expertly welled up in his eyes.

Instantly some switch in Egan seemed to click and he looked fiercely at the rest of the class. "That's how it happened. Right? Right, Scully? Right, Lynch? Cos we're all in it now," he said in a low voice.

"Right then. Turn on the waterworks and go for help,"

he added brightly, then ran out the door and down the corridor. "Help! Help! Quick! Help!" His footsteps and the tears in his voice echoed through the monastery and covered the shriek of twisting wood as the stairs in the bell tower writhed and torqued.

28

The bowels of the earth," intoned Mr. Pollock, hefting the hunk of rock in his palm. He walked distractedly to the window and looked out into the haze. "On a clear day you can see Moscow from here." This was his token gesture to what was supposed to be Geography class. "What did I say, Mr. Leake?"

There was silence. Mr. Pollock spun around on his crepe-heel with a squeak and glowered at where Leake was all too obviously not sitting.

"And where might our friend Mr. Leake be today? Some snooker hall? Police custody?"

"His ma died last night," said McDonagh from the back of the class.

"Ah, I see," murmured Mr. Pollock as if this was all part of some childish plot to make him look stupid. "Well then, Mr. McDonagh, perhaps you would like to tell us what I said?"

"And where might our friend Mr. Leake be today? Some snooker hall? Police custody?" repeated McDonagh.

"No, Mr. McDonagh, sor, before that."

McDonagh looked blankly at the teacher. He had not been paying the slightest attention.

"Hmmmm," mused Mr. Pollock, giving the signal for a free-for-all.

"Sir, sir, sir, sir, sir, sir, sir, sir, sir, sir, sir, sir, sir, sir,

sir, sir, sir, sir, sir, sir, sir, sir, sir, sir, sir, sir, sir, sir, sir, sir," hissed the boys in counterfeit eagerness to answer as they waved their hands around in the air.

"Well, Lynch. It is not often we see your hand above your head except when you are throwing stones at passing buses. Pray enlighten us, sor."

Lynch stood up, hands by his sides like some well-behaved Dickens urchin, and barked: "The bowels of the earth. On a clear day you can see Moscow from here, sor!" What Mr. Pollock could not see was the sheet of paper Lynch had stuck to his own arse that said *Fuck Pollock* in bright red letters.

"Very good, sor. You may sit down."

"Thank you, sor!" replied Lynch, and sat down.

Brother Cox came to the door and tapped gently on the glass panel. The teacher nodded back conspiratorially.

Mr. Pollock then beckoned silence. "We will be going to the oratory now to pay our respects to Brother Kennedy, so I want no blackguardism. We will make our way up the stairs in silence and then you will wait for me at the oratory door."

The boys stood outside the closed double doors of the oratory in a disorderly huddle. Mr. Pollock squeaked up the stairs so slowly that there was barely a trace of movement in his gown. When he got to the landing he held his arms up over his head to part the boys in front of him. They shuffled back and let him through. He opened the door a crack and peered inside.

"We shall be entering shortly," he announced to the boys as if they were waiting expectantly for every tiny development in this outing. While they waited Mr. Pollock weaved his way through, ordering the tucking in of a shirt here, the tightening of a tie there, the straightening of unruly hair here, the removal of a smirk from the face there.

"As if the dead shite is going to be looking," muttered Scully under his breath.

The door opened and Brother Cox's red leather face peered round it. Mr. Pollock pushed the boys nearest the door back to allow for the egress of those inside the oratory. Brother Cox stood back from the door and watched his charges file out.

"Is it a good show?" whispered McDonagh to one of the boys leaving.

"Deadly. Laugh a minute," whispered the other boy and rolled his eyes skyward.

Mr. Pollock stood by the door and ushered the boys in with a flourish of his right arm. They filed in and stood there in an uncertain maul.

"You will be seated in the pews," called Mr. Pollock from the doorway.

The seating options were severely limited by the ragged scaffolding that Conall McConnell had erected to repair the ceiling. Out of deference to Brother Kennedy's lying in state, repairs to the oratory had been suspended and all of McConnell's tools gathered safely away under lock and key in the basement. Of the pews that were left in place, the backmost ones filled first. Only the physically weak or the devout ended up in front.

Before the altar stood Brother Kennedy's open coffin on a shiny liturgical-looking trolley. From a seated position you could just make out Kennedy's red nose peeking above the edges of the coffin. It did not look as red as usual, more like a wax apple in a window than the nose of a bad-tempered reformed boozer.

Mr. Pollock stood beside the coffin and blessed himself

ostentatiously. At the signal the boys knelt down in the pews, surprised by the unusual softness of the kneelers.

"We will say a decade of the rosary for the repose of the soul of dear departed Brother Kennedy," announced Mr. Pollock.

He rattled on, followed by the ragged response of the boys. As if lulled by the sounds of Erse devotion to the Blessed Virgin, Finbar found himself staring at the end of the coffin and putting his eyes out of focus. When he was younger he had been able to drift deep into himself by fixing his stare like this. The room would grow larger and more distant while the detail of the fixed point would sharpen to an almost microscopic intensity. It sometimes used to feel like he was floating and sailing downward into an ever-expanding self and receding from the growing world. As he stared at Brother Kennedy's coffin now, the only effect it had was that his eyes watered and he had to blink. There was no drifting away from the reality of this moment. His stomach tightened and he began to twitch his right leg rapidly. He found himself praying; at first half-heartedly mouthing the words and then gradually seizing on the broad vowels and the hard consonants in the hope of riding away on their sound to somewhere that was not here and sometime that was years from now when all of this was some faded memory.

Scully's mind drifted through the blur of words around him and down the front of Sharon McGoldrick's blue bank clerk's uniform. There it dwelt on the alluring bulges of her soft, heavy-looking breasts. For two weeks now he had been dawdling on his way home to run into her. She wore lipstick and high heels when she went out on Saturday nights, clattering down their grim little street and away into the mysterious world that her three years of seniority over Scully and a job entitled her to. Despite all evidence to the contrary, Scully still harboured the fantasy that, with a little persistence, he could get her to go down to the canal with him.

Lynch was busy picturing himself in front of Stone's lumberyard. The gate was wide open and there was no one in sight. The box of matches in his pocket sang with promise and joy. His mouth watered at the imagined smell of burning resin. He could almost taste the sweet wood smoke already.

Brian Egan sat tight-lipped and pushed hard with his stomach muscles. This was something he had become good at. The panic and the shouting would well up inside him and he would push it back down with his diaphragm. Smalley Mullen counted the three warm pennies in his palm over and over, and McDonagh wondered if God was listening and, if so, did he speak Irish. Through all the activity, the closest thing to prayer was Finbar's fervent wish that none of it was really happening. Finally the decade of the rosary was over.

Just when the boys were ready to get up and go, Pollock announced: "We will now pause in silence and pay our respects to our dear departed Brother in Christ."

He moved toward the back of the room. Craftily he pulled up his jacket sleeve: ten-fifteen. If he could drag this out for a few more minutes he could avoid that awful too-short-to-actually-teach-anything-too-long-to-just-kill-time period back in the classroom.

"I will be outside on the landing, I wish to have a word with Brother Cox. Let there be no carry-on or you will know all about it."

He stepped out onto the empty landing, leaving the oratory door ajar behind him. Brother Cox was nowhere to be seen. Fifteen little squeaks of his brothel-creepers took him out onto the fire escape overlooking the empty cloistered garden. He lit a cigarette and inhaled deeply, rejoicing in the brisk early-spring air and the mournful calling of crows in the nearby trees.

Scully lay on the floor and peered through the crack in the door. "Gone for a smoke," he whispered to the others.

This was not exactly the ideal set-up for mischief. What could you get up to in an oratory with a dead body lying out in state? That was what Finbar thought, anyway. Lynch, however, would not have agreed. Mischief might not have been the exact word in Lynch's head, but like every other time he had been left unsupervised something cloudy was humming in his head. Solemnly he approached the coffin. He stood at its head and joined his hands in front of himself in prayerful attitude. The low buzz of conversation that had begun just after Mr. Pollock's departure dwindled and died into silence.

"And pray tell us what you might be doing, Mr. Lynch, sor? It is not often we see your hands joined except to wield a crowbar." Finbar couldn't help it. The impression of Pollock just spilled out of him in a nervous overflow. A couple of boys laughed and Finbar felt a tiny satisfying glow inside.

Lynch turned and Finbar caught the tiniest hint of an approving smile in his look. The boys fell silent again. Then Lynch turned, bowed his head reverently, and began to speak: "Kennedy, ye aul dead bastard, ye're dead aren't ye?"

The silence darkened a little. How far would Lynch go with this?

"And we're here to give ye a big sendoff. So . . ." Lynch reached out and took Brother Kennedy's right hand from where it laid over his left one on his chest. He shook hands with the corpse. "Couldn't happen to a nicer vicious aul fucker," he said cheerfully.

There was a collective sigh of relief as Lynch moved to sit down. Most of them really just wanted this over with. They had put him in the box and that was more than enough to deal with.

Brian Egan stood up suddenly, as if compelled by some invisible force. He walked slowly and deliberately up the aisle. Lynch stared at him questioningly as they passed each other. Egan ignored him and walked on. He stopped beside the head of the coffin and stood uncertainly. He seemed to be collecting his thoughts from somewhere deep inside himself.

"Well, have a nice time in Hell, ye fucker! How about a smoke before ye go? Can't do ye any harm now, cos ye're DEAD!"

Egan reached into his pocket and withdrew a crumpled cigarette. The silence was now thick with disbelief and coloured bright red around its edges with something unnameable. Egan took the cigarette and forced it between the dead man's lips.

"Want a light?" he asked, and moved Brother Kennedy's head roughly in a grotesque parody of an enthusiastic nod. "Well ye can't have one, ye slimy bastard!" Egan whipped the cigarette from the cold lips and put it back in his pocket. He hawked deep in his throat and drew up a big mouthful of phlegm. The silence coloured to a fiery red.

"Sketch!" hissed Scully from the door where he was keeping watch. In a flash Egan was back in place in his pew. He leaned down and spat loudly on the carpet.

When Mr. Pollock entered, he noticed the silence but failed to detect any of its colouring. He took it to be the usual silence concealing prior moments of messing and telling jokes. He walked to the coffin and again blessed himself. One quick "Hail Holy Queen" directed to the Irish-speaking Blessed Virgin Mary, and then it was done. Mr. Pollock walked to the door, opened it theatrically just as the bell for small break rang, and congratulated himself on his perfect timing.

29

Brendan Kennedy sat in the late-night gloom of Brother Loughlin's office and impatiently tapped his good tweed cap on his arthritic left knee. He was tired after his bus and train journey from Knockpaltry-on-Fergus. He had never been east of the River Shannon in his life and though he would have been quite happy to keep it that way, he felt he owed it to his only brother to attend his funeral despite the fact that they had not spoken in over forty years.

The office door opened and Brother Loughlin entered, his face now even more solicitous than when he had met Brendan at Kingsbridge Station.

"We're ready now," he said softly.

Brendan Kennedy glanced at his watch and shook his head in disbelief. There was something really unnatural and unwholesome about conducting a funeral in the middle of the night. He followed Brother Loughlin across the dark yard, up the monastery stairs, and into the oratory.

The Brothers were already in their pews sucking on the mouthfuls of ashes prescribed by tradition. These were the last ashes from the pyre of the late Brother Bell's possessions, so it was fortunate that they would now get to replenish their supply. It had over the years become a belief of the Brother General Superior that it was a good practice for the Brothers to savour some ashes at the passing of a confrere as both a tribute and a memento mori. The Brothers did their best to ignore the scaffolding and the gaping hole in the ceiling that loomed above them in the candlelight, an ugly beacon of mockery and menace.

Brother Loughlin motioned Brendan Kennedy to a straight-backed chair in the centre aisle. The latter sat down and peered about him in the surrounding gloom. The only light came from the four tall candles at the corners of his brother's coffin where it still rested on the trolley. Barely discernible against the altar railings stood the plain lid of the coffin, the light reflecting dully off the lead plaque that bore the name and dates of Brother Matthew Kennedy.

Brendan looked around at the Brothers, their faces drawn and empty-looking in the dim light. These were his brother Matthew's companions. These were the empty souls with whom he had shared his last sixty years.

Loughlin walked to the front of the oratory, took his place at the head of the coffin, and drew his rosary beads from his pocket. Immediately the oratory was filled with the reciprocal clacking and rattling of the Brothers' beads.

Brendan opened the time-softened leather pouch that contained his First Communion beads and draped them from his hands in a prayerful fashion. He focused on the candle flame nearest him and drifted into the murmur around him. He shivered suddenly and Brother Loughlin's hand on his shoulder brought him back to the here and now of Matthew's funeral.

"If you would like to take your leave of, ahem . . ." stumbled Loughlin.

Brendan stood up and moved to the side of the coffin. He blessed himself and stared down at the inert features of his dead brother. He was shocked by how much yet how little his brother's face had changed. It looked like the face of the sixteen-year-old boy he had known with the lines of sixty years carved onto it by some amateur hand. He racked his brains for something to say or think or some last thought to impart to his brother, but nothing came, just a hazy sense of regret for a life thwarted and wasted. He blessed himself again and sat down heavily.

Brother Loughlin moved silently to the side of the coffin, tapped Brother Kennedy's cold forehead three times with the small liturgical lead hammer, and then took the candles from the holders and passed them out: one to Brother Mulligan, one to Brother Boland, and one to Brendan Kennedy. Taking the last one himself, he led the way out of the oratory down the stairs to the garden.

"This is the weirdest job I've ever had. I didn't know it was part of janitoring. This is a right pain in the arse," grumbled McRae.

"Shut up and help," hissed Conall McConnell as they waited on the landing above the oratory for the last of the Brothers to move down the stairs. "Come on now."

McConnell led the way to the oratory and began manoeuvring the trolley toward the door. "Open the fire escape door for me," he said.

"The two of us are going to get that down the stairs? You must be joking!" protested McRae.

"No. No. We just leave it at the top of the fire escape. The Brothers will take it down to the garden. It's part of their thing. That's what I was told and that's all I know."

"Creepy, that's what it is, this lugging dead bodies around in the middle of the night."

"Just get the door for me, can't you!"

McRae held the door open while McConnell positioned the coffin trolley on the metal landing of the fire escape and stepped back in, closing the heavy door softly.

* * *

Brendan Kennedy stared blankly at Brother Loughlin, unable to believe what he had just heard. "Come again?" he said icily.

". . . To defray some of the funeral costs. I hate to ask, but you know we are not a wealthy congregation. Of course, you also get this." Brother Loughlin held out the small liturgical lead hammer.

Brendan Kennedy's face paled with rage: "Get away with you and take that creepy thing away from me! The funeral was all paid for up front when Matthew joined! Well do I remember my poor sainted father, God be good to him, lamenting that he had to fork out eighteen shillings for a shroud and a box for his perfectly healthy sixteen-year-old son. Don't come the poor mouth with me, Loughlin! It was all paid for fair and square and well you know it!"

Leaving a stunned Brother Loughlin standing on the platform, Brendan Kennedy climbed into the three a.m. mail train and took a seat on the far side where he wouldn't have to look at the man. After witnessing his only brother being perfunctorily buried in an unmarked grave in the monastery garden at midnight while his cassock, sandals, and personal possessions were ritually burned, Brendan had had quite enough of the Order of the Brothers of Godly Coercion.

Had he the courage to acknowledge it, he would probably have admitted that he was plagued by guilt and by a sense of the tragedy of Matthew's end: his only brother buried a stranger to him and the only other mourners a shower of moribund relics who seemed to almost envy the relief of the grave. It wasn't his fault, there was only enough farm for one of them and his parents had decided Matthew was the brighter one and should go to the Brothers. Brendan recoiled from thought, took out the *Farmer's Sentinel*, and plunged himself into "Bovine TB: the Curse of Progress?" The doors slammed, the porter blew his whistle, and the train shuddered and creaked out from under the dark canopy of Kingsbridge Station to begin its long haul through the night to Limerick Junction.

30

The morning after the funeral, Brother Loughlin could still taste the ashes in his mouth. He slammed the phone back into its cradle with tight-lipped fury. As if he didn't have enough to do with things breaking all the time and only that incompetent janitor and his fool apprentice to fix them! This was the last straw! He had been fobbed off by Cardinal Russell's personal secretary's assistant, then by some nameless drone at the office of the Bishop of Spokes and Duggery, then by the personal secretary of Father Sheehan, Mulvey's boss, and finally, to add insult to injury, by Mulvey's damn insolent housekeeper. The woman even had the audacity to tell him to stop telephoning all the time, that it was doing his cause no good at all. It was *his* school! It was *his* miracle! They should be falling over themselves to talk to him!

"I'll show them I mean business," he bellowed. "I'll show them I know how to manage a miracle site! Mrs. Broderick! Take a letter!"

"Come in!" called out Mr. Pollock before there was even a knock. The door opened and in strode Anthony, the large-lugged first year who seemed to have become the messenger boy for the whole school. "What is it, Mr. Antney, sor?" he asked, ever ready to mock the boy's accent.

"It's a note from de Head Brudder, sir."

"And who is the Head Brother?"

"Brudder Loughlin."

"That is right, sor."

Mr. Pollock imperiously took the letter from Anthony and read through it before pursing his lips approvingly.

"You boys! Attention. This is a letter from Brother Loughlin, so listen and listen carefully:

All boys and all teachers are hereby informed that, in view of the increased importance of the school as a site of a miracle now under investigation by the Diocesan Investigator's office, there will be no toleration of sinning—mortal, venial, or otherwise—within the school boundaries. All manner of sin by word, deed, or thought, whether committed alone or with others, will be mercilessly punished while we keep the site of this miraculous occurrence pure and free of stain. Tally sticks will be issued to all boys to keep count of their sins. Beating and confession will be administered after school each day. Every step will be taken to keep all boys in a perpetual state of Grace.
—Brother Loughlin, Principal

Copies to Bishop of Spokes and Duggery, Father Thomas Sheehan, S.J., Father Martin Mulvey, S.J.

Mr. Pollock glowered at the boys meaningfully and returned the note to Anthony without looking at him.

Tally sticks. The words echoed coldly in each boy's guts. They knew about them but always figured they were something from dark times long ago. Brother Loughlin well understood this. There was no real extra efficiency in using tally sticks, but they were potent symbols. The humiliation of wearing them and their associations of repression were powerful tools against the boys.

31

The air of the Limping Gunman was rife with the ammoniacal smell of cleaning as Spud Murphy sat heavily at the end of the bar and pinched the bridge of his nose. The consumptive regulars at the other end of the bar ignored him completely. He was only an amateur drinker as far as they were concerned.

"Rough morning, Mr. Murphy?" asked Tom Stack, the barman, glancing up from his copy of the *Daily Horse & Hound.*

"Yeah. You could say that."

"I'm sure those young fellahs down there can be a bit much betimes."

Spud smiled ruefully at the naïve notion that the boys were the problem but said nothing.

"So what'll you have?" asked Stack without missing a beat.

"A large bottle and maybe one of them ham sandwiches."

"No bother," said Stack, and placed the morning paper on the counter beside the teacher.

Spud glanced at it but could not seem to get beyond the headlines. His mind was a roiling tempest of anger and disgust. Jesus H. Christ! What had become of them at all? It was enough trying to teach and keep yourself out of the loony bin without this new madness.

He could still not fully believe it. Suffering shite! He had spent the last class handing out tally sticks to the boys and explaining how they worked: any boy who was seen sinning would have a notch carved in his stick, and at the end of the day would receive one belt of the strap for each notch. These were things from bad times when children were forced to learn English and got a notch every time they spoke Irish. But for Irish people to use them on one another was vile and sickening in a deep, disturbing way.

The street door opened and Mr. Laverty stood uncertainly in the doorway before sitting down at a small round table. He had not seen Spud.

"For fuck sake, don't sit over there like some blushing debutante, come over here and have a drink," called Spud.

Laverty crossed the bar hesitantly and sat down on the stool next to his fellow teacher.

"Bet you're glad you did the extra course in Tally Stick Administration at university," remarked Spud.

"Oh yeah. Very handy."

They nodded together, both painfully aware of their hollow attempts to dilute the whole thing with sarcasm.

Stack placed the large bottle and sandwich on the bar and took the money Spud had left out.

"You can get my friend here a large bottle out of that too, Tom."

"Thanks," mumbled Laverty.

"No problem. Fucked if I can find a good reason not to drink this lunchtime."

"They've really gone over the edge this time."

"They have. And they're getting more vicious too."

"I get this sick feeling in my stomach every day when I walk in to the place. It's like I'm a schoolboy myself again. It's fucking awful."

"I'm just hoping they'll run out of steam on this one and it'll go away."

"But the miracle . . ."

"Miracle, my arse! Ceiling fell on Boland. They've been dying for a miracle for years. There was a water stain on the gym ceiling four years ago. They claimed it looked like Saint Patrick."

Stack returned with Laverty's drink. "D'youse want raffle tickets?" he asked.

"What for?"

"To raise money for the pilgrimage to Knock. First prize a twenty-pound voucher for Hennessey's on Crimea Street."

"Eh, no. Not today, thanks," answered Spud coldly.

"Fair enough. Another day maybe."

"Don't hold your breath," said Spud.

Stack retired to the other end of the bar and his *Horse & Hound*. Spud glanced at his watch. They had three-quarters of an hour before they had to go back to that madhouse. In unison he and Laverty poured the porter carefully into their glasses.

"Tally sticks! Have they no clue at all? They have their glue if they think I'm going to waste me lunchtime patrolling for sinners and notching tally sticks," declared Spud as he watched his porter settle.

"I'll drink to that! Sláinte!" replied Laverty.

Together they drained their glasses.

"Same again?" called Stack from the other end of the bar.

Mouths still full of porter, Spud and Laverty nodded enthusiastically.

"You, boy! Spotty boy with the buckteeth. Come here."

The spotty-faced boy in question moved away from his friends and warily approached Brother Cox.

"What were you laughing at?"

"Nothing, Brother."

"Do you usually laugh at nothing?"

"No, Brother."

"Then what were you laughing at?"

"Something he said," replied the boy, shrugging in the general direction of his friends.

"So you were laughing at something?"

"Yes, Brother."

"So you lied to me. *Thou shalt not bear false witness.*" Brother Cox grabbed the tally stick that hung around the boy's neck and clipped a notch out of it with his toenail clippers. "And one for whatever you were laughing at," he added, making a second notch. "Now, behave yourself!

"You, boy! You with the limp! Where's your tally stick?" Cox moved across the yard with surprising speed in search of more retribution. He had been hoping to slip out to the Limping Gunman or one of the shady pubs on the docks for a quick one at lunchtime. Now that tally stick duty had ruined his plans, someone was going to pay.

In the small shed Mr. Hourican was busy checking for sins of thought, deed, or omission, committed alone or with others, and on the far side of the yard stood Brother Walsh with what looked like a small pair of binoculars.

"Come on, let's go down to Hutton's. They're on the warpath here," said Scully.

Scully, McDonagh, and Lynch got up off the windowsill they had been sitting on and started toward the gate. Finbar, who had just come downstairs with his bag of sandwiches, moved to sit on the vacated sill.

"You coming or what?" asked McDonagh.

"Oh yeah, right," said Finbar, surprised.

"What's in your sandwiches?" asked Scully.

"Meat paste."

"Jaysus! Hate that!" said McDonagh.

"Giz one," said Lynch unconditionally.

Finbar opened the bag and handed Lynch a sandwich. He watched in wonder as Lynch crammed the whole thing into his mouth and seemed to swallow without chewing.

At the gate Larry Skelly stopped them and checked for tally sticks. "Ye'll be searched coming back," he needlessly informed them.

"Fuck sake! It's like fucking Colditz," muttered Scully as they walked up the lane to Werburgh Street.

Lynch grabbed a passing first year, pulled out his penknife, and in a flash left a neat little notch on the unfortunate boy's tally stick.

"Ye big bastard!" shouted the boy, running away and straight into Larry Skelly who gave him another notch for swearing. Scully and the others hurried round the corner out of sight before the boy could point them out.

They stopped in their tracks about twenty yards from Fanny Hutton's and stared in disbelief. Mr. Pollock was standing outside it marshalling boys into an orderly line.

"For fuck sake! They're gone mad—" Scully stopped abruptly when Finbar elbowed him in the ribs.

"Moody!" whispered Finbar urgently, indicating with a move of his eyes the sinister figure of Brother Moody on the other side of the street walking back toward the school.

"IRA shop!" said Scully decisively, and picked up the pace.

They passed by Hutton's and gaped in at the lack of mayhem as if it were something sacrilegious and unnatural, an affront to their collective sense of right.

At the IRA shop they found Brother Tobin presiding over the same sickening lack of chaos.

"Ah, bollix! Mary's then," said Lynch.

They crossed the West Circular Road and headed down Stanhope Gardens. Mary's fish-and-chip shop sat uneasily between the burnt-out shell of the bookies and the boarded-up Dundalk Dairy. Brother Mulligan stood at the door admitting boys in twos and threes, eliminating the usual life-threatening crush that was the main challenge and attraction of buying chips at Mary's. Certainly no one went there for the quality of the food. Disgustedly they got on the back of the line and waited their turn to go in.

Like sharks to blood on the sea, Mr. Pollock and Brother Moody were drawn toward Brother Cox where he was haranguing a group of four second years who had been trying to get their penny ball off the roof of the small shed.

"Who told you you could get up on that roof?" bellowed Brother Cox.

Before the boys had any chance to muster up an answer, he repeated the question even louder. He was stalling while he racked his brains to find a way to make thinking about climbing on the shed into a sin.

"What's this? What's this then?" snapped Mr. Pollock, drawing up behind Cox.

"About to climb up on the shed," Cox informed him.

"They were now, were they?" dissembled Mr. Pollock. He too found difficulty pinpointing the actual sinful content of this transgression.

Within seconds Brother Moody sidled up beside Pollock. Moody could smell a kindred spirit, even through the fug of occasional matrimonial congress that surrounded the lay teacher in Brother Moody's moral smellscape. He was glad of this new development, as patrolling Hutton's Lane had lost its allure once the boys realised what he was like. That was always the problem: once they knew you were out to get them, they started behaving and then you had to try harder to find reasons to punish them.

"I can't see that boy's tally stick!" exclaimed Brother Moody, pointing at one of the smaller boys through the space between Pollock and Cox.

"Indeed and you can't!" concurred Brother Cox, sensing that here might be a whole new tack. "Where's your tally stick, boy?"

The poor boy who found himself on the wrong end of Brother Moody's accusing finger searched around inside the back of his sweater where the exertions of kicking a football had sent his tally stick.

"Come on, boy, we don't have all day!" snapped Pollock.

"It's supposed to be visible at all times," sneered the Iago-within of Brother Moody.

"True for you. Sure that's probably a sin in itself, hiding your tally stick like that," observed Cox hopefully.

Finally the boy retrieved his stick and brought it out of his pullover.

"Let me see that!" demanded Brother Cox, grabbing it and almost toppling the unfortunate boy.

"Look at that! Not a mark on it!" cried Brother Cox, now formulating something resembling a plan in his head. "Explain yourself, boy!"

"I, I, I didn't do any sins, Brother."

"Didn't sin? Do you mean to tell us that you are without sin? Do you mean to imply that you are Christlike? Is that what you mean? Who made you?" barked Brother Moody.

"God made me. But I didn't do any sins. That's why there's no marks on me stick."

"I didn't COMMIT any sins. There ARE no marks on MY stick." Mr. Pollock wondered momentarily if bad grammar and diction could be interpreted as bearing false witness. "Out with your sticks the rest of you!"

One by one the shed climbers held up their unmarked tally sticks.

"So you're all as pure as the driven snow then?" Pollock raised himself up on his toes and back down as he spoke.

Gradually the very unmarkedness of the sticks began to worry the boys. The sands were shifting under their feet. They could feel the quagmire of adult logic ripple and swell under them.

"Not a sin among ye, eh?" sneered Brother Moody.

"Comparing yerselves to Our Lord then, are ye?" spluttered Brother Cox.

The boys nodded uncertainly, then shook their heads slowly. *Yes* and *no* had turned into equally wrong answers no matter what the question was.

"Think ye're perfect then, do ye?" added Brother Moody.

Again the boys shook their heads, then nodded, then shook their heads again. They were lost.

"I'd say we have some prideful sinners on our hands here, wouldn't you, Brothers?" said Mr. Pollock.

"One of the Seven Deadly Sins, that," chimed Brother Cox.

Moments later Spud Murphy and Mr. Laverty, and a few yards behind them Scully and the others on their way back from their dispiriting trip to Mary's, turned into the yard to witness Pollock, Cox, and Moody thrashing the group of second years.

"Such bastards! They turn my stomach," Scully and the others heard Spud mutter to Laverty as they passed the ugly scene.

The two teachers walked despondently to the staff room while Larry Skelly half-heartedly searched the boys for instruments of destruction and checked they were wearing their tally sticks.

Once past Skelly the boys skirted the beating scene lest they get sucked into it.

"I'll be back in a sec," said Scully suddenly. He handed his chips to Finbar and darted into the school.

Sucking at the pieces of stewed apple stuck between his teeth, Brother Boland bustled along the corridor from his cell.

At the main entrance he reached into the cubbyhole behind the door. His hand grasped at unexpected emptiness and he pulled the door back to let some light in. What touch had told him, the paltry light in the hallway now confirmed: the handbell was not there.

His handbell stolen! The nerve of it! Was nothing sacred? Not a second too late had they introduced the tally sticks. Boland bustled into the yard and danced furiously in front of Finbar, Lynch, and McDonagh, who happened to be standing near the door.

"Get to your classes! Don't you know the time? Get up to your classes!"

"But Brother, the bell . . ." protested Finbar.

Boland felt his blood boil and a powerful urge to throttle the boy surged up within him. Instead he turned on his heel and ran through the downstairs lab and into the monastery. "Bell? I'll give them bell!" he screeched as he ran.

"I told ye. He's completely off his head," said Finbar.

In the musty custard-nuanced postprandial gloom of the monastery stairwell, Brother Boland grabbed the bell rope. "I'll put an end to your lunchtime of acting the blackguard and sinning all over my miracle!"

He pulled on the rope sharply and it was only when he heard the muted hurt inside the bell's peal did he realise what he had done. Powerless to stop what he had started, Boland dropped the bellrope as if burned, clasped his hands over his ears, and held his breath. He could not bear to listen to the wrongness inside the bell's tones. Gradually its peals grew weaker and further apart and the Brother could breathe again. He listened to the dying echoes and sensed them penetrate the walls, the glass of the windows, every crevice and crack of the building.

Behind him he heard a gentle tapping from the refectory. He moved toward it, drawn by some irresistible need to bear witness. From the doorway he stared at the high centre window and listened to its laboured creaking. There was a sudden snap as the sash ropes gave way inside the casement. The top half of the window slammed down under its own weight and splattered the floor with shards of stained glass.

Brother Boland stared at the mess. What had once been a carefully executed resurrection scene now covered the floor in a chaos of coloured splinters.

"Jesus, Mary, and Joseph!" he exclaimed, and ran off to find Brother Loughlin.

32

Mr. Laverty, we're here to check the tally sticks," announced Mr. Pollock as he strode into the class just after lunch. Behind him followed a flushed and sweaty Brother Moody, who had his sleeves rolled and his leather warmed up and at the ready. Clearly they couldn't wait until the end of the day.

Laverty sighed and sat on the windowsill staring down into the yard while Pollock walked through the class inspecting the sticks.

"Outside."

"But sir, there's no mark," whined Smalley Mullen.

"Outside, sor! I know a counterfeit tally stick when I see one! You're in right trouble now, me bucko!" Mr. Pollock grabbed the boy by the shirt collar and pulled him out of his chair.

"Don't drag your feet like that, you little gurrier!" snapped Brother Moody as Smalley shuffled out the door.

"Where's your stick, boy?"

"It must've fallen off," answered Bradshaw as he searched frantically on the floor under his desk.

"Outside!"

"Mr. Scully, outside!"

"But sir, there's no mark. It's the real stick."

"Mr. Scully, you are a guttersnipe, a bowsie, and an incorrigible miscreant, and I am sure you deserve a beating.

Outside! Now! And that goes for your cohorts too: McDonagh, Lynch, Sullivan! Outside!"

Finbar could not believe his ears. "But sir . . ."

"At least one of you sinned at lunchtime and the others were there so you are all guilty of collusion. Guilty one, guilty all! Outside, the lot of ye!"

Finbar followed McDonagh out the door and smelt Brother Moody's acrid sweat as he passed him.

"Thank you, Mr. Laverty. You may continue with your lesson," said Mr. Pollock, and swept out of the classroom with the eager Brother Moody in tow.

Mr. Laverty looked at the dozen or so who were left out of the thirty.

"Youse can do yizer homework or go to sleep. I don't care," he said tiredly over the sounds of beating and chastisement from the corridor outside.

"Ring that bell properly, damn you! They'll never hear that!" scolded Brother Loughlin.

He stood behind Brother Boland and waited. Boland turned around and stared emptily. He bit his lip and trembled but otherwise refused to move.

"That's what broke the window in the refectory," he protested.

"Don't talk rot! That was woodworm. Give me that!" snapped Brother Loughlin, and grabbed the bellrope from Boland's hands. He gave it a sharp tug, and to his satisfaction the bell above wheeled round and pealed the start of the last class.

"What in the name of God is wrong with you now?" shouted Loughlin above the noise of the bell.

Boland was cowering and had his hands clamped over his ears again. "It's wrong! All wrong! There is a mouldering!"

He fled up the stairs to his cell. *Dam-Age, Dam-Age, Dam-Age*, the bell tolled in his head.

"Don't come back down! You are confined to your cell. I'll find someone responsible and willing to undertake bell duty! Do you hear?" yelled Loughlin. He harrumphed dismissively and gave the bellrope another pull for good measure before striding off to check on McConnell's progress on the oratory repairs. Now he needed him to fix the refectory window too.

The monastery bell announced the end of the last class. Brother Boland got up from his cot and paced nervously around the narrow confines of his cell. He went to the window and stared down. He breathed in and out rapidly through his nose, the nasal hairs fluttering about like kite tails. In the distance he heard the dull murmur of the boys in the school corridors, and through it, cutting into his mind like a scream, came the sound of the monastery bell once again. It was being rung by a harsh, uncaring hand, a hand with no sense of echoes or resonances. It was being rung by that damned blow-in Moody! He could feel it! Boland moved to the window and gripped the sill to steady his trembling hands.

He shrank from the bell's internal discord. Behind its peal he could hear the swelling hum of protest. The inaudible grace notes of wrongness nested in his chest and squirmed inside him. He stood up from his cot, sat down again, stood up again, and went again to his small window.

He watched the boys below pour out of the school and across the yard. The grey tide flowed slowly out into the world beyond. He looked through the grimy glass at the school building across the yard. He peered at its outline and held his breath. Was there an answer to the bell's wrongness in there? He pressed his floppy ear against the glass and listened, its quiet coldness for a moment calming him.

He saw Conall McConnell lock the gate behind the last stragglers and walk back toward the monastery. Boland leaned his forehead against the glass and closed his eyes. The wind gusted and the window sashes above his head rattled within the frame. He breathed deeply through his nose. Patiently he waited for the light to fade. He soon opened his eyes again and watched the cross on the spire of Saint Werburgh's away to his left. Slowly it faded into the growing darkness. Somehow he figured the darkness would make it easier to sense the inner tremors of the school.

He went to his cell door and listened to the late-afternoon silence. He opened it a crack, half expecting to find Brother Tobin or Brother Walsh outside on sentry duty. Evidently Brother Loughlin had forgotten to post anyone. He slid out through the door and closed it silently behind him. He stood still and the sparse fuzz of what was left of his hair tensed and flickered. He looked like a very worried peach.

The wrongness was all around him now. It was sourceless, omnidirectional. He had no idea where to look for it. He had to go to the bell tower to get a better sense of it or he would never find it in time.

Suddenly, a wave of the wrongness made manifest boomed and whooshed through Boland's understanding. Barely able to stay upright, he scuttled along the corridor toward the stairs to confront the unease howling down from the attic.

"Be careful not to splatter that all over the place."

Conall McConnell looked down at the floor beside his bucket and saw Brother Loughlin's boots peeking out from under the hem of his cassock. As if the shit work wasn't enough, he had to put up with orders from this fat fuck.

"Yes, Brother," he replied tonelessly.

"So, how's the work coming along?" shouted Loughlin up at McConnell's legs and arse at the top of the ladder. The rest of him was out of sight inside the hole in the oratory ceiling.

"Fine," answered McConnell's muffled voice. Some of the joists were quite rotten but he was certainly not mentioning that.

Before Loughlin could make any more comments he was silenced by a dull thump and resultant explosion of dust that blew out from the hole in the ceiling. McConnell almost fell off the ladder and clambered down spluttering and coughing and covered in sooty black filth.

"Holy Mother of . . ."

This time the rumble was louder and longer and the oratory was completely filled with soot and dust that billowed out from the hole in the ceiling.

"Merciful hour, what on earth is going on now?" cried Loughlin fearfully as he felt the floor shudder and jerk under his feet.

"Go on in there and ask your father if he would have a match for a weary traveller," the stranger had said. Brother Comiskey had gone inside to get his father. When his father saw Michael Collins at the gate he had erupted with laughter. Brother Comiskey remembered how Michael Collins had patted him on the head and gave him a penny still warm from his pocket. He could still hear the two men's voices talking low into the small hours of the morning.

Brother Comiskey was so lost in himself that he failed to notice the bare bulb over his head start to swing in a tiny arc unnatural to light fixtures on dry land. His wizened hands picked and pulled nervously at his white hair.

Brother Talbot closed his eyes and mused on his calling to the Brotherhood. "Be good, son, and make us proud. This is all for the best. You'll get a proper education this way. The Holy Ghost will help you." Talbot could see his mother standing at the gate of their small farm, his eight younger brothers and sisters clustered in the doorway of the small cottage. His father must have been somewhere inside. Byrne, the carter, had cleared his throat impatiently and spat onto the ground. He'd muttered darkly about missing the train to Thurles. Brother Talbot had stood up on the cart and waved to his mother until she and the gate and the farm disappeared out of sight behind the brow of Mish Hill. He was thirteen. He did not see his mother again until she was laid out for her wake.

"Ah, Christ! Where did I leave those damned glasses? I can't find me slippers without them!" Brother McGovern patted the blanket on his cot searching for the glasses that sat atop his bald head. Without their aid he stood no chance of apprehending the unusual bulging of the ceiling above his door.

Moira Brady was the only girl Brother Garvey had ever loved. When she ran away with that British Army officer he never recovered. He still remembered the day he'd made the driver stop that bus in Longford and had run down the street thinking he'd seen her. He had been nearly forty then and was still not sure what had possessed him to join the Brothers.

He sat on his straight-backed chair and sighed heavily.

A tear ran from his one good eye and trickled down his unshaven cheek. He was completely unaware that the only thing holding up the ceiling was the closed door in the overburdened load-bearing wall between his cell and the corridor.

"Our Lady of Indefinite Duration, pray for us sinners who have recourse unto thee," mumbled Brother O'Toole softly as he lit another candle at the tiny makeshift altar beside his bed. Unable to kneel, he braced himself in veneration on his walking sticks and stooped nearer the floor than usual. A pious man, being confined to his cell with only Father Flynn's communion visits for spiritual sustenance had left him hungering for more. He had therefore fashioned himself a little straw statue of Our Lady of Indefinite Duration and surrounded it with homemade earwax candles. His whispered prayers were just loud enough to obscure the ominous creaking of joists above his head.

That little pup Sheridan. Oh yes, he had seen through Sheridan all right. Spotted him as a wrong one from the start. And wasn't he right? Didn't the pup grow up to move to London and land in jail for killing a girl with a hammer? Wasn't he right when he said Sheridan was a wrong one? Oh yes, you couldn't pull the wool over Brother Galvin's eyes in those days.

Galvin felt his cot rattle and gaped in horror as his tiny floor-level dormer window buckled at the sides, shattered, and popped out into the yard far below. His bath chair rolled across the room and crashed into the door.

It happened so quickly that there was no time for any last-minute thoughts of dying. The ancient relics were drooling and mulling over what was left of their past lives and suddenly there was noise, darkness, and then silence: terrible, irreversible silence. Simultaneously the two end walls of the attic folded inward and the roof collapsed and buried the ancient Brothers under an avalanche of masonry, wood, and slates.

Brother Loughlin took the stairs two at a time. Conall McConnell tried to keep his eyes anywhere but on the heaving bulk of Loughlin's arse that preceded him up the stairs.

At the top they found a frantic confusion of Brothers.

"The roof fell in! I tried to warn them! It told me it was coming!" shouted Brother Boland. He was covered in dust and stood shivering with shock.

Loughlin elbowed Boland out of the way and ran straight into the pile of rubble that blocked the final flight of stairs to the attic. "Jesus, Mary, and Joseph!"

"Is it another miracle?" asked Brother Tobin excitedly.

"What are we to do?" asked Brother Boland fearfully.

Loughlin ran his intelligence twice round the narrow limits of his mind and snapped his fingers decisively. "Mr. McConnell, you will stay here and make sure no one touches anything. The rest of you, back downstairs. It could be dangerous here."

"Aren't we going to rescue the elder Brothers?" asked Brother Tobin nervously.

"Is it those little bastards again?" called Brother Moody as he ran up the stairs to join them.

"I'll take care of it! Brother Moody, please take Brother Boland back to his cell and make sure he stays there," snapped Loughlin, and clumped back down the stairs with all haste.

Moody took Boland roughly by the arm and led him down.

"I think you should all go back downstairs now," said McConnell.

The Brothers reluctantly headed down, a multilimbed knot of fear.

"Yes, Brother Loughlin here. I need to speak to Father Mulvey immediately . . . No, madam, I will not phone back later. Tell him this is an emergency."

Brought Loughlin waited.

"Father Mulvey . . . Yes, I know, but I think you should get over here as soon as you can. We have a spot of bother . . . I'd rather not say. I think you should come over right away. You might want to bring that Father Sheehan with you . . . Yes, I am serious . . . Yes, I do . . . Right then."

Loughlin hung up the phone and sat back in his chair. He picked up the brass figure of Venerable Saorseach O'Rahilly that presided over his desk. He weighed it in his hand and smiled with satisfaction at the little catch he had heard in Father Mulvey's voice. Not quite fear but something other than total composure, and it had pleased him to no end. Briefly it clouded the fact that he had not the slightest idea what to do about this new development. Before he could fully relish this sweet moment to its fullness, his door burst open and McRae stumbled in.

"Brother, Brother, ye have to come! Mr. McConnell sent me! Quick! Fire!"

"Mother of God! Where?"

"In the attic rubble somewhere."

"Fierce the way these old buildings go all of a sudden. A cousin of mine moved into a lovely little corporation house up above in Phibsboro near where the railway is. Painted her up like new. Repointed the brick himself, he did. Very handy, so he is. Grand little house. Little yard out the back for the greyhound and all. First thing you know, day after the Annunciation, one of the window sashes goes and nearly takes one of his little boys' head off and him out the window watching the Sodality parade. Next thing you know the cousin discovers dry rot on the stairs. Before you can say *who stole me hat*, he finds a crack in the supporting wall and the back door won't close. One thing after another it is. Has a lad out from Dublin Corporation to look at it and he scratches at his clipboard and says the cousin had been neglecting the place and says they could evict him. Strange, though, the way once one thing starts to go and all the others start to follow. Feast or a famine, I suppose."

Brother Loughlin stopped in his tracks while McRae continued on in front of him across the yard. Against the dark sky he watched aghast as tiny flames started to spring from the collapsed attic roof.

"Will you shut up and get everyone out, you fool!" he shouted at McRae. "Go ring the bell and get them all out of there!"

In the distance Loughlin heard the wail of the approaching fire brigade. He stood helplessly watching the tiny flames grow bolder and more playful as they flitted and danced through the crushed attic. Behind him he heard the rasping and whining of a motor being brought to a halt by inexpert hands and he turned round. There, like a thickening bulge in the darkness, he saw a pristine black Morris Minor pull up. It was ageless, in perfect condition, and reeked of care. It stopped just beside him and through the driver's window he saw the troubled face of Father Mulvey. Next to him in the passenger seat was a large, imposing figure, presumably Father Sheehan.

As if propelled by some unseen force, McRae was

suddenly holding Father Sheehan's door open like one of the flunkies outside the Shelbourne Hotel.

"Thank you, my good man," baritoned Sheehan. He stepped out of the car and Brother Loughlin caught his first glimpse of the next step after Mulvey on the long ladder of authority that led all the way to the Vatican.

Father Sheehan stood about six-foot-two and his athletic figure filled his perfectly pressed black suit. His hair was silvery grey and neatly swept back without a parting to show his high forehead. He had aquiline features and deep-set eyes that glinted with something that in the dark Loughlin could not clearly identify. It could have been mirth, it could have been anger, or it could have been the reflection of the flames now making merry in the rubble of the attic.

"Brother Loughlin, Father Sheehan; Father Sheehan, Brother Loughlin."

Loughlin took Sheehan's outstretched hand and pressed it firmly, hoping thereby to give himself an air of self-confidence. "A pleasure to make your acquaintance, Father," he beamed.

Sheehan smiled and ended the handshake with an adroitness that conveyed a perfect mixture of disdain and amity and left Loughlin feeling respected and slighted at the same time. He felt like he had just shaken hands with someone who knew just how the world ran and exactly how long it could be expected to continue doing so.

"So, Brother Loughlin, this is your spot of bother, is it? You would seem to have quite the penchant for the understatement. Wouldn't you agree, Father Mulvey?"

"Yes, well, it was, when I rang Father Mulvey, it was," replied Loughlin brightly, hoping his bonhomie might distract them from the fact that part of his school was currently aflame. He was saved the embarrassment of further dithering by the arrival of the fire brigade.

"I think you might want to move my car out of the firemen's way now, Father Mulvey," commented Sheehan with the assurance of one accustomed to never needing the imperative mode to have his bidding done.

Loughlin shifted his weight from foot to foot. "Perhaps we should go to my office while the firemen tackle this," he suggested, thinking his weight might rest more easily if he put his arse in a chair.

"Yes. I don't think we can be of much help to the fire brigade by standing here in their way," said Father Sheehan, deftly stepping aside to avoid the ashen-faced Brother Boland who had just bolted out of the monastery pursued by Brother Moody.

McRae's brutal tolling of the monastery bell brought out the rest of the Brothers who gathered in an anxious knot in the middle of the yard.

Brother Tobin broke away from the group and ran toward Loughlin. His eyes were rolling in his head and he sweated profusely. "He cradled her ample bosom! Caressed! Embrace! Moist buttocks! Stimulate! Fairness beguiling! Burgeoning aches flamed in her loins! Noisily swiving! Smooth thighs against his! She moaned! Rosy-fingered dawn! Pulsing shaft! Carefully her mouth slid! Bodice! Slowly mounting! Enflamed! Inwardly downwardly! Tangle of limbs! Yes! Again! Again! Yes! Yes!" All the slivers of filth that Tobin had censored and eaten over the years boiled up inside him and spewed out in one shocked flood.

"This way, please, Fathers," said Loughlin, ignoring Tobin as best he could. He led Sheehan and Mulvey across the yard toward his office.

33

"What the hell is that?"

Finbar looked down at his chest where his father's horrified finger was pointing.

"It's what we have to wear at school. It's a tally stick."

"I know damn well it's a tally stick! *Have to*? Have to wear at school?"

Finbar shot a glance at Declan, who shook his head almost imperceptibly and fixed his stare down on his teacup.

"Yeah, they make us wear them," replied Finbar nervously.

"Who makes you wear them?"

"I don't know. They sent a note around. Something to do with the miracle and the sins going on and the miracle and—"

"Miracle? What miracle? What are you talking about?"

Finbar looked at his father with alarm. He had never seen him like this. It was as if someone had lit a fuse inside him that no one knew existed. Sweat was beading on his forehead and he was frantically restless as if under attack from some unknown adversary. No sooner did he stand at the kitchen table with his hand resting on the back of a chair than he was off over to the fireplace. After a couple of moments there it seemed like the only safe place in the room was in the doorway to the hall.

"There was some kind of miracle. In the oratory. Statue

fell and started bleeding. They said it was a miracle. They—"

"So they're making you wear tally sticks because of some sort of miracle?"

"I don't know. That's what they said." Finbar was very uncertain as to what exactly was going on. He glanced toward the hall. Maybe his mother would appear and soften whatever it was that he appeared to have done wrong.

"Does everybody have to wear them?"

"Yeah. Well, not the Brothers or the teachers but all of us. Yeah."

"Jesus wept!"

"What's going on in here? Ye can be heard all the way down the street?" called Mrs. Sullivan coming in from the scullery.

"Finbar, Declan, take your tea up to your room and finish it there," ordered Mr. Sullivan.

Knowing better than to question this, Finbar and Declan obediently tromped up the stairs and closed the bedroom door loudly. A moment later they silently reopened the door and Finbar tiptoed back down the stairs until he was level with the hall ceiling. He sat with his knees tucked against his chin in a small listening ball. Declan stood at the head of the stairs and craned to hear as well.

"Get back in your room, you two!" shouted Mrs. Sullivan.

The boys tiptoed back into the bedroom.

"And shut that door!"

Finbar resignedly pushed the door closed.

"So? Jack? What was all that commotion about? Do you want to tell me?"

"A tally stick! They're making him wear a tally stick! They're making my son wear a fucking tally stick! Did you know about this?"

With his ear pressed against the bedroom floor, Finbar

could hear his mother clear her throat uncertainly. This was not good. Normally when his father got himself worked up about the Black and Tans or the North or the Spanish Civil War, she could smack him down with ease. This was different. He could tell that she did not know what to say, and in her own way was as apoplectic as he was.

"Jesus, Mary, and Joseph! Why would they be doing such a thing?" asked Mrs. Sullivan in a plaintive tone.

"Damned if I know, but I'm damn well going to find out. No son of mine is going to be subjected to this. It's not for the likes of that that my father got shot into an open grave. It's not for that that—"

"Easy, easy, easy, pet. Don't go getting yourself all worked up over it. You'll do yourself a mischief. Why don't you go down and see Brother Loughlin and he'll explain it to you? He seems a nice holy man, so he does."

"To hell with Brother Loughlin! I'll not talk to the monkey when I can talk to the organ grinder. I'll write straight to the Department of Education. And I'll write to Morris Barry, that's what I'll do. He was in school with me. He's a county councilor. I'll have the president himself down on that Loughlin like a ton of bricks. No son of mine—"

"Jack, pet, for God's sake, go easy, won't you? You don't want to start any trouble."

"Trouble? You think we should just take this lying down? Over my dead body! You think writing letters is starting trouble? Can't you see the madness of this?"

Their voices abruptly dropped below the pitch that Finbar could possibly hear through the floor.

"What are they saying?" whispered Declan.

"I can't hear. They've gone all quiet," answered Finbar.

They heard the rattle of the kitchen doorknob.

"Don't try to fob me off! Fuck writing letters! I'm sick

of it, I tell ye! Tally sticks, for crying out loud! These bloody religious and their maniac carry-on! Haven't they already done enough to this family? Didn't we keep quiet and let them put Sheila Barry away? Shameful! I'll do more than write to some fucking pen-pusher! And you making excuses for them! Have you lost all sense? Is there no fight left in you, woman?"

The hall door opened and shut and Mr. Sullivan's footsteps receded down the empty street. Finbar could almost hear the slow fuming of his mind in the heavy deliberateness of his footfalls.

"What was all that about?" asked Finbar.

Declan looked squarely at Finbar but did not answer.

"What?" pressed Finbar.

"Nothing."

"Come on! What?"

"Nothing. I said nothing."

"No, come on. You know something. What?"

Declan sat down heavily on his bed. "Do you remember years and years ago Dad and Uncle Francie took us out to visit Na-Na Sullivan's grave out by Four Mile Cross?"

"I don't know. Sort of. The day the red car broke down and it was all sunny and we walked back and we caught the frog in the stream?"

Declan nodded and almost smiled at the childish images Finbar recalled. He had forgotten about the frog.

"Well?"

Declan shifted his feet under him and turned to face his brother, half sitting, half kneeling on the edge of his bed. "What else do you remember?"

"I don't know. Dad cut the grass on Na-Na's grave with the hedge shears and we put some flowers in a jam jar and set it on top."

"Do you remember going to another grave?"

Finbar thought hard but could recall nothing more. He just remembered it being very sunny and warm and walking in his short wool trousers and the way they chafed his legs. He shook his head.

"You were small. Only four or so. We went over to this other part of the graveyard. There were no stones, just an open bit of the graveyard. Dad and Francie were talking. They were spelling words so I wouldn't understand, but I got some of it. I asked Uncle Francie about it a couple of years ago at Eileen's wedding. He hemmed and hawed but I told him I knew there was something. He made me promise never to tell Dad that he told me."

"What? What?" hissed Finbar impatiently.

"Dad and Francie had a younger brother Joseph. When they were all little, Granda Sullivan died in the troubles. They were sent to an orphanage cos Na-Na didn't have enough money to keep them. Joseph was only eight and he used to piss his bed and get in trouble for it. The head nun got tired of beating him so she started making him wear a tally stick. Every time he wet the bed or cried or got in trouble she put a notch in his tally stick, and then on Sunday morning she would leather him for all the notches. He got so many notches all the time that she started making him wear a big huge tally stick like a broom handle around his neck, and then she would beat him with it and make him sand down the notches.

"This went on for a couple of years and Joseph started to stutter and got all blinky in the eyes and they used to give him notches for all of it. Francie turned sixteen and was let go because the county wouldn't pay for him anymore, and the next year Dad left. They were both working on farms when they heard that Joseph was dead. One of the nuns who was a decent woman got word to them. But it was after they had buried Joseph and they never knew exactly where the grave was. So Dad and Francie put some stones down beside the wall near Na-Na's grave and called it Joseph's. They never knew what happened, but then one of the other boys in Joseph's dormitory told Francie one time that Joseph hanged himself with the tally stick."

Declan let out a sigh and lay back on his bed. Finbar sat on the edge of his bed looking down at his trembling hands.

"I never knew."

"And you don't now. You say anything and I'll beat the shite out of you. Do you hear me?"

Finbar nodded and then shook his head sadly. "Fuck sake," he whispered.

"Yeah. So that's why the tally stick set him off. But don't say anything—not to him, not to Mam. Right?"

"All right."

Finbar picked up his comic book and started flicking through it. He was not paying any attention to what was in front of him but he needed to do something that felt some way normal. Things like that could not have happened to his family. *Destitute*, *Orphans*, the words rang in Finbar's ears. His father had been destitute. His father had been in an orphanage. His father had this and how many other stories that Finbar would never know?

"Promise you won't say anything," repeated Declan quietly.

"Promise," whispered Finbar, and listened hard for some meaningful break in his mother's heavy silence downstairs.

34

"Go in peace to love and serve the Lord." Father Flynn hastily concluded the morning mass. By now he was used to saying mass in the refectory, but the oppressive air that hung over the school this morning was almost unbearable. During the mass the Brothers had barely responded, each one seemingly locked in his own cocoon of all-consuming trepidation. The air smelt of charred wood and dampness.

Father Flynn quietly closed his missal and left. The Brothers sat on as if unsure what was supposed to happen next. None of them had seen Brother Loughlin since the previous night and each to some extent now felt the same directionless fretful uncertainty. How could they just treat this day like any other? They had spent the night sleeping on gym mats on the refectory floor.

"Our Lady of Indefinite Duration . . ." called Brother Boland hollowly.

"Pray for us!" responded a few of the Brothers.

"Saint Loman of Perpetual Paucity . . ." called another reedy voice.

"Pray for us!" chorused the Brothers, this time with added voices.

"Saint Drommod of the Holy Undershirt . . ."

"Pray for us!"

"Venerable Saorseach O'Rahilly . . ."

"Pray for us!"

"Blessed Vincent of Edenderry . . ."

"Pray for us!

"Blessed Conor of the Tattered Shroud . . ."

"Pray for us!"

"Blessed Imelda of Immoderate Mystery . . ."

"Pray for us!"

The Brothers slowly began to look at one another in the ensuing silence with dazed, puzzled expressions.

The fire inspector said there would have to be a safety inspection of the upper floors of the monastery before any of them would be allowed back to their cells.

How could this have happened? What did any of it mean? One by one they got up from their chairs and moved like sleepwalkers in search of someone who would gently wake them up and point them in the right direction of where the day should go.

Mrs. Broderick was surprised to find Brother Loughlin's office unlocked, and even more so to find him behind his desk already on the telephone.

"Is everything all right, Brother?" she asked, her usual acid tone softened by the sense of something out of the ordinary taking place.

"Everything is fine, Mrs. Broderick. Just fine," said Loughlin sternly. He stood up, gently ushered her back out of his office, and closed the door on her.

He sat down and picked up the phone again. "I'm sorry about that, Mr. DePaor. Yes, I understand the department's point of view but I just thought . . . I see." Brother Loughlin replaced the phone in its cradle. An inspection! That was all he needed. He got up and yanked the door open: "Mrs. Broderick, get Brother Moody! I want to see him immediately."

* * *

"Stupid fucking PE class!" muttered Lynch.

"The bastards could've given us the day off for the fire," complained Scully.

The boys stood in front of the stage in their white T-shirts and shorts, arms folded and jumping up and down trying to keep warm. The hall was cold and they had to try to distract themselves from the fact that even here indoors their breath steamed in front of them. Finbar stood quietly to one side. His father had still not come home.

The dispirited near silence was abruptly shattered by a loud bang from the back of the hall. They turned to see Brother Moody standing there with two sacks of hurling sticks at his feet.

"Right now! One hurley each! Get them now and line up over there against the wall! Don't crowd, there's one for everyone!"

Brother Moody's warning was a needless caution to the sluggish group that traipsed down to the end of the hall and reluctantly took one heavy ash stick each.

"Right then! There will be no more pointless PE. Take the base of the hurley in your right hand and rest the handle against your right shoulder like this."

Moody stood to attention and demonstrated how to hold the hurley like a soldier ready to march with his rifle on his shoulder. He moved along the row of boys correcting and adjusting until he had what he desired: a line of young men ready to charge into the future to bring about one Holy United Catholic Ireland. He stomped his feet and shouted in time: "Left! Right! Left! Right! Lift those feet!"

The boys marched in approximate time to Brother Moody's exhortations.

"What have we suffered? Eight hundred years of

oppression! When is the time? The time is now! The time for what? One Holy United Catholic Ireland! What do we do with Planters? Drive them back to Scotland!" Brother Moody stopped in front of Bradshaw. "What have we suffered?" he barked.

"Eh, eight hundred years of depression?" ventured Bradshaw.

"*Oppression*, you fool, do you know nothing?" He drew his hurley back and went to hit Bradshaw with it. Clumsily Bradshaw drew his hurley down but failed to block the swing. He fell to the floor clutching his knee.

Moody moved on down the line: "What have we suffered?" he barked at Lynch

"Six hundred years of impressions," mumbled Lynch.

Brother Moody walked on and suddenly turned and swung at Lynch. The boy moved in a flash and not only deflected the swing but also drew back ready to strike. Moody deftly shifted to block Lynch's swing. He leaned into the boy and stared at him hard. "Try it, you little thug, and you know where you'll end up," he hissed.

The boy very slowly lowered his hurley without taking his eyes from Moody's face.

"Good! That's what I like to see! A bit of fight," crowed Brother Moody, and moved on down the line of marching boys. "Mind your legs!" he shouted at McDonagh a split second before he swung his hurley.

McDonagh turned awkwardly and mostly blocked Brother Moody's swing, but took a sharp blow to the ankle.

"You must be ever vigilant! You must be ready to act! The heroes of Ireland did not lay down their lives so that you could laze around like corner boys. There is still work to be done! There is still Ireland's work to be done!"

"Brother Loughlin wants to see you," came a small voice at Moody's back.

The Brother swung around and almost skulled Anthony with his hurley. The boy ducked and handed Moody the note.

"Right, twenty laps of the yard and ten decades of the rosary! Consecutive, not concurrent. I'll be back," promised Moody, and left the hall.

35

Father Sheehan slowly relit his pipe and turned over another page of the sheaf that lay before him on his immaculately polished walnut desk. He read by the pale midafternoon light that did its best to fill the room through the two tall arched windows overlooking the well-tended gardens of Loyola House.

Aside from the soft sucking noise of Sheehan's pipe, the only other sound in the office was the precise metronomic tennis match of the pendulum clock that stood beside the door. Father Mulvey was too busy holding his breath to add anything to the soundscape.

Sheehan quietly cleared his throat and Father Mulvey drew in another sharp breath to add to the chestful of anxious air he was already harbouring. He could not read this ambiguous sound from Sheehan. Was it a chuckle, a sound of disapproval, of approbation? He uncrossed and recrossed his legs and fixed his eyes on the fingers of Sheehan's left hand where they drummed lightly and soundlessly on the small pile of pages he had already read.

Sheehan stopped suddenly and looked up. He took his pipe from his mouth, noted with indifference that it had gone out again, and laid it softly in the purple tin ashtray to his right. "Mr. Madden seems to be working prolifically," he said softly.

"Oh yes, Father, he is," blurted Father Mulvey, glad

for the long-awaited opportunity to exhale. "He is most enthusiastic about this undertaking. I believe he is afire with the light of faith. Almost inspired, you might say!"

"So how much longer do you think it will take Mr. Madden to finish the revised *Life of O'Rahilly*?" asked Father Sheehan casually. He took out his pocket watch and checked it against the pendulum clock.

"Well, at the back there you have the drafts he brought me this morning for the chapters that bring the story up to date, including the collapse of the oratory and the bleeding statue."

"I must say, this is fascinating, truly fascinating," said Father Sheehan as he flipped through the pages.

Mulvey felt his unease take wing and soar away into a huge blue yonder of future prestige.

From under the sheaf of papers Sheehan took that morning's *The Way Forward*. It was opened to an inside page. He glanced at it distractedly and shook his head sadly. "Tragic. Shocking," he said, almost in an undertone.

"What's that, Father?" inquired Mulvey brightly.

"Chap found hanged this morning."

"Oh, the Lord bless us and save us," hushed Mulvey, and quickly crossed himself.

"Would you listen to this: *Citizens of Howth were shocked and saddened by the discovery this morning of a hanged man on the channel marker at the southeast entrance to the harbour. The man was found at 5:15 this morning by Mr. Fergus Stokes who was taking his boat out. The county coroner was immediately called to the scene.*"

Sheehan paused and looked carefully at Mulvey, who shook his head ruefully: "One has to feel sorry for someone who will go to such terrible lengths as to take his own life. Surely the poor man couldn't have been in full possession of his wits."

Sheehan selected another illuminating tidbit from the article: "'*He was fond of a pint, but no, I don't think that was anything to do with it really, though he had seemed to be a little down of late,' said Patrick Iveagh, an acquaintance of the deceased.*"

"Oh, the drink is a curse upon this troubled, benighted nation," said Mulvey vehemently.

"It is, Father Mulvey, it is," concurred Sheehan softly. "But you know what puzzles me most about this case?" He read again in the same measured, mildly curious tone as before: "*The deceased, Marcus Madden, B.A., was best known for his* Life of Venerable Saorseach O'Rahilly, *the founder of the Brothers of Godly Coercion. He had in recent years fallen on hard times and was believed to have taken to the drink.*"

Mulvey's apprehension swooped back out of the wide blue future and collapsed around him like a wet tarp thrown from a third-floor window.

"I believe you have a little bit of explaining to do, Father Mulvey," Sheehan said softly, and held the newspaper across the desk, lest Mulvey should for a moment doubt the veracity of Marcus Madden's sudden, brief, and surprising resurgence into the public eye.

"Well, Father Sheehan. This is an unexpected pleasure, I have to say. Tea, Father? No? Fine. You can leave us, Mrs. Broderick."

The woman pointedly sniffed her distaste for Loughlin's haughty tone and left the office.

"Please, Father, have a seat. What can I do for you? Father Mulvey is not joining us?"

"Father Mulvey has some urgent internal administrative matters to attend to."

Sheehan sat down in front of Brother Loughlin's desk without taking off his coat. He placed his black felt hat carefully on his right knee and listened carefully to the ticking of the clock on the wall, and to Loughlin's silence.

"Brother Loughlin, it has come to my attention that Father Mulvey's researches with Mr. Madden were somewhat unorthodox, to say the least. I trust you saw today's *The Way Forward*?"

"I'm afraid I didn't really get a chance to look at it."

"Then it might interest you to know that it carried the grim story of Mr. Marcus Madden's demise. The unfortunate man apparently hanged himself from a channel marker in Howth Harbour last night."

"God bless us and save us, but that's terrible. The poor man!"

"It is a sad event. It may also interest you to know that Father Mulvey delivered to me some pages of the revised *Life of the Venerable Saorseach O'Rahilly* which Mr. Madden had given him only this morning. A curious occurrence given that Mr. Madden hanged himself at least twelve hours before allegedly giving these pages to Father Mulvey. One would imagine that receiving written pages from a corpse at the end of a rope would be the type of thing one would comment on to one's superior, would one not?" Sheehan smiled mirthlessly.

Loughlin stared straight into the priest's small, intelligent eyes. They gave no indication of how much or how little he actually knew, but the overall impression was one of deep wells of information and knowledge that he would share or not according to his wider purposes. The Brother's armpits grew hot and sticky under his cassock.

"I'm sure you would agree, Brother Loughlin, that this is a disquieting development in the preparation of a disposition for a miracle. It is, how could one put it, suspicious at best, would you not agree?"

Loughlin scurried through the twisted half-lit passageways of his mind hoping to find some appropriate response. Indignation? Angry shock? Hurt and shock at being deceived by Mulvey? He turned briefly into a dead end of dissimulated righteous rage and helplessly backed out of it.

"Uhm, yes indeed, Father," he managed.

Sheehan nodded solemnly. He picked an invisible piece of lint from the band of his hat and dropped it to the floor. "Did you know that Mr. Madden had turned into a disreputable drunkard and Father Mulvey himself had taken on rewriting *The Life of Venerable Saorseach*, Brother?"

"I had no idea!" rued Brother Loughlin, delighted with the chance to say something truthful that could only damage someone else.

Again Sheehan nodded. "Did you know that Brother Boland cut his hand on the night of the oratory incident?"

Loughlin detected a derisory italicising of the words *oratory incident* that made him very uneasy. He looked carefully at the figure of Venerable Saorseach O'Rahilly on his desk as if trying to remind himself of exactly how he had broken the statuette and smeared it with his own blood. He wanted to be clear on exactly what he was concealing from Sheehan.

"I can't say that I noticed. We were all very perturbed. In a panic, shock, you know, like."

"I am certain you were," replied Sheehan. He joined his hands as if for prayer and put the tips of his index fingers to his lips. "I am not quite sure how to say this, Brother Loughlin, but say it I must. I believe that there is more, or rather less, of a divine nature to this so-called miracle than meets the eye. I should not like to have to defend it in front of the Bishop. I would be duty bound to voice my misgivings about the authenticity and, well, if there were an antagonistic investigation, who knows where it might lead?"

Loughlin shifted uncomfortably under Sheehan's unwavering gaze. Did he know or was he fishing? Would it be best to own up now or try to brave it out? What if Sheehan were to have an accident? Would the process go ahead then? Even if they let the whole thing slip back into the quiet, would Sheehan come after him for his part in falsifying it? What had he already done to Mulvey? What the hell was that racket outside?

The office door burst open and Brother Loughlin and Father Sheehan were treated to the bizarre spectacle of Brother Mulligan struggling into the office while Mrs. Broderick did her best to restrain him.

"Get your hands off me, woman! This is important!"

With astonishing strength for his ancient frame, Mulligan shrugged the woman off and pushed her gently but firmly out the door. He grabbed a chair and wedged it against the door handle to keep her out.

"Brother Mulligan! What do you think you . . . ?" Loughlin fell silent under the glare from Mulligan.

"Whisht!" hissed Mulligan, and raised his right palm toward Loughlin with a flourish of authority and determination that impelled him back into his chair. Mulligan carefully circled Father Sheehan, who sat unperturbed, patiently waiting for this embarrassing interlude to end. The Brother leaned down and stared into Sheehan's face from very close. Sheehan shifted a little in his seat and cleared his throat. Mulligan stopped his circling and stood to Sheehan's left.

"It's him," he said to Brother Loughlin conclusively.

"Him? Who him? What are you talking about, you old

fool?"

"Sheehan. He's a Sheehan. I'd know them anywhere!" With this Brother Mulligan seemed to reach a pitch of fury that threatened to burst him. He launched himself at Sheehan, who was forced to stand up and remove the Brother's hands from around his throat with some considerable effort. Loughlin moved from behind his desk and grabbed Mulligan by the elbows. "What on earth do you think you are at?"

"He's one of them Sheehans. His father informed to the Black and Tans. Well I'd know the face. Think I don't know ye, Sheehan? Well I do! Went to Jesuit school on Civil War blood money, ye did! Ye hid long enough, but now that I know who ye are, ye'll not rest easy till I have me revenge! I know plenty of people who'd be interested to know who you are and where you came from! I'm sure you know Archbishop Ryan's father was shot by the Black and Tans. That'd put a halt to your gallop quick enough if he found out."

"Brother Mulligan, Father Sheehan is here about the miracle. He's no one's informer. That's all in the past now." Loughlin nodded to Sheehan, who removed the chair and opened the door. "Go back to your duties, Brother. I need to have a good talk with Father Sheehan. I will handle this."

Mulligan glared at Sheehan and exited with slow dignity, leaving the door open behind him. Loughlin watched him leave Mrs. Broderick's outer office and then closed the door softly.

"Have a seat, Father. I think, in light of Brother Mulligan's information, we have some more things to discuss, don't you? I think there might be some mutually beneficial agreement we might reach about these, ehm, how shall we say, revelations," he grinned.

Father Sheehan smiled wanly. He was intelligent enough to realise that he had lost all advantage and a trade of his silence for Loughlin's was the best he could hope for. The miracle investigation would go through the motions and then quietly disappear and no one would ever accuse anyone of trying to fake anything.

36

The boys lined up by class and year and Brother Loughlin and Mr. Pollock walked up and down the rows inspecting each boy carefully. From time to time they stopped and conferred in urgent whispers before: "You, boy! Over to the other side."

Each boy selected trotted over to the other side of the yard to Brother Cox beside the grotto of Our Lady of Indefinite Duration. Whatever their fate, the grotto at least offered temporary shelter from the biting wind that sheared across the rest of the yard.

"What are they doing?" whispered Finbar.

"No idea," answered Scully. His mind was whirring as he tried to figure out what was going on and whether he should concentrate his efforts on getting himself sent to the other side or on being left where he was. There seemed to be no rhyme or reason to the selection process. Some of the quietest and some of the worst boys were being sent to the other side. He could not figure out the underlying plan. That made him very uneasy.

Finbar looked up and down the fifth year row where he stood. There was a nervous uncertainty in the air. To his left Smalley Mullen was shaking. It could have been the cold, but the way he kept looking from side to side told Finbar that the boy was very nervous.

"Eyes front!" barked Mr. Pollock suddenly. Finbar

snapped his gaze forward. Brother Loughlin and Mr. Pollock were in the third year row in front of him. They had stopped beside a very tall third year. Brother Loughlin moved the boy's head from side to side and peered at his face.

"Walk up and down for me," said Loughlin. The boy stepped forward and moved along the space between the rows of boys. Loughlin and Pollock exchanged meaningful glances as the boy's left foot made a harsh dragging sound on the gravel.

"Lift your feet when you walk, boy!" ordered Pollock.

"I can't, sir. It's my leg."

"Then get over to the other side with you," barked Loughlin.

They moved on along the row. Soon they would get to Finbar.

"Psssst!"

Finbar turned to see Smalley Mullen gesticulating wildly. It was clear he wanted to know what was going on.

I don't know, mouthed Finbar back at him.

Smalley waved him to lean back. He wanted Scully's opinion, not Finbar's.

Scully shrugged his shoulders at Smalley. *No fucking idea*, he mouthed.

Brother Loughlin and Mr. Pollock were now at the beginning of the fifth year row and coming toward them. They stopped in front of Lynch.

"Are those your only shoes?" asked Brother Loughlin.

"Yes, Brother," mumbled Lynch, looking down at his scuffed and broken shoes to see what the problem might be.

"Other side!"

Lynch slouched across the yard with an air of complete indifference. It was all the same to him; middle of the yard or beside the grotto, none of it mattered a shite. His gait as much as said so.

"And hurry on with you!" Loughlin snarled after him.

Finbar tensed as they moved closer. They stopped at Bradshaw on the other side of Scully. Loughlin motioned Pollock, who reluctantly leaned forward and sniffed at the boy. He recoiled sharply and nodded to Loughlin.

"Other side!"

They slowly passed Finbar and Scully, moved down the row, and stopped at Smalley.

"Stop that shaking, boy!"

Smalley pulled his arms tightly about himself in an attempt to stop shivering.

"What on earth is the matter with you?"

"Cold, Brother," struggled Smalley between his chattering teeth.

"Cough," instructed Mr. Pollock.

"What, sir?"

"I said cough."

Puzzled, Smalley let out a small *ahem-ahem*.

"None of your messing. Cough properly!"

Smalley coughed a little harder and then doubled over in a violent fit of genuine coughing.

"I thought as much. Other side!"

By the time Brother Loughlin and Mr. Pollock finished their inspection, some eighty boys had been sent to the other side of the yard. Brother Cox was concentrating very hard on remembering the instructions Loughlin had given him. He divided the boys into two even groups. With a nod from Loughlin he sent one group back to stand behind all the other boys. Then Loughlin sent half the boys from his side of the yard to stand in front of Cox's boys. They formed two groups on each side of the yard like some press-ganged guard of honour with the offending handpicked boys at the back of each group.

"Is the Pope coming or what?" asked McDonagh quietly as he stood between Finbar and Scully.

As if in answer to McDonagh's question, two black cars pulled into the yard between the battalions of boys.

Brother Loughlin and Mr. Pollock stepped forward to meet the occupants of the vehicles when they stepped out.

"Ah, Mr. DePaor, how nice to see you again!" Brother Loughlin greeted. "I believe you already know our vice principal, Mr. Pollock."

DePaor perfunctorily shook hands with Loughlin and Pollock. "Let me introduce my colleagues." He gestured to the man and woman who had just emerged from the other car.

"I don't believe you have met Mr. Nolan from the Department of Schools, Reformatories, and Borstals, and this is Miss Moloney from the Department of Waifs, Strays, and Orphans. They will be joining our inspection."

Inspection. The word rippled through the boys like a forest fire, igniting sensations of fear always associated with inspectors, followed quickly by the euphoric realisation that they, the boys, were not the subject of the inspection—it was the school and the staff.

"That's what it was!" whispered Finbar suddenly.

"What?" hissed Scully.

"They put all the sick and dirty-looking fellahs at the back for the inspection."

"The sly bastards! They must be worried."

"Very nice to meet you both!" called Brother Loughlin as he bustled round the car to shake hands with Mr. Nolan and Miss Moloney.

They each took his hand for an instant and nodded curtly. Mr. Nolan went back to the car and retrieved a very thick file. Brother Loughlin eyed it suspiciously, wondering where on earth Nolan could have got so much information on his school.

"May we begin?" asked Miss Moloney in a brittle, impatient voice.

"Oh yes. Of course. Of course. This way, please!" beamed Loughlin. Pollock nodded and smiled nervously at Mr. Nolan and Miss Moloney.

Mr. Nolan turned from the group and approached the boys to his left. He flinched slightly when he saw the boys recoil en masse as he came near.

"What's your name, young man?"

"Martin Wardick, sir."

"My name's Martin too. Isn't that funny?" Mr. Nolan smiled. Wardick stood blinking and bewildered. "Do you like school, Martin? Are you happy here?" he asked kindly.

Wardick continued to stare at the man. The incongruity of being addressed by his first name, combined with the alien concepts of liking or being made happy by school, succeeded in paralysing his mind completely. He gawked helplessly and repeated: "Martin Wardick, sir."

Mr. Nolan smiled painfully at the boy and moved to join the rest of the inspection team. He caught Brother Loughlin's ingratiating eye and a dark scowl clouded his normally serene face.

"Mr. Nolan has just returned from investigating the Deargalstown Reformatory fire," announced Mr. DePaor while the inspection team moved toward the school.

Brother Loughlin's blood ran cold as he suddenly made the connection: this was the Mr. Nolan who had excoriated the nuns at Deargalstown when his investigation found that so many girls had died in the fire because the nuns insisted that they change out of their nightgowns before fleeing the building. The Mother Superior had said she'd been afraid their virtue might be put at risk. Nolan had scathingly concluded in his report that the nuns deemed it better that a girl be burned to death than risk an occasion of immodesty. It was creating quite a controversy.

"I thought we'd begin with a quick tour of our laboratories. I'm sure Mr. Nolan will find our school a very different proposition to Deargalstown," Brother Loughlin informed the group as he ushered them into the school.

"It is clearly not a girls' reformatory, but the rest remains to be seen," replied Mr. Nolan coldly.

"The rest of you, back to your classes!" shouted Brother Cox once Brother Loughlin and Mr. Pollock had taken the inspectors into the lab.

Finbar's sense of excitement mounted: "They're the ones in trouble. Not us!" he explained eagerly to Scully on the stairs. "Did you see the way Loughlin was licking up to them? They're shitting bricks."

They walked into the classroom to find Brother Moody waiting for them. He was not supposed to be there. They were supposed to have Civics with Larry Skelly.

As the boys entered, Moody handed each one a rag: "There are tins of polish in that sack. You will work four to a tin and you will begin with this corridor. Now get to work! And put your backs into it, you lazy guttersnipes!"

The Brother walked along the corridor inspecting the boys' work. Wherever he saw a missed patch he ground his foot on it to make it worse and told them to do it again. Suddenly Smalley Mullen sneezed and, his hands being otherwise occupied with polishing, delivered a generous dollop of snot onto the floor.

In a flash Brother Moody was beside him: "Lick that up, you disgusting little savage."

Smalley looked up at him. "I can get a hanky and wipe it up, Brother."

"You could, but what did I say?"

"You said lick it up, Brother."

"That's what I said. Are you about to defy me?" Moody clenched his thin pale fingers into a fist and then unfurled them into their individual crab-leg glory again. "Come on now, Mr. Mullen. It's not like it's anything new to you. Every time I turn around I see you with half your fist up your snotty little nose excavating some morsel out of there. Lick it up!"

Smalley stayed immobile on his hands and knees vainly hoping that this moment would just go away. He stared up at Brother Moody's pinched, bitter face and then glanced down at the glob of snot on the parquet. Before he could look up again, Brother Moody had grabbed his hair and pushed his face against the floor. "Lick it up!"

In the cupola of the bell tower two resting pigeons raised their heads off their breasts and looked up suddenly. There was a disturbance somewhere within the air. They roused themselves and flew out of the tower into the light southwest wind that would take them to the canal.

As Brother Moody rubbed Smalley Mullen's face in his own snot, an accelerated shudder ran through the whole school. In one tremulous instant the sense memory of a hundred years relieved itself in every brick and lintel, vibrated through every cracked course of mortar, hummed through every pipe, tap, and cistern, fizzled simultaneously along every copper wire and into every clunky Bakelite switch and socket, tiptoed along every beam and rafter, and finally sighed itself out through every plughole, urinal, toilet bowl, and drain into the sewers below the school and out to sea. In that bewildering instant the school reverberated to the lofty words of Thomas Breen as he laid the foundation stone one hundred years before:

> *We are gathered together on this auspicious day to lay not just the foundation stone of one school but the cornerstone of a network of schools throughout this land. This State, with the able help of the men of the cloth, will cherish each and every child and provide them with an education that will be the envy of the world. We are embarking on a noble endeavor. We have set our sights high and we will not fail. We will not fail those who toiled and sacrificed to make this endeavor possible, nor will we fail those to come whose future formation has been entrusted to us. We will be tireless in our work to produce good citizens, good scholars, and good servants of the Lord Our God.*

With a lurch of tired despair the school settled heavily on its foundations, and the foundation stone bearing Breen's words cracked right down the middle and scowled at the world with its shattered visage.

The inner tremors of the school were replaced by a silence new and absolute. The institution had given up its central governing spirit. The will to endure had left it. It stood like a house of cards, held up only by bad workmanship, the haphazard arrangement of substandard building materials, and a kind of rigor mortis. Every weakness, every crack and fissure, every stress point and loose shingle had only to will itself and it could put an end to its sorry lot of bearing witness to the daily enactment of a vision twisted and thwarted that now blighted everyone and everything in its ambit.

There was an imperceptible shift within the tower and the ornamental rosette that adorned the top of the four-sided cupola let go of its hold and dropped. It hit the beam supporting the bell, and broke into two pieces, each of which crashed against the bell, bringing forth two jagged staccato peals before falling on down to smash into powder at the bottom of the spiral stairs.

The humming of the bell died down and was replaced by a gentle but constant pitter-patter as first tiny then slightly more substantial flakes of paint and plaster drifted onto the bell. The tower was softly filled with each of these sounds blending and swirling like so much glass being smashed in the distance.

"That stupid Boland, ringing the bell like that for no reason," muttered Moody under his breath. "Should have had him committed years ago." He turned his attention back to Smalley Mullen, whose drool and blood were now mixed with his snot on the parquet floor. "Go and get a mop and clean up your mess, you disgusting little bastard!" He released Smalley's hair and the boy slowly picked himself up. He stood facing the Brother.

From where he was polishing Finbar looked up to see what was going to happen next in this grotesque dance of power and punishment.

"What are ye looking at? Get back to yer polishing!" snapped Moody.

Smalley's lower lip was cut and trembling, and his eyes welled with tears that he struggled to fight back. He took one deep breath and his eyes seemed to glaze over. He hopped awkwardly onto his left foot and with surprising agility managed to pivot himself in midair to put all the weight of his body and anger behind his right foot as he swung it hard into Brother Moody's crotch. "Fucking bollix!" he shouted as his foot made contact.

Moody took a second to comprehend what had just happened before he buckled in pain and clasped one hand to his testicles and one to his knee to keep himself upright. Smalley stared around him at the strange new world he had just created for himself. The Brother groaned and then vomited noisily on his boots.

"Go!" Scully hissed to Smalley.

Smalley stood for a moment as if trying to grasp what he had just done. He peered down at Moody and drew his foot back once more and swung it again at the man's hands covering his crotch. Moody buckled and groaned again and Smalley turned and ran, first hesitantly, then with more decision.

Sensing that Brother Moody's vomiting was over, the boys backed out of striking distance and waited. This was a strange and wonderful moment, the like of which they had never in their wildest dreams thought they would see, but they knew one thing: someone was going to pay for it.

"And this is our Biology laboratory. The Chemistry laboratory is above us on the second floor and Physics on the third."

"Indeed. You seem to be very low on equipment despite spending," Mr. Nolan consulted his file, "three hundred pounds on laboratory supplies last summer. Of course, considering the number of boys you have sent off to industrial schools over the last couple of years, you probably don't need so much equipment," observed Mr. Nolan acidly.

"Uhm, there was a slight accident."

"Was there now?" Mr. Nolan made a quick note in his file.

Brother Loughlin did his best to ignore the man's hostile tone and directed himself as much as possible to Mr. DePaor and Miss Moloney. "Shall we move on and begin our tour of the classrooms? We have three-quarters of an hour before lunchtime."

Without waiting for an answer he walked out of the lab, leaving Pollock to take up the rear and usher the inspectors along.

Brother Moody retched and spat into the puddle of vomit at his feet. He stood up carefully and looked round him, searching for Smalley Mullen's face.

"Cowardly little bastard," he snarled. "You! You there! Go get a mop and a bucket and clean up this corridor."

"Me, Brother?" asked Scully.

"Yes, you."

Scully's mind raced. "But Brother, I don't know where they do be keeping the mops," he answered, while he gently nudged Finbar.

Before Finbar knew what he was saying, he blurted: "I'll help him, Brother. I know where they are."

Too pained to perceive or speculate about any ulterior motives Finbar might have, Moody nodded his permission and waved the two boys down the stairs. Then he returned his attention to the two most pressing matters at hand: "The rest of you, back to polishing that floor! Which way did that little bastard Mullen go?"

The boys leapt back to their polishing, all jostling for a spot as far away from Moody and his puddle of vomit as possible. Just as the Brother was about to pick one of them for interrogation about Smalley's escape, there was a rumble from the bathroom at the end of the corridor followed by a loud screeching of metal.

"The stupid little bastard. He's cornered himself," laughed Moody, and strode down the corridor to the toilets leaving a trail of little vomit footprints on the newly polished floor. "I'm going to make you wish you'd never been born, Mullen."

When he pushed open the toilet door, a thick jet of rusty water hammered him square in the face. He fell backward into the corridor with its force and the toilet door slammed shut again.

"One of you, run and get McWhatsisname, the janitor," spluttered Moody, as he lay drenched and stunned on the floor.

A charge ran through the boys as each one independently decided this was a great opportunity to get away. Before Moody could react they were all clattering down the stairs and out of earshot.

"I said *one* of you!" he shouted weakly after them.

Smalley Mullen inched toward the door that led to the yard and peeped out cautiously. He was completely out of breath. He had to get away or they'd catch him and he'd be disappeared off to Drumgloom before anyone knew what was happening. He was about to make a break for it across the yard to the gate when he heard voices and saw Brother Loughlin, Mr. Pollock, and the inspectors emerge from the Biology lab and walk toward him. Without thinking he turned and burst through the next nearest door.

He stared in shock to find he had entered the staff room. He hesitated but, seeing no one, closed the door behind him and leaned against it trying to catch his breath. At that moment the exterior door to the yard opened. Smalley's heart contracted to a walnut and he turned to open the connecting door again.

"I think we'll proceed upstairs to the second year classes," he heard Brother Loughlin's voice announce outside.

Smalley froze with his hand on the doorknob.

"By the sounds of it, I don't think you'd want to be going out there right now," Spud Murphy's voice advised him softly from the far side of the staff room. "They're all a bit edgy right now."

Smalley turned around to look at the teacher.

"Ah, for fuck sake! What did they do to you now?" exclaimed Spud when he saw the blood on Smalley's face.

"Brother Moody . . . I sneezed . . . pushed me on the floor . . . kicked him in the bollix," stammered Smalley before his chest tightened and he dissolved into tears.

"Shhh. Come here. It's all right," said Spud, and gently led the boy to one of the ratty armchairs by the window. "Just take deep breaths. That's it. Let it out. You'll be all right. Don't worry. Take your time." He handed Smalley his handkerchief.

Just then Mr. Laverty walked in. Spud motioned him to stay quiet. "Just keep watch and make sure no one comes in." Laverty hesitated. "Just make sure no one comes in! It's not hard!"

Laverty nodded nervously.

In the third-floor toilets one pipe after another gave way. The floor was awash; the trough urinal overflowed and the water began to seep out under the door. The cisterns gurgled painfully and the toilet bowls in the stalls churned and bubbled, then suddenly emptied with a heaving, choking sound.

The plaster in the ceiling, sodden by the upward spray of the broken pipes, flaked and fell. The ceiling bulged and creaked and then all the water stopped and there was nothing but an ominous dripping silence.

Drawn to the silence and still believing that Smalley Mullen was inside, Brother Moody carefully opened the toilet door. The farthest stall was closed.

"I'm going to give you a beating you will never forget," Moody said calmly as he advanced toward it. He reached into his pocket and withdrew his leather just as the ceiling came down on top of him.

"What are we doing?" called Finbar.

"Looking for Smalley. We can hide him in McConnell's shed." Scully pushed open the door of the second-floor Chemistry lab. "Oh, sorry sir," he said, and abruptly closed the door.

"Where could he go?" asked Finbar.

"Don't know. The gates are locked and those inspectors are wandering around all over the place. Maybe the monastery."

"Don't be insane!"

"The main exports of West Germany are steel, coal, and cars," parroted the second year, handpicked to display his learning for the inspectors.

Before Brother Loughlin could attempt to elicit any praise for this wonderful feat of rote learning, the classroom shook with a sudden thump.

"Merciful hour! What was that?" shrieked Miss Moloney.

"Uhm, that's just our janitor working on the ceiling in the oratory," ventured Pollock.

Loughlin nodded his agreement and cranked his face

into a carefree smile.

"But isn't the oratory that way?" asked Mr. Nolan, pointing in the opposite direction to the seeming origin of the thump.

"Mr. McConnell is doing some very extensive work on the joists," explained Brother Loughlin with an air of great patience while the sweat ran freely down the fleshy folds of his back.

"Is he indeed?" remarked Mr. Nolan, and made another note in his file.

Finbar and Scully crept carefully into the entrance hallway of the monastery. To their left the bellrope swung gently in a tiny arc beside the staircase. Ahead of them the refectory door stood open.

"Let's try in there first," suggested Finbar.

"Smalley? You there?" hissed Scully as loudly as he dared.

There came in response the sound of hurried feet on the stairs above them.

"Quick! In here! Might not be him," whispered Finbar, and pulled Scully into the alcove under the stairs.

From their hiding place they heard the footsteps accelerate and approach and then saw Brother Boland flash by, waving his arms distractedly and shaking his head.

"Asunder! Corruption! Breached! It's a weakening! Ruptures! Fissures everywhere! A rent in the fabric! Decomposition! Crispations through everything! A horrible yielding!" Boland ran into the refectory and darted from one side to the other as if searching for something. He stopped and stared at the plastic sheeting that covered the broken main window and quickly blessed himself. He took one more look round the refectory and ran back past where Finbar and Scully hid in the shadows. "CA-TAS-TRO-PHE!"

The man's footsteps stopped momentarily and then they heard him rattle back up the stairs.

"He's completely cracked now," said Scully. "Come on!" He led Finbar back toward the school.

"Wait! I thought we were looking for Smalley."

"We will, but we need to get the word out. This is it. This is the big one. We are going to fuck their inspection up."

They rounded the corner and ran straight into the rest of their classmates.

"What the fuck?"

"Moody sent us to look for McRae."

"All of ye?"

"Well, sort of."

"Right. Forget that. Listen. Split up and go round the whole school. Make noise. Break things. Get yerselves caught. Go mad. Ye'll get leathered but it'll be worth it. This is the big blackout! Spread the word. Right?"

"What're youse going to do?" asked Lynch.

"We're going to find Smalley."

"What about me? Why can't I come?" asked Lynch icily.

"Lynch, you need to get everyone to act the bollix and get leathered. This inspection is fucked! Biggest blackout ever! Whole school! Okay? You're running it."

Lynch stared at Scully and his eyes slowly narrowed to two points of brittle energy. "Fucking deadly," he said softly, and ran out into the yard pulling a none-too-reluctant Brian Egan after him. There was some shouting and then the sound of breaking glass.

"Sorry, Bollix Loughlinnnnnnn. Me hand slipped," rang Lynch's voice round the yard.

"Go!" shouted Scully to the rest of them, and they scattered off to spread the action.

37

Brother Boland stood rooted to the spot in the oratory. Sweat was running down his face and he struggled to catch his breath. The two bulky radiators on the side wall were shaking and rattling violently.

"Stop! Stop! No!" he pleaded. The shaking and rattling intensified and a piercing hiss filled the room. Boland turned and ran, slamming the oratory door shut behind him.

"*. . . And a small cabin build there, of clay and wattles made: nine bean rows will I have there, a hive for the honey bee, and live alone in the bee-loud glade . . .*"

"Very good! Very good! Thank you! You can stop now! You can all sit down again," Mr. Nolan hastily told 3-B. In the few brief moments of listening to the jog-trot class recitation of *The Lake Isle of Innisfree* he fully grasped why W.B. Yeats couldn't bear hearing it read in unison by three thousand boy scouts. Had Mr. Nolan stopped it a line earlier he would surely have heard glass breaking and Lynch shouting in the yard.

"Very good. Thank you, Brother Walsh," smiled Mr. Pollock.

"Perhaps we could move on to the attic and the oratory," suggested Miss Moloney.

Mr. DePaor and Mr. Nolan nodded in agreement.

"Ah yes, right, the attic. Right so," answered Brother Loughlin hesitantly.

"That is, after all, our main reason for being here," said Mr. Nolan with an unmistakable impatience creeping into his voice.

"Right then. Thank you, Brother Walsh. You may proceed with your lesson," said Loughlin curtly, and opened the classroom door.

"Brother! Brother! Brother! Brother!" shrieked Lynch and Egan as they burst in.

"What on earth is this carry-on?"

"A message, Brother."

"From Mrs. Broderick, Brother."

"It's urgent, Brother."

"Yes, yes! What is it then?" snapped Loughlin.

"She says you have to come quick."

"She can't wait."

"It's an emergency."

"Out with it!" snarled the Brother.

"She needs . . ."

"A long . . ."

"Hard . . ."

"Deep . . ."

"Shag . . ."

"On your desk . . ."

"From behind . . ."

"Now!"

For a moment Brother Loughlin was completely stunned. It was only when he heard the giggles from the boys of 3-B did he really believe his ears. He drew his leather and grabbed Egan who was nearest.

"How dare you? You filthy-mouthed little cur!" The whole class fell silent. Still, the reality of the moment persisted, percolating from disbelief into something akin to hysteria. One of the boys at the back could stifle his laughter no longer and burst into uncontrollable giggles.

"Come up here, you boy!" called Mr. Pollock, pushing his way past Mr. Nolan to get to work quicker.

"Hurry up with that polishing," barked Brother Cox, and glanced at his watch. He should have got more than three classes of boys to polish the school hall. A temporary lunch table had been set up for the inspectors and now it was nearly lunchtime. He jumped as the doors flew open but was relieved to see that it was only a boy.

"Mr. Pollock wants to see Tony Begley, Brother," said McDonagh respectfully.

"Hah! Begley, in trouble again?" Cox administered two perfunctory belts of the leather before waving Begley out the door with McDonagh.

Outside in the hall McDonagh turned to Begley: "Wait here a couple of minutes and then go back in. We're going for the big blackout. Biggest ever. The whole school. Pass it on." McDonagh then darted back across the yard toward the school.

It took ten minutes of phony messages like McDonagh's, chance meetings in corridors, and furtive signals while passing classroom doors for all the boys to be aware of the big blackout. Simultaneously across the school stammers were developed in midsentence, geometry sets galore crashed to the floor, repetitive stupid questions were asked, tremendous feats of farting and belching were accomplished, idiotic answers to the simplest of questions were ventured. Every imaginable annoyance was brought to bear in one united front of provocation. Fearful of being surprised by the inspectors in the middle of a beating, the teachers and Brothers reacted swiftly and furiously, doling out quick, vicious leatherings in an attempt to restore order as soon as possible.

Brother Boland burst into his cell. There, too, the radiator was hissing and shaking like a thing possessed. He grabbed his rosary beads from the washstand where they hung and fled the room. He ran down the main stairs and then up the back stairs to the bell tower, feverishly fingering his beads.

"As you can see, the damage is quite extensive." Brother Loughlin motioned to the wreckage around him. He stood on what had been the attic but now amounted to little more than a flat roof of rubble atop the monastery.

"Were the victims' remains recovered?" asked Mr. DePaor.

"Yes. The fire brigade brought them to the city morgue. They will be returned to us for burial when they have finished with them."

"Are you sure this is safe now?" asked Mr. Nolan.

"It is safe but we need to do a lot of work to clear it, and it is slow work."

"Slow? Why?"

"Well, since the, uhm, miracle we haven't been dealing with any outside contractors."

"But I heard the miracle investigation was suspended. I heard that Father Sheehan, the Chief Diocesan Investigator, was reviewing it," countered Mr. Nolan.

"Ah yes, indeed, that's true all the same, temporarily suspended all right," babbled Loughlin.

"I think what Brother Loughlin means to say," interrupted Mr. Pollock smoothly, "is that we are still considering working with Father Sheehan and hope to find a new biographer for Venerable Saorseach O'Rahilly, and as such we need to preserve the miracle site from outside hands."

"I see," murmured Miss Moloney a split second before the whole building shook with a series of distant impacts.

"Jesus Christ! What was that?" cried Mr. Nolan

"I have no idea. Must be that damned janitor again," said Brother Loughlin as casually as he could.

They all stood amazed as the monastery shook and trembled, and suddenly the rubble at the other end of the roof shot up to allow passage to a radiator that flew fifty feet into the air before falling with a crash into the yard below.

"That's enough, Brother Loughlin. Evacuate the school!" shouted Mr. DePaor.

"But—"

"This instant, Brother Loughlin! Something is very wrong here."

"Smalley! Smalley! Where are you?"

"Come on, Scully. We already looked in there."

Scully had just turned away from the refectory door when there was a deafening blast. The radiator under the window shot off the wall and hurtled down the corridor. It narrowly missed him and skidded past Finbar, making shreds of the parquet floor before smashing through the main door and coming to rest in the yard.

"Fuck sake! Come on!" shouted Scully.

As they neared the door they heard the commotion of many feet outside. There was a lot of yelling and some screaming. "Where is McConnell?" they heard Spud Murphy shouting above it all. "Who has the key to the gate?"

A shadow fell across the doorway and a figure stepped over the mangled radiator into the hallway.

"Leave me for dead, would ye, ye little bastards?"

Brother Moody, covered in dust and bleeding heavily from the forehead, advanced on them. In his right hand he held a jagged length of brass pipe that he swung wildly in front of him. "I'll break every bone in your poxy little bodies!"

Finbar and Scully backed down the corridor, flinching at each tiny sound, fearing another radiator might fly at them from somewhere. Scully stumbled on a clump of fallen masonry and Moody was on him in a flash. Finbar stared in horror as the Brother raised the pipe above his head and swung down hard. Scully turned away reflexively but still took a blow to the ribs. Finbar launched himself at Moody and grabbed him round the neck and kicked at him for all he was worth. Moody threw himself backward and smashed Finbar against the wall.

Winded and stunned, Finbar slid to the floor. Moody swung the pipe drunkenly and caught Finbar on the arm he raised to protect his head. There was a sickening crack and Finbar saw white and felt a biting pain.

"What on earth is going on, Brother Moody?"

Moody turned to see Brother Loughlin stepping in through the shattered doorway.

"I caught these two skulking around in here. They're up to something. I just know they are. They're behind all this."

Brother Loughlin gaped in incomprehension at the scene before him. "But what happened to you?"

"Ceiling collapsed in the toilets upstairs. These little bastards left me for dead. And this one is the ring leader, I'll bet." Moody slapped Scully in the small of the back with the pipe.

Loughlin jumped as Moody's blow was answered by an explosion and another window in the refectory fell in. "Hit him again," he said.

Moody willingly obliged and this time the fuse box

under the stairs burst into flames. Loughlin's eyes narrowed as the appalling realisation of the building's ailment settled into his brain.

"The little bastards!" he screamed, and dragged Scully up from the floor. "If you want to bring this school down, you have to be prepared to go with it. Are you prepared to do that, you little bastard?"

"Noooooooooooooooooooooooooooooooooo!" came a thin voice from above.

Scully leapt aside, and a second later Brother Boland, clinging to the school bell, crashed through the stairwell onto Brother Loughlin. Boland was flung to the ground and lay there stunned. Loughlin twitched, then did not move; he lay under the bell with his head at a very peculiar angle to his trunk.

"Boland, you mad bastard! You and your precious fucking bell. Look what you've done," howled Moody. He advanced on Boland, his eyes afire with hate and violence.

Finbar crawled up to where Scully lay. "He'll kill him," he whispered.

"So what?" groaned Scully.

Brother Moody struck out wildly at Brother Boland but jammed the pipe into the broken fuse box instead. He froze and then shuddered as the current coursed through him. Boland lashed out with his foot and kicked Moody's legs from under him. Moody fell to the floor twitching.

"I'm going to do for ye all," sneered Moody, and tried to stand up. The staircase shook and seemed to wrench itself off the wall. Finbar grabbed Scully and dived toward the doorway. The air was filled with noise and dust, and then just dust. As it cleared they saw Brother Moody pinned under a huge beam and Brother Boland trapped under the other end of it.

"Help me! Help me!" pleaded Brother Moody.

Finbar and Scully stood uncertainly at the doorway.

"Go! Save yourselves!" croaked Brother Boland. "What a terrible waste of a life! Diseased, terrible waste. Leave me. Leave him too. He doesn't deserve to be saved. His like should never be let near decent people. Run! Save yourselves. The school is sick and must die. Save yourselves. You have to try to understand . . ."

A tremendous rumble from the floors above drowned out Brother Boland's voice.

"Run! And keep running!" shouted Finbar, and pushed Scully out the door in front of him. They heard the crash and crunch behind them and were enveloped in a cloud of choking dust. They veered to their left and emerged in the middle of the yard, which was deserted and littered with rubble, desks, slates, pipes, broken glass.

"The gate's open! Keep going!" screamed Scully, who limped on ahead. They dashed out the gate, up the lane, and turned onto Werburgh Street. At the top of the street they saw everyone else and ran toward them, then turned to look back and saw what the crowd was staring at numbly.

Windows were popping and smoke was rising. With each thump and shudder the school seemed to exhale more dust and smoke.

"Look! The tower!" someone shouted.

All eyes locked on the bell tower. It was listing. It seemed to regain stability for a moment and then gently folded in on itself and lay down with a huge stony sigh. Some of the boys cheered.

"Where's Smalley?" Scully asked Lynch.

"Over there with Spud Murphy and Laverty."

Scully turned to see the boy standing behind Spud Murphy, who was shouting furiously at Mr. Pollock: "You and your fucking miracle and your fucking school! I'll hang you, Pollock. I don't care what it takes. You are a vicious, twisted little fucker and not fit to be near animals, no mind say young people. You're a sick bastard and I will see you pay for this!"

As if to echo Spud's words, the top floor of the monastery building collapsed completely.

"It'll be your word against mine, Mr. Murphy."

"It will not." Mr. Laverty stood in front of Pollock. "I'll back him up. I will make it my life's work to see you get what's coming to you. Come on, Mullen, let's get you cleaned up and I'll drive you home. Away from this vicious fucker."

"Where the hell were you until now? We were . . ." Mrs. Sullivan yanked the front door open and her breath caught when she saw Finbar, Scully, and Spud Murphy standing on the doorstep. Finbar's arm was in a sling and Scully's head was heavily bandaged.

"Holy Mother of God! What happened to you, Finbar?"

"They're fine, Mrs. Sullivan. Do you think we might come in? They've had quite a day. I'm Mr. Murphy, Finbar's History teacher," said Spud softly.

"Oh God, of course! I'm sorry. I was worried sick."

"What the . . . ?" Finbar froze in the sitting room doorway. His father was there on the sofa with Declan. Sheila Barry sat in the armchair with a baby on her lap. Mr. Sullivan met Finbar's mystified look and shook his head gently to say that this was not the time. How he got Sheila and the baby back would be a story for another day.

Scully stood awkwardly in the hall behind Finbar. "Eh, maybe I should go home."

"You will do no such thing, young man! You'll have

something to eat and then Finbar's father will take you home," commanded Mrs. Sullivan, and steered Scully into the parlour and onto the other armchair.

"Sheila, do you need anything?"

The young woman met Mrs. Sullivan's eyes for a moment and then shook her head: "I'm grand, thanks."

"Finbar, get your friend something to drink. There's some of that orange squash in the fridge."

"His name is Francis, Ma. Francis Scully."

Finbar went into the kitchen and opened the tall cupboard to get some glasses. From the parlour he heard Spud Murphy's voice but could not make out the words. Then he heard his father laugh nervously: "I'm bloody glad! I wouldn't let him go back to that kip of a school even if it hadn't fallen down. Finbar, come in here! You have to meet your niece. She's awake now. And bring a bottle of stout in from the shed for Mr. Murphy! And see if there are any biscuits in the tin for your friend Francis here."

Finbar glanced at his reflection in the scullery window.

"Fin, I hid the biscuits behind the tea caddy," called Declan's voice from the parlour.

Finbar smiled at his reflection and felt a comforting sense of crowdedness seep through him as the tiny chuckling of the baby and the warm murmur of voices from the parlour wafted over him like the soft mizzle of a summer shower.

38

One lone crow sat in the dead tree that stood over the gatehouse of Drumgloom Industrial School. It seemed to be waiting and listening for something. Its tiny black eyes darted in the direction of the Victorian hulk of Drumgloom itself. The bird stretched its wings, cawed harshly at the dying light of the day, and opened its beak wide. *All fall! All fall!* it seemed to cry.

"Sooner or later we will find the culprit," declaimed Brother Benedict MacAeongus, Principal of Drumgloom, as he strode toward the grand staircase of the erstwhile mental asylum. "Make no mistake about that. You know who you are. You can make it easier on yourself and own up now and take the chance to be a man about it, or we can punish you all until we find who it was. It is no skin off my nose. I can stay here all night if I have to!"

All along one side of the stairs and along the corridors knelt boys dressed only in their underpants. Their arms were outstretched parallel to the floor and in each hand they held ball bearings the size of large apples.

With his leather MacAeongus tapped one of the boys at the elbow: "Arms straight! This is your personal cross!"

He passed on up the stairs and along the corridor to the dormitories of the youngest boys, some of them little older than seven.

"Stop quivering, boy!"

Before MacAeongus had a chance to further berate the child, there was the sound he had been waiting for, the heavy clunk of a ball bearing dropped on the bare floorboards.

"Just what do you think you're at, you disobedient little cur?" he shouted as he hurried in the direction of the offending noise.

In his haste he brushed against another boy's outstretched arm, causing the ball bearing to roll out of his upturned palm.

"You clumsy little bastard!" screeched MacAeongus, and hit the boy a stinging blow on the ear with his leather.

Near the head of the stairs MacAeongus saw a hand reaching into the middle of the corridor to lift its fallen ball bearing. He picked up his pace and arrived just in time to place his foot on the boy's hand.

"Maher! The cripple from Werburgh Street who says he was sent here for no reason! I might have known! Well, boy, is that an admission of guilt for the hall window or did you just drop the ball?"

"I just dropped the ball, Brother. Me arm was—"

"I'll tell you what your arm was, me bucko! Lazy, that's what it was. Banjaxed legs and lazy arms, you're hopeless! Good for nothing! Do you think these floors are here for you to destroy them dropping ball bearings on them? Is that what you think? Is it?"

"No, Brother."

"Well then, why did you drop the ball, eh, eh? I'll tell you why. Because you're a disobedient, useless little cur!"

MacAeongus picked Maher up by the arm and marched him to the stairs, swiping with his leather at the backs of his thighs below the brace straps.

"I'll learn you to go dropping ball bearings on our good floors!" spat MacAeongus.

Trying to shield his legs, Maher dropped the other ball bearing he was holding. MacAeongus stood on it, slipped, and flailed for the banister to right himself. With a rending screech the banister gave way and MacAeongus fell to the polished parquet floor of the main hall twenty feet below.

The boys got up from their knees and rushed to see what was happening. MacAeongus was lying dazed on the floor. A hush of indecision hovered over the boys, only to be dispelled by a loud splintering as the ceiling above the prone figure of MacAeongus unburdened itself of the spiked chandelier that it had unwillingly supported for so long. In a few moments the awful weight was gone and the central spike severed MacAeongus's carotid artery and buried itself deep in the parquet floor.

Small tremors shuddered out from Drumgloom, through the ready earth, and added to the after-hum of Werburgh Street's collapse. They found many willing resonances. The long-suffering cracked ceiling of Saint Agnes of Birr Home for the Wanton seized the vibrations of this new call to action and collapsed with a relieved sigh on top of visiting confessor Father Cafferty's furtive groping of one of the girls. The girl escaped without a scratch. The loose staircase of the Poor Sisters of the Threadbare Cowl Boarding School for Foundlings hummed to the pulsations and pitched itself into the vestibule, causing irreparable damage to two load-bearing walls and the immediate decease of Sister Assumpta, who had just returned from caning one of the new girls. The gable wall of the Brothers of the Venerable Lacerations Home for the Unhinged threw itself into the vegetable garden, leaving the roof to hover uneasily before it too unmoored itself. Obdurate Heart Convent tossed all caution to the wind and shook itself to the ground while the nuns were on the playing fields hosing the girls down with vinegar. Saint Rathlin's Reformatory burst a gaspipe, took a deep breath, and struck a match. In the Jezebel Laundry outside Dullow, Sister Delia, furiously searching the washing room for Sheila Barry, was scalded and then crushed by a falling vat of dirty underclothes just before the roof caved in.

Day after day, for the next three weeks, the country rumbled as one institution after another gave in to the effects of years of corrosive viciousness. Damage was extensive, fatalities and injuries among staff widespread, but not one child was so much as scratched.

Epilogue

Where's that Head Brother, whatsisname, ehm, Loughlin? He needs to sign me docket." Matt waved the paperwork that was now fully in order with today's date on it and accounted for the sixty radiators and eight hundred feet of pipe filling the three trucks he was waiting to lead back to the depot.

Mr. Pollock and the knot of Brothers behind him tried to move away.

"One of yiz needs to sign," insisted Matt.

"Brother Loughlin is deceased," said Pollock coldly as he scrawled a signature across the docket.

"Ah, the Head Brother is a Dead Brother. That's a shame, I suppose, but I have to say he didn't look too well last time we saw him. Blood pressure, I would have said. Looked like a man with a short temper. Good luck now. Enjoy the rest of yer day," said Matt, swinging himself up into the cab of the truck.

The Brannigan Brothers scrap metal trucks hauled themselves up the street. Once they were clear, the siren bawled out its three-minute warning and the police moved everyone to the top of Werburgh Street away from the school.

The crowd around the Brothers fell suddenly silent and parted to reveal Maher making good headway on crutches followed by his docker father. Even the police flanking

Pollock stood back fearfully as Mr. Maher placed his formidable bulk right in front of Pollock.

"You, you vicious little fucker! I could rip your poxy head off with my bare hands, but I won't. Some other fucker just like you will be sitting on a judge's bench waiting to ruin my life. You should have known better! These fucked-up Brothers maybe have some excuse cos half of them were fucked up themselves and never lived anywhere but in some shithole school or orphanage or seminary, but you should know better! You live in the real world. But I bet you don't even remember being a kid.

"What I have to say to you is this: May the rest of your life be a barren, painful waste. May you die roaring, alone and far from the sight of your God and your fellow man, and may your name be forgotten as soon as you are cold in the box."

With that, Mr. Maher turned and gently shepherded his son back through the crowd. Ashen-faced, Pollock stared after them and looked like he would have preferred if Maher had ripped his head off.

The siren bawled its long final warning. The crane bearing *Brannigan Brothers Demolition* revved its engine and the air filled with sweet diesel fumes. Men shouted from under their hard hats. The crane swung. The wrecking ball broke through a high window of the condemned school with a dull thump. From the top of the street at the main road there came a wild shrieking cheer.

"Callous, ungrateful little bastards!" muttered Brother Tobin, shaking his nicotine-tinted head sadly.

Brother Mulligan quivered and flinched beside him. Brother Tobin tightened his supporting grip on Mulligan's forearm. Mulligan's slight frame seemed barely able to support the lolling of his shorn head. Beside them Mr. Pollock and Brother Cox stood in grim silence.

More glass crunched and more masonry caved in like so much damp sand. So soon. So quickly the top floor of the school began to look like something unfinished and ailing, its identity wrenched from it.

"No, no, no, no," gibbered Brother Mulligan feebly. His home since the age of fourteen, almost sixty-five years, buckled and crumbled with each slow, methodical assault of the wrecking ball. Each swing of the crane drove him deeper into his frailty.

"We should go, Brother. There's no sense staying to watch this," said Tobin softly.

"They took it away from me! They destroyed my world!" rasped Mulligan.

Tobin led Mulligan up the street toward the West Circular Road where the barricades had blocked off the traffic onto Greater Little Werburgh Street, North. A loud booing broke out among the crowd of boys behind the barricade and Tobin slowed his steps. He stopped about twenty yards from the barricade and waited, Mulligan quaking and shuddering beside him. A half-eaten apple sailed through the air from the back of the crowd and splattered on the street near Tobin's feet.

The crowd of jeering bodies parted and three policemen came forward. There was a short silence while the booing tried to decide how to react to this new development. One of the policemen escorted Tobin and Mulligan to a nearby car where the Brother Superior General was waiting to take them to the Saorseach O'Rahilly Hospice for Unhinged Brothers. The other two policemen walked toward Pollock and Cox. A slow dawning of understanding spread through the crowd of boys and the silence burst into a new bloom of jeering, whistling, and cheering. They were taking them away! They were going to lock the bastards up!

A dull, gut-trembling rumble drowned out the cheering as the wall of the school fell in on itself, taking the two narrower side walls with it. Brannigan Brothers did good work. The cheering redoubled to greet the cloud of dust that belched out of the erstwhile four-storey block.

Brother Cox lowered his head as the police put him in the backseat of the squad car. He closed his eyes tightly and hummed one long, hoarse note to try to drown out the banging on the roof of the vehicle as the boys made their gleeful and malevolent farewells. Mr. Pollock slid into the backseat beside him just as a rotten tomato exploded stingingly against the side of his face.

"How did you like that, sor?" called a familiar voice.

Pollock wiped the mess from his face and glared at the faces that crowded in around the police car. Smalley Mullen stood there staring defiantly at him with another tomato at the ready.

"Imeacht gan teacht ort, sor! May you go and never return, ye louse!" grinned Smalley. Before Pollock could pull the door closed, the boy mashed the second tomato into the teacher's face, then walked away.

The crowd moved forward to read the notice that one of the Brannigan Brothers men hung on the railings:

We, Fionn and Patrick Sweeney, hereby make known our intention to build on this site (Lot # 867-3D/9A, Folio 4287 of the Register of Freeholds) a storage and warehouse facility in compliance with City Ordinances 44-J, 22-B5, and 221-F. Approval of Planning Permission granted—docket 112-4K-12-28. Plans will be available for viewing at 18 Danegild Street between the hours of 10:00 and 10:55 on weekdays or by appointment. Construction will begin on August 18 at 9 a.m. sharp.

Acknowledgments

As my personal experience was only a glimpse of the tip of the iceberg, for the larger cultural context that informed this fiction I am indebted to the extraordinary *Suffer the Little Children: The Inside Story of Ireland's Industrial Schools* by Mary Raftery and Eoin O'Sullivan, and to *Church and State in Modern Ireland, 1923–79* by J.H. Whyte. Whenever my energy waned, I needed only the briefest look at the findings of the Commission to Inquire into Child Abuse, available online at http://www.childabusecommission.ie/.

I thank my brothers Peter and John for their irreverence and stories, my dear friends Paul McDermott and Brian Brady whose company and resilient humour made the actual process of secondary education bearable and who encouraged the writing of this story. I thank Tom Cayler, the late Beverly Jensen, Jenifer Levin, Tim Ledwith, Paul Power, and Frank Spain, who have generously read and offered suggestions on parts and versions of this over the years.

Thanks to Claudio Berghenti, Madeline Boughton, Paddy Breathnach, Randy Finch, Henry Dunn, Bethany Fiore, Jason Fogelson, Ruth Gallagher, Ed Kadysewski, Merle Lefkoff, Karin McCully, John McDermott, Peter McDermott, Kieran McEvoy, Belinda McKeon, Liz Morrissey, Éanna Ó Lochlainn, Marie O'Riordan, Rob Walpole, and Feargal Whelan for their seemingly inexhaustible support, advice, and goodwill, and to Joseph O'Connor for his years of unflagging guidance, help, and encouragement.

At No Exit thanks to Ion Mills for his commitment and hard work on this edition, Claire Watts for her attention to the text and Chris Burrows, assisted by Alexandra Bolton, for their PR expertise.

At Akashic I thank Johanna Ingalls, Ibrahim Ahmad, Zach Pace, and of course Johnny Temple for his courtesy, editorial care, thoroughness, and risk-taking.

Underlying and yet above all, special thanks to my mother and late father who stood up for us, and to my beloved wife and most painstaking reader Lisa Diamond and our son Leo without whose patience, support, and love this book would never have come to completion.